Praise for the Trylle Trilogy by Amanda Hocking

'Her character-driven books, which feature trolls, hobgoblins and fairy-tale elements, and keep the pages turning, have generated an excitement not felt in the industry since Stephenie Meyer or perhaps even J. K. Rowling' ***New York Times***

'A fast-paced romance . . . addictive' ***Guardian***

'In terms of page-turning immediacy, they are unrivalled' ***Daily Telegraph***

'Has a resonance that I found compelling' ***Daily Mail***

'Drew me in and kept me hooked . . . cracking pace' ***Sunday Express***

'A well-told, simple fantasy story . . . You can have fun and get lost in a world' ***Irish Independent***

'Amanda Hocking is one of the most experienced and successful first-time novelists around' ***SFX***

'Enough surprises to keep even a paranormal-romance sceptic interested, and the writing is briskly paced and casual enough to make reading fast and fun' ***We Love This Book***

'[*Switched*] is full of adventure, tense moments – the sort of "what is going to happen next" moments, a romance and a great plot . . . I will definitely be looking out for the next book in the series ***kReviews.me.uk***

'Short chapters, punchy sentences and [a] penchant for cliff-hangers . . . it is easy to devour this book in one sitting'

TheUpComing.co.uk

'The voices and inner thoughts of each character come through loud and clear . . . Amanda Hocking sets the bar in more ways than one' ***Lunch.com***

'[*Switched*] was a page-turner. I devoured the thing and stayed up late to finish it . . . I'll be grabbing the sequels to read fairly sharpish, just as soon as I can' ***BartsBookShelf.co.uk***

'I thoroughly enjoyed this book . . . I just can't wait for the next part to come out. Read it!' ***BookBlitz.co.uk***

'I couldn't put this book down . . . The story gives an original spin to the Troll folklore and feels fresh and magical at the same time' ***OneMorePage.co.uk***

Ascend

Amanda Hocking

TOR

First published 2012 by St Martin's Press, New York

First published in Great Britain 2012 by Tor
an imprint of Pan Macmillan, a division of Macmillan Publishers Limited
Pan Macmillan, 20 New Wharf Road, London N1 9RR
Basingstoke and Oxford
Associated companies throughout the world
www.panmacmillan.com

ISBN 978-1-4472-1031-3

1 3 5 7 9 8 6 4 2

A CIP catalogue record for this book is available from
the British Library.

Printed and bound by CPI Group (UK) Ltd, Croydon, CR0 4YY

To all the readers—thank you for all your support.

Ascend

ONE

amnesty

I had my back to the room as I stared out the window. It was a trick I'd learned from my mother to make me seem more in control. Elora had given me lots of tips the past few months, but the ones about commanding a meeting were the most useful.

"Princess, I think you're being naive," the Chancellor said. "You can't turn the entire society on its head."

"I'm not." I turned back, giving him a cool gaze, and he lowered his eyes and balled up his handkerchief in his hand. "But we can't ignore the problems any longer."

I surveyed the meeting room, doing my best to seem as cold and imposing as Elora always had. I didn't plan to be a cruel ruler, but they wouldn't listen to weakness. If I wanted to make a change here, I had to be firm.

Since Elora had become incapacitated, I'd been running the day-to-day activities of the palace, which included a lot of meetings. The board of advisers seemed to take up a lot of my time.

The Chancellor had been voted into his position by the Trylle people, but as soon as his term was up, I planned to campaign against him as hard as I could. He was a conniving coward, and we needed somebody much stronger in his position.

Garrett Strom—my mother's "confidant"—was here today, but he didn't always attend these meetings. Depending on how Elora was doing that day, he often chose to stay and care for her instead.

My assistant Joss sat at the back of the room, furiously scribbling down notes as we talked. She was a small human girl who grew up in Förening as a mänsklig and worked as Elora's secretary. Since I'd been running the palace, I'd inherited Joss as my own assistant.

Duncan, my bodyguard, was stationed by the door, where he stood during all the meetings. He followed me everywhere, like a shadow, and though he was clumsy and small, he was smarter than people gave him credit for. I'd grown to respect and appreciate his presence the last few months, even if he couldn't completely take the place of my last guard, Finn Holmes.

Aurora Kroner sat at the head of the table, and next to her was Tove, my fiancé. He was usually the only one on my side, and I was grateful to have him here. I didn't know how I would manage ruling if I felt completely alone.

Also in attendance were Marksinna Laris, a woman I didn't

particularly trust, but she was one of the most influential people in Förening; Markis Bain, who was in charge of changeling placement; Markis Court, the treasurer for the palace; and Thomas Holmes, the head guard in charge of security and all the trackers.

A few other high-ranking officials sat around the table, all of their expressions solemn. The situation for the Trylle was growing increasingly dire, and I was proposing change. They didn't want me to change anything—they wanted me to support the system they'd had for centuries, but that system wasn't working anymore. Our society was crumbling, and they refused to see the roles they played in its breakdown.

"With all due respect, Princess," Aurora began, her voice so sweet I could barely hear the venom underneath, "we have bigger issues at hand. The Vittra are only getting stronger, and with the truce about to end—"

"The truce," Marksinna Laris snorted, cutting her off. "Like that's done us any good."

"The truce isn't over yet," I said, standing up straighter. "Our trackers are out taking care of the problems now, which is why I think it's so important that we have something in place for them when they return."

"We can worry about that *when* they return," the Chancellor said. "Let's deal with saving our asses right now."

"I'm not asking to redistribute the wealth or calling to abolish the monarchy," I said. "I am simply saying that the trackers are out there risking their lives to save us, to protect our changelings, and they deserve a real house to come back to. We should be setting aside money *now* so that when this is over, we can begin building them real homes."

"As noble as that is, Princess, we should be saving our money for the Vittra," Markis Bain said. He was quiet and polite, even when he disagreed with me, and he was one of the few royals whom I felt actually wanted to do what was best for all the people.

"We can't pay the Vittra off," Tove interjected. "This isn't about money. This is about power. We all know what they want, and a few thousand—or even a few *million*—dollars won't matter to them. The Vittra King will refuse it."

"I will do everything in my power to keep Förening safe, but you are all correct," I said. "We have yet to find a reasonable solution for the Vittra. That means this might very well turn into a bloody fight, and if it does, we need to support our troops. They deserve the best care, including adequate housing and access to our healers if they're injured in wartime."

"Healers for a tracker?" Marksinna Laris laughed, and a few others chuckled along with her. "Don't be ridiculous."

"Why is that ridiculous?" I asked, working to keep the ice from my voice. "They are expected to die for us, but we aren't willing to heal their wounds? We cannot ask more of them than we are willing to give ourselves."

"They are lower than us," Laris said, as if I didn't understand the concept. "We are in charge for a reason. Why on earth should we treat them as equals when they are not?"

"Because it's basic decency," I argued. "We may not be human, but that doesn't mean we have to be devoid of humanity. This is why our people are leaving our cities and preferring to live among the humans, letting their powers die. We must offer them some bit of happiness, otherwise why would they stay?"

Laris muttered something under her breath, keeping her steely eyes locked on the oak table. Her black hair was slicked back, pulled in a bun so tight her face looked strained. This was probably done on purpose to draw attention to her strength.

Marksinna Laris was a very powerful Trylle, able to produce and control fire, and something that strong was draining. Trylle powers weakened them, taking some of their life and aging them prematurely.

But if the Trylle didn't use them, the abilities did something to their minds, eating at their thoughts and making them crazy. This was especially true for Tove, who would appear scattered and rude if he didn't find constant outlets for his psychokinesis.

"It is time for a change," Tove said, speaking up when the room had fallen into annoyed silence. "It can be gradual, but it's going to happen."

A knock at the door stopped anyone from offering a rebuttal, but from the beet-red color of the Chancellor's face, it looked like he had a few words he wanted to get out.

Duncan opened the door, and Willa poked her head in, smiling uncertainly. Since she was a Marksinna, Garrett's daughter, and my best friend, she had every right to be here. I'd extended an invitation for her to attend these meetings, but she always declined, saying she was afraid she would do more harm than good. She had a hard time being polite when she disagreed with people.

"Sorry," Willa said, and Duncan stepped aside so she could come in. "I didn't mean to interrupt. It's just that it's after five, and I was supposed to get the Princess at three for her birthday celebration."

I glanced at the clock, realizing this had dragged on much longer than I'd originally planned. Willa walked over to me and gave the room an apologetic smile, but I knew she'd pull me out kicking and screaming if I didn't put an end to the meeting.

"Ah, yes." The Chancellor smiled at me with a disturbing hunger in his eyes. "I'd forgotten that you'll be eighteen tomorrow." He licked his lips, and Tove stood up, purposely blocking the Chancellor's view of me.

"Sorry, everyone," Tove said, "but the Princess and I have plans this evening. We'll pick up this meeting next week, then?"

"You're going back to work next week?" Laris looked appalled. "So soon after your wedding? Aren't you and the Princess taking a honeymoon?"

"With the state of things, I don't think it's wise," I said. "I have too much to get done here."

While that was true enough, that wasn't the only reason I'd skipped out on a honeymoon. As much as I'd grown to like Tove, I couldn't imagine what the two of us would do on one. I hadn't even let myself think about how we would spend our wedding night.

"We need to go over the changeling contracts," Markis Bain said, standing up in a hurry. "Since the trackers are bringing the changelings back early, and some families decline to do changelings anymore, the placements have all been moved around. I need you to sign off on them."

"Enough talk of business." Willa looped her arm through mine, preparing to lead me out of the room. "The Princess will be back to work on Monday, and she can sign anything you want then."

"Willa, it will only take a second to sign them," I said, but she glared at me, so I gave Bain a polite smile. "I will look them over first thing Monday morning."

Tove stayed behind a moment to say something to Bain, but he caught up with us a few moments later in the hall. Even though we were out of the meeting, Willa still kept her arm through mine as we walked.

Duncan stayed a step behind us when we were in the south wing. I'd gotten talked to many, many times about how I couldn't treat Duncan as an equal while business was being conducted and there were Trylle officials at work around us.

"Princess?" Joss said, scampering behind me with papers spilling out of her binder. "Princess, do you want me to arrange a meeting on Monday with Markis Bain for the contracts?"

"Yes, that would be fantastic," I said, slowing so I could talk to her. "Thank you, Joss."

"You have a meeting at ten A.M. with the Markis of Oslinna." Joss flipped through the appointment section of the binder, and a paper flew out. Duncan snatched it before it fell to the floor and handed it to her. "Thank you. Sorry. So, Princess, do you want to meet Markis Bain before or after that meeting?"

"She'll be going back to work just after getting married," Willa said. "Of course she won't be there first thing in the morning. Make it for the afternoon."

I glanced over at Tove walking next to me, but his expression was blank. Since proposing to me, he'd actually spoken very little of getting married. His mother and Willa had done most of the planning, so I hadn't even talked to him about what he thought of colors or flower arrangements. Everything had been decided for us, so we had little to discuss.

"Does two in the afternoon work for you?" Joss asked.

"Yes, that would be perfect," I said. "Thanks, Joss."

"All right." Joss stopped to hurriedly scribble down the time in the binder.

"Now she's off until Monday," Willa told Joss over her shoulder. "That means five whole days where nobody calls her, talks to her, or meets with her. Remember that, Joss. If anybody asks for the Princess, she cannot be reached."

"Yes, of course, Marksinna Strom." Joss smiled. "Happy birthday, Princess, and good luck with your wedding!"

"I can't believe how much of a workaholic you are," Willa said with a sigh as we walked away. "When you're Queen, I'll never see you at all."

"Sorry," I said. "I tried to get out of the meeting sooner, but things have been getting out of hand lately."

"That Laris is driving me batty," Tove said, grimacing at the thought of her. "When you're Queen, you should banish her."

"When I'm Queen, you'll be King," I pointed out. "You can banish her yourself."

"Well, wait until you see what we have planned for you tonight." Duncan grinned. "You'll be having too much fun to worry about Laris or anybody else."

Fortunately, since I was getting married in a few days, I'd gotten out of the usual ball that would happen for a Princess's birthday. Elora and Aurora had planned that the wedding would take place immediately after I turned eighteen. My birthday was on a Wednesday, and I was getting married on Saturday, leaving no time for a massive Trylle birthday party.

Willa insisted on throwing me a small party anyway, even though I didn't really want one. Considering everything that was happening in Förening, it felt like sacrilege. The Vittra had set up a peace treaty with us, agreeing not to attack us until I became Queen.

What we hadn't realized at the time was the specific language they had used. They wouldn't attack *us*, meaning the Trylle living in Förening. Everyone else was fair game.

The Vittra had started going after our changelings, the ones that were still left with their host families in human society. They'd taken a few before we caught on, but as soon as we did, we sent all our best trackers to bring home any changeling over the age of sixteen, including most of the trackers serving as palace bodyguards. For anyone younger than that, our trackers were supposed to stand guard and watch them. We knew the Vittra would avoid taking them because they couldn't do so without setting off an Amber Alert. Still, we felt that every precaution must be taken to protect the most vulnerable among us.

That left us at a horrible disadvantage. To protect the changelings, our trackers had to be in the field, so they couldn't be here guarding the palace. We would be more exposed to an attack if the Vittra went back on their part of the deal, but I didn't see what choice we had. We couldn't let them kidnap and hurt our children, so I sent every tracker I could out into the field.

Finn had been gone almost continuously for months. He was the best tracker we had, and he'd been returning the changelings to all the Trylle communities. I hadn't seen him since before Christmas, and sometimes I still missed him, but the longing was fading.

He'd made it clear that his duty came before everything else and I could never be a real part of his life. I was marrying someone else, and even though I still cared about Finn, I had to put that behind me and move past it.

"Where is this party happening anyway?" I asked Willa, pushing thoughts of Finn from my mind.

"Upstairs," Willa said, leading me toward the grand staircase in the front hall. "Matt's up there putting on the finishing touches."

"Finishing touches?" I raised an eyebrow.

Someone pounded violently on the front door, making the door shake and the chandelier above us tremble. Normally people rang the doorbell, but our visitor was nearly beating down the door.

"Stay back, Princess," Duncan said as he walked over to the entrance.

"Duncan, I can get it," I said.

If somebody hit the door hard enough to make the front hall quake, I was afraid of what they would do to him. I made a move for the door, but Willa stopped me.

"Wendy, let him," she said firmly. "You and Tove will be here if he needs you."

"No." I pulled myself from her grip and went after Duncan, to defend him if I needed to.

That sounded silly, since he was supposed to be my bodyguard, but I was more powerful than him. He was really only meant to serve as a shield if need be, but I would never let him do that.

When he opened the door, I was right behind him. Duncan meant to only partially open the door so he could see what waited for us outside, but a gust of wind came up, blowing it open and sending snow swirling around the front hall.

A blast of cold air struck me, but it died down almost instantly. Willa could control the wind when she wanted to, so as soon as it blew inside the palace, she raised her hand to stop it.

A figure stood before us, bracing himself with his hands on either side of the doorway. He was slumped forward, his head hanging down, and snow covered his black sweater. His clothes were ragged, worn, and shredded in most places.

"Can we help you?" Duncan asked.

"I need the Princess," he said, and as soon as I heard his voice, a shiver shot through me.

"Loki?" I gasped.

"Princess?" Loki lifted his head.

He smiled crookedly, but his smile didn't have its usual

bravado. His caramel eyes looked tired and pained, and he had a fading bruise on his cheek. Despite all that, he was still just as gorgeous as I remembered him, and my breath caught in my throat.

"What happened to you?" I asked. "What are you doing here?"

"I apologize for the intrusion, Princess," he said, his smile already fading. "And as much as I'd like to say that I'm here for pleasure, I . . ." He swallowed something back, and his hands gripped tighter on the door frame.

"Are you all right?" I asked, pushing past Duncan.

"I . . ." Loki started to speak, but his knees gave out. He pitched forward, and I rushed to catch him. He fell into my arms, and I lowered him to the floor.

"Loki?" I brushed the hair back from his eyes, and they fluttered open.

"Wendy." He smiled up at me, but the smile was weak. "If I'd known that this is what it would take to get you to hold me, I would've collapsed a long time ago."

"What is going on, Loki?" I asked gently. If he hadn't been so obviously distressed, I would've swatted him for that comment, but he grimaced in pain when I touched his face.

"Amnesty," he said thickly, and his eyes closed. "I need amnesty, Princess." His head tilted to the side, and his body relaxed. He'd passed out.

TWO

birthday

Tove and Duncan had carried Loki up to the servants' quarters on the second floor. Willa went back to help Matt so he wouldn't worry, and I sent Duncan to get Thomas because I had no idea what we should do with Loki. He was unconscious, so I couldn't ask him what had happened.

"Are you going to give him amnesty?" Tove asked. He stood next to me with his arms folded over his chest, staring down at Loki.

"I don't know." I shook my head. "It depends on what he says." I glanced over at Tove. "Why? Do you think I should?"

"I don't know," he said finally. "But I will support any decision you make."

"Thank you," I said, but I hadn't expected any different from him. "Can you see if there's a doctor that will look at him?"

"You don't want me to get my mother?" Tove asked. His

mother was a healer, meaning she could put her hands on someone and heal almost any wound that person might have.

"No. She would never heal a Vittra. Besides, I don't want anyone to know that Loki is here. Not yet," I said. "I need an actual doctor. There is a mänks doctor in town, isn't there?"

"Yeah." He nodded. "I'll get him." He turned to leave but paused at the door. "You'll be okay with the Vittra Markis?"

I smiled. "Yes, of course."

Tove nodded, then left me alone with Loki. I took a deep breath and tried to figure out what to do. Loki lay on his back, his light hair cascading across his forehead. Somehow he was even more attractive asleep than he was awake.

He hadn't stirred at all when they'd carried him up, and Duncan had jostled and nearly dropped him many times. Loki had always dressed well, and while his clothes looked like they had once been nice, they were little more than rags now.

I sat down on the edge of the bed next to him and touched a hole in his shirt. The skin underneath was discolored and swollen. Tentatively, I lifted his shirt, and when Loki didn't wake, I pushed it up more.

I felt strange and almost perverse undressing him, but I wanted to check and make sure there weren't any life-threatening contusions. If he was seriously injured or appeared to have any broken bones, I would summon Aurora and make her heal him, whether she wanted to or not. I wouldn't let Loki die because she was prejudiced.

After I pulled his shirt over his head, I got my first good look at him, and my breath caught in my throat. Under ordinary circumstances, I was sure his physique would be stunning, but that wasn't what shocked me. His torso was covered with bruises, and his sides had long, thin scars on them.

They wrapped around, so I lifted him a bit, and his back was covered with them. They crisscrossed all over his skin, some of them older, but most of them appeared red and fresh.

Tears stung my eyes, and I put my hand to my mouth. I'd never seen Loki shirtless before, but I knew there had never been scars on his forearms. Most of this had happened since I'd seen him last.

Worse still, Loki had Vittra blood. Physically, he was incredibly strong, which was how he'd pounded at the door so hard it shook the front hall. That also meant he healed better than most. For him to look this terrible, somebody really had to have beaten the hell out of him, over and over again, so he wouldn't have time to heal.

A jagged scar stretched across his chest, as if someone had tried to stab him, and it reminded me of my own scar that ran along my stomach. My host mother had tried to kill me when I was a child, but that felt like a lifetime ago.

I touched Loki's chest, running my fingers over the bumps of his scar. I didn't know why exactly, but I felt compelled to, as if the scar connected us somehow.

"You just couldn't wait to get me naked, could you, Princess?" Loki asked tiredly. I started to pull my hand back, but he put his own hand over it, keeping it in place.

"No, I—I was checking for wounds," I stumbled. I wouldn't meet his gaze.

"I'm sure." He moved his thumb, almost caressing my hand, until it hit my ring. "What's that?" He tried to sit up to see it, so I lifted my hand, showing him the emerald-encrusted oval on my finger. "Is that a wedding ring?"

"No, engagement." I lowered my hand, resting it on the bed next to him. "I'm not married yet."

"I'm not too late, then." He smiled and settled back in the bed.

"Too late for what?" I asked.

"To stop you, of course." Still smiling, he closed his eyes.

"Is that why you're here?" I asked, failing to point out how near we were to my nuptials.

"I told you why I'm here," Loki said.

"What happened to you, Loki?" I asked, my voice growing thick when I thought about what he had to have gone through to get all those marks and bruises.

"Are you crying?" Loki asked and opened his eyes.

"No, I'm not crying." I wasn't, but my eyes were moist.

"Don't cry." He tried to sit up, but he winced when he lifted his head, so I put my hand gently on his chest to keep him down.

"You need to rest," I said.

"I will be fine." He put his hand over mine again, and I let him. "Eventually."

"Can you tell me what happened?" I asked. "Why do you need amnesty?"

"Remember when we were in the garden?" Loki asked.

Of course I remembered. Loki had snuck in over the wall

and asked me to run away with him. I had declined, but he'd stolen a kiss before he left, a rather nice kiss. My cheeks reddened slightly at the memory, and that made Loki smile wider.

"I see you do." He grinned.

"What does that have to do with anything?" I asked.

"*That* doesn't," Loki said, referring to the kiss. "I meant when I told you that the King hates me. He really does, Wendy." His eyes went dark for a minute.

"The Vittra King did this to you?" I asked, and my stomach tightened. "You mean Oren? My father?"

"Don't worry about it now," he said, trying to calm the anger burning in my eyes. "I'll be fine."

"Why?" I asked. "Why does the King hate you? Why did he do this to you?"

"Wendy, please." He closed his eyes. "I'm exhausted. I barely made it here. Can we have this conversation when I'm feeling a bit better? Say, in a month or two?"

"Loki," I said with a sigh, but he had a point. "Rest. But we will talk tomorrow. All right?"

"As you wish, Princess," he conceded, and he was already drifting back to sleep again.

I sat beside him for a few minutes longer, my hand still on his chest so I could feel his heartbeat pounding underneath. When I was certain he was asleep, I slid my hand out from under his, and I stood up.

In the hall, I wrapped my arms around myself. I couldn't shake the heavy feeling of guilt, as if I somehow shared responsibility for what had happened to Loki. I'd only spoken to Oren once, and I had no control over what he did. So why did I feel like it was my fault that Loki had been so brutally beaten?

I wasn't in the hall for long when Duncan and Thomas approached. I'd wanted to alert as few people as possible to Loki's presence, but I trusted Thomas. Not just because he was the head guard and Finn's father. He'd once had an illicit affair with Elora, so I thought he was good at keeping secrets.

"The Vittra Markis is in there?" Thomas asked, but he was already looking past me into the room where Loki slept.

"Yes, but he's been through hell," I said, rubbing my arms as if I had a chill. "He's going to be out for a while."

"Duncan said he asked for amnesty." Thomas looked down at me. "Are you going to give it to him?"

"I'm not sure yet," I said. "He hasn't been able to talk much. But I'm letting him stay here for now, at least until he heals and we can have a conversation."

"How do you want us to handle this?" Thomas asked.

"We can't tell Elora. Not right now," I said.

The last time Loki had been here, he'd been held captive. We didn't have a real prison, so Elora had used her telekinesis to hold him in place, but that had weakened her so much it nearly killed her. In fact, she hadn't recovered from it yet, and there would be no way she could do it again.

Besides that, I didn't think Loki was really capable of causing trouble. Not in his present state, at least. And he'd come to us of his own free will. We didn't need to hold him.

"We need a guard stationed outside his door at all times,

just to be safe," I said. "I don't think he's a threat, but I won't take any chances with the Vittra."

"I can stand watch now, but somebody will have to relieve me of my post eventually," Thomas said.

"I can take over later," Duncan offered.

"No." Thomas shook his head. "You stay with the Princess."

"Do you have any other guards you can trust?" I asked.

Most of the guards seemed to be gossips, and when one of them heard something, they all knew it. But there were very few guards around to tell anymore, since most of them were out protecting changelings.

Thomas nodded. "I know of one or two."

"Good," I said. "Make sure they know they cannot tell anybody about this. This all needs to stay quiet until I figure out what I'm going to do. Is that clear?"

"Yes, Your Highness," Thomas said. It always felt strange hearing people refer to me as *Highness.*

"Thank you," I told him.

Tove arrived shortly after that with the mänks doctor. I waited outside the room while he examined Loki. He woke up for it, but offered very little explanation for his injuries. When the doctor was done, he concluded that Loki didn't have any serious ailments, and he gave him medication for pain.

"Come on," Tove said, after the doctor had gone. "He's resting now. There's nothing more you can do. Why don't you go enjoy your party?"

"I'll let you know if there's any change with him," Thomas promised.

"Thank you." I nodded, and walked down the hall toward my room with Tove and Duncan.

I hadn't felt like having a party before Loki crashed the palace, and I felt even less like having one now. But I had to at least try to have fun so I wouldn't hurt Willa's or Matt's feelings. I knew they had gone to a lot of trouble, so I would play the part of the happy birthday girl for them.

"The doctor thinks he'll be okay," Duncan said, responding to my solemn expression.

"I know," I said.

"Why are you so worried about him anyway?" Duncan asked. "I know that you two are friends or something, but I don't understand. He's a Vittra, and he kidnapped you once."

"I'm not worried," I said, cutting him off and forcing a smile. "I'm excited for the party."

Duncan directed me to the upstairs living room. It had been Rhys's playroom when he was little, and they'd converted it into a place to hang out when he became a teenager. But the ceilings still had murals of clouds and childish things, and the walls were lined with short white shelves that still held a few of his old toys.

When I opened the door, I was bombarded by streamers and balloons. A banner with the words "Happy Birthday" in giant glitter letters hung on the back wall.

"Happy birthday!" Willa shouted before I could step inside.

"Happy birthday!" Rhys and Rhiannon said in unison.

"Thanks, guys," I said, pushing a helium-filled balloon out

of my face so I could go in. "You guys know my birthday isn't actually until tomorrow?"

"Of course I know," Matt said, his voice a little high from inhaling helium. He had a deflated balloon in his hands, and he tossed it aside to walk over to me. "I was there when you were born, remember?"

He'd been smiling, but it faltered when he realized what he'd said. Rhys and I had been switched at birth. Matt had actually been there for Rhys's birth, not mine.

"Well, I was there when you came home from the hospital anyway," Matt said and hugged me. "Happy birthday."

"Thank you," I said, hugging him back.

"And I definitely know your birthday," Rhys said, walking over to us. "Happy birthday!"

I smiled. "Happy birthday to you too. How does it feel to be eighteen?"

"Pretty much exactly the same as it does being seventeen." Rhys laughed. "Do you feel any older?"

"No, not really," I admitted.

"Oh, come on," Matt said. "You've matured so much in the past few months. I hardly even recognize you anymore."

"I'm still me, Matt," I said, shifting uneasily from his compliment.

I knew that I'd grown up some. Even physically I'd changed. I wore my hair down more now because I'd finally managed to tame my curls after a lifetime of struggling with them. Since I was running a kingdom now, I had to play the part and wear dark-colored gowns all the time. I had to look like a Princess.

"It's a good thing, Wendy." Matt smiled at me.

"Stop." I waved my hand. "No more seriousness. This is supposed to be a party."

"Party!" Rhys shouted and blew into one of those cardboard horns they use on New Year's.

Once the party got under way, I actually did have fun. This was much better than if I'd had a birthday ball, since most of the people here wouldn't be able to go.

Matt wasn't even supposed to live in the palace, and since Rhys and Rhiannon were mänks, they would never be allowed to attend a ball. Duncan would be let in, but he'd have to work. He wouldn't be able to laugh and goof around like he did now.

"Wendy, why don't you help me cut the cake?" Willa suggested while Tove attempted to act out some kind of clue for charades. Duncan had guessed everything under the sun, but judging by Tove's comically frustrated response, he wasn't even close.

"Um, sure," I said.

I'd been sitting on the couch, laughing at everyone's failed attempts, but I got up and went over to the table where Willa stood. A cake sat on a brightly colored tablecloth, next to a small pile of gifts. Both Rhys and I had specifically asked for no gifts, but here they were.

"Sorry," Willa said. "I didn't mean to drag you away from the fun, but I wanted to talk to you."

"Nah, it's okay," I said.

"Your brother made the cake." Willa gave me an apologetic

smile as she sliced through the white frosting. "He insisted that it was your favorite."

Matt might be a very good cook, but I wasn't sure. I dislike most foods, especially processed ones, but Matt had been trying hard to feed me for years, so I pretended to like a lot of things I didn't like. My annual chiffon birthday cake was one of them.

"It's not horrible," I said, but it kind of was. At least to me, and Willa and all the other Trylle.

"I wanted to let you know that I didn't tell Matt about Loki." Willa lowered her voice as she carefully put pieces of cake on small paper plates. "He would just worry."

"Thank you," I said and looked back over at Matt, laughing at the ridiculous miming Tove was doing. "I suppose I'll have to tell him eventually."

"You think Loki will be around for a while?" Willa asked. She'd gotten some frosting on her finger, and she licked it off, then grimaced.

I nodded. "Yeah, I think he will be."

"Well, don't worry about it now," she said quickly. "This is your last day to be a kid!"

I tried to push all of the fears and concerns I had about the kingdom, and Loki, from my mind. And eventually, when I let myself, I had a really good time with my friends.

THREE

scars

My dreams were filled with bad winter storms. Snow blowing so hard I couldn't see anything. Wind so cold I froze to the bone. But I had to keep going. I had to get through the storms.

Duncan woke me up a little after nine the next morning. Usually I got up at six or seven to get ready for the day, depending on what time my first meetings were. Since it was my birthday, I'd slept in a bit, and it felt nice but strange.

He wouldn't have woken me at all, except Elora had requested to eat breakfast with me today since it was my birthday. I didn't mind being woken up, though. Sleeping in that late made me feel surprisingly lazy.

I didn't even really know what I would do with the day. It'd been so long since I'd had a full day that was free of plans. Either I was working on things for the kingdom, helping Aurora with the wedding plans, or spending time with Willa and Matt.

I met Elora in her bedroom for breakfast, which was usually where I saw her. She'd been in decline for a while, but even before Christmas she'd been on bed rest. Aurora had tried healing her a few times, but she was only staving off the inevitable.

On my way to Elora's chambers in the south wing, I walked past the room Loki was staying in. His bedroom door was closed, and Thomas stood guard outside. He nodded once as I walked by, so I assumed everything was still going all right.

Elora's bedroom was massive. The double doors to her room were floor-to-ceiling, so they were nearly two stories high. The room itself could easily fit two of my bedrooms in it, and my room was quite large. Making the room look even larger was a full wall of windows, although she kept the shades drawn most of the time, preferring the dim light of a bedside lamp.

To fill the space, she had several armoires, a writing desk, the largest bed I'd ever seen, and a sitting area complete with a couch, two chairs, and a coffee table. Today she had a small dining table with two chairs set up near the window. It was all laid out with fruit, yogurt, and oatmeal—my favorite things.

The last few times I'd visited with her, Elora had been in bed, but she sat at the table today. Her long hair had once been jet-black, but it was now silver-white. Her dark eyes were clouded with cataracts, and her porcelain skin had wrinkled. She was still elegant and beautiful, and I imagined she always would be, but she'd aged so much.

She was pouring herself tea when I came in, her silk dressing gown flowing behind her.

"Would you like some tea, Wendy?" Elora asked without looking up at me. She'd only recently begun calling me Wendy. For a long time she refused to call me anything but Princess, but our relationship had been changing.

"Yes, please," I said, sitting across from her at the table. "What kind is it?"

"Blackberry." She filled the small teacup in front of me, then set the teapot on the table. "I hope you're hungry this morning. I had the chef whip us up a feast."

"I'm quite hungry, thank you," I said, and my stomach rumbled as proof.

"Go ahead." Elora gestured to the spread. "Take what you'd like."

"Aren't you eating?" I asked as I got myself a helping of raspberries.

"I'm eating some," Elora said, but she made no move to get a plate. "How is your birthday?"

"Good, so far. But I haven't been awake that long."

"Is Willa throwing you a party?" Elora asked, picking absently at a plum. "Garrett told me something about it."

"Yeah, she had a little party for me last night," I said between bites. "It was really nice."

"Oh, I assumed she would have it today."

"Rhys had plans today, and I don't have that many friends, so she thought it would be better to do it last night."

"I see." Elora took a sip of her tea and said nothing more for several minutes. She only watched me as I ate, which would've made me self-conscious before, but I was starting to realize that she just enjoyed watching me.

"How are you feeling today?" I asked.

"I'm moving about." She gave a small shoulder shrug and turned to look out the window.

The shades were open slightly, letting the brilliant light shine in. The treetops outside were covered in a heavy blanket of snow, and the reflection made the sun twice as bright.

"You look good today," I commented.

"You look nice today too," Elora said without turning back to me. "That's a lovely color on you."

I glanced down at my dress. It was dark blue with black lace designs over it. Willa had picked it out for me, and I did think it was really beautiful. But I still hadn't gotten used to Elora complimenting me.

"Thank you," I said.

"Did I ever tell you about the day you were born?" Elora asked.

"No." I'd been eating vanilla yogurt, but I set the spoon down on a plate. "You only told me that it was hasty."

"You were early," she said, her voice low, as if she were lost in thought. "My mother did that. She used her persuasion, and convinced my body to go into labor. It was the only way we could protect you, but you were two weeks early."

"Was I born in a hospital?" I asked, realizing I knew so little about my own birth.

"No." She shook her head. "We went to the city your host

family lived in. Oren thought I was interested in a family that lived in Atlanta, but I'd chosen the Everlys, who lived in northern New York.

"My mother and I stayed in a hotel nearby, hiding out in case Oren came after us," Elora went on. "Thomas watched the Everlys closely until he saw the mother go into labor."

"Thomas?" I asked.

"Yes, Thomas went with us," Elora said. "That's how I met him, actually, when we were on the run from my husband. Thomas was a new tracker, but he'd already proven to be very resourceful, so my mother chose him to help us."

"So he was there when I was born?" I asked.

"Yes, he was." She smiled at the thought. "I gave birth to you on the floor of a hotel bathroom. Mother used her powers on me, induced labor, and made it so I wouldn't scream or feel pain. And Thomas sat at my side, holding my hand and telling me it would all be fine."

"Were you scared?" I asked. "Giving birth like that?"

"I was terrified," she admitted. "But I had no choice. I needed to hide you and protect you. It had to be done."

"I know," I said. "You did the right thing. I understand that now."

"You were so small." Her smile changed, and she tilted her head. "I didn't know you would be so tiny, and you were so beautiful. You were born with a dark shock of hair, and these big dark eyes. You were beautiful and you were perfect and you were mine."

She paused, thinking, and a lump grew in my throat. It felt

so strange to hear my mother talking about me the way a mother talks about her children.

"I wanted to hold you," Elora said at length. "I begged my mother to let me hold you, and she said it would only make it worse. She held you, though, wrapping you in a bedsheet and staring down at you with tears in her eyes.

"Then she left," she continued. "She took you to the hospital to leave you with the Everlys, and brought home another baby that wasn't mine. She wanted me to hold him, to care for Rhys. She said that it would make it easier. But I didn't want him. *You* were my child, and I wanted you."

Elora turned to look at me then, her eyes looking clearer than they had in a while. "I did want you, Wendy. Despite everything that happened between your father and me, I wanted you. More than anything in the world."

I didn't say anything to that. I couldn't. If I did, I would cry, and I didn't want her to see that. Even as open as she was being, I didn't know how she would react to me weeping outright.

"But I couldn't have you." Elora turned back to the window. "Sometimes it seems to me that that's all my life has been, a series of things that I loved deeply that I could never have."

"I'm sorry," I said in a small voice.

"Don't be." She waved it off. "I made my choices, and I did the best I could." She forced a smile. "And look at me. This is your birthday. I shouldn't be whining to you."

"You're not whining." I wiped at my eyes as discreetly as I could and took another sip of my tea. "And I'm glad you told me."

"Anyway, we need to talk about switching the rooms around," Elora said, brushing her hair back from her face. "I plan to leave most of my furniture in here, unless you'd like to change it, which is your prerogative, of course."

"Switching what rooms?" I asked, confused.

"You're taking my room after you get married." She motioned around us. "This is the wedding chamber."

"Oh, right. Of course." I shook my head to clear the confusion. "I've been so busy with everything else that I'd forgotten."

"It's no matter," she said. "It shouldn't be much work to move things around, since it will only be personal items we're moving in and out. I'll have some of the trackers move my things out Friday, and I'll be staying in the room down the hall."

"They can move my things in then," I said. "And Tove's things too, since he'll be sharing the room with me."

"How is that going?" Elora leaned back in her chair, studying me. "Are you prepared for the wedding?"

"Aurora is certainly prepared for it." I sighed. "But if you're asking if I'm prepared to be married, I'm not sure. I guess I'll wing it."

"You and Tove will be all right." She smiled at me. "I'm certain of it."

"You're certain?" I raised an eyebrow. "Did you paint it?" Elora had the ability of precognition, but she could only see her visions of the future in static images.

"No." She laughed, shaking her head. "It's mother's intuition."

I ate a little more, but she only picked at the food. We talked, and it was strange to think that I'd miss her when she was gone. I hadn't actually known her for very long, and most of that time our relationship had been cold.

When I left, she was climbing back in bed and asked me to send someone up to clean the mess from breakfast. Duncan had been waiting outside the door for me, so he went in to take care of it.

While Duncan was busy with the dishes, I stopped by Loki's room to see how he was feeling. If he was better, I wanted to find out what was going on.

Thomas was still outside, so I knocked once and opened the door without waiting for a response. Loki was in the middle of changing clothes as I came in. He'd already traded his worn slacks for a pair of pajama pants, and he was holding a white T-shirt, preparing to put it on.

He had his back to me, and it was even worse than I'd thought.

"Oh, my god, Loki," I gasped.

"I didn't know you were coming." He turned around to face me, smirking. "Shall I leave the shirt off, then?"

"No, put the shirt on," I said, and I closed the door behind me so nobody could see or overhear us talking.

"You're no fun." He wrinkled his nose and pulled the shirt over his head.

"Your back is horrific."

"And I was just going to tell you how beautiful you look today, but I'm not going to bother now if you're going to talk that way." Loki sat back down on his bed, more lying than sitting.

"I'm being serious. What happened to you?"

"I already told you." He stared down at his legs and picked at lint on his pants. "The King hates me."

"Why?" I asked, already feeling indignation at my father for doing this to him. "Why in god's name would he do something so brutal to you?"

"You clearly don't know your father," Loki said. "This isn't that brutal for him."

"How is it not brutal?" I sat down on the bed next to him. "And you're nearly a Prince! How can he treat you this way?"

"He's the King." He shrugged. "He does what he wants."

"But what about the Queen?" I asked. "Didn't she try to stop him?"

"She tried to heal me at first, but eventually that became too much for her. And there's only so much Sara can do to counter Oren."

Sara, the Queen of the Vittra, was my stepmother, but she'd once been betrothed to Loki. She was more than ten years older than him, and it was an arranged engagement that ended when he was nine. They were never romantic, and she had always considered Loki more of a little brother and protected him as such.

"Did he personally do that to you?" I asked quietly.

"What?" Loki looked up at me, his golden eyes meeting mine.

He had a scar on his chin, and I was certain he hadn't had that before. His skin had been flawless and perfect, not that the scar detracted in any way from how handsome he was.

"That." I touched the mark on his chin. "Did he do that to you?"

"Yes," he answered thickly.

"How?" I moved my hand, touched a mark he had on his temple. "How did he do this to you?"

"Sometimes he'd hit me." Loki kept his eyes on me, letting me trace my fingers on his scars. "Or he'd kick me. But usually he used a cat."

"You mean like a living cat?" I gave him an odd expression, and he smiled.

"No, it's actually called a cat-o'-nine-tails. It's like a whip, but instead of one tail, it has nine. It inflicts more damage than a regular whip."

"Loki!" I dropped my hand, totally appalled. "He would do that to you? Why didn't you leave? Did you fight back?"

"Fighting back wouldn't do any good, and I left as soon as I was able," Loki said. "That's why I'm here now."

"He held you prisoner?" I asked.

"I was locked up in the dungeon." He shifted and turned away from me. "Wendy, I'm glad to see you, but I'd really rather not talk about this anymore."

"You want me to grant you amnesty," I said. "I need to know why he did this to you."

"Why?" Loki laughed darkly. "Why do you think, Wendy?"

"I don't know!"

"Because of you." He looked back at me, a strange, crooked smile on his face. "I didn't bring you back."

"But . . ." I furrowed my brow. "You asked to go back to the Vittra. We bartered with the King so he could have you."

"Yes, well, he still thought you would come around." He ran a hand through his hair and sat up straighter. "And you didn't. It was my fault for letting you go in the first place, and then for not bringing you back." He bit his lip and shook his head. "He's determined to get you, Wendy."

"So he tortured you?" I asked quietly, trying to keep the tremor from my voice. "Over me?"

"Wendy." Loki sighed and moved closer to me. Gently, almost cautiously, he put his arm around me. "What happened isn't your fault."

"Maybe. But maybe this wouldn't have happened if I'd run away with you."

"You still can."

"No, I can't." I shook my head. "I have so much I need to do here. I can't just leave it all behind. But you can stay here. I will grant you amnesty."

"Mmm, I knew it." He smiled. "You'd miss me too much if I left."

I laughed. "Hardly."

"Hardly?" Loki smirked.

He'd lowered his arm, so his hand was on my waist. Loki was incredibly near, and his muscles pressed against me. I knew that I should move away, that I had no justifiable reason to be this close to him, but I didn't move.

"Would you?" Loki asked, his voice low.

"Would I what?"

"Would you run away with me, if you didn't have all the responsibilities and the palace and all that?"

"I don't know," I said.

"I think you would."

"Of course you do." I looked away from him, but I didn't move away. "Where did you get the pajamas, by the way? You didn't bring anything with you when you came."

"I don't want to tell you."

"Why not?" I looked sharply at him.

"Because. I'll tell you, and it will ruin this whole mood," Loki said. "Can't we just sit here and look longingly into each other's eyes until we fall into each other's arms, kissing passionately?"

"No," I said and finally started to pull away from him. "Not if you don't tell me—"

"Tove," Loki said quickly, trying to hang on to me. He was much stronger than me, but he let me push him off.

"Of course." I stood up. "That's exactly the kind of thing my fiancé would do. He's always thinking of other people."

"It's just pajamas!" Loki insisted, like that would mean something. "Sure, he's a terrifically nice guy, but that doesn't matter."

"How does that *not* matter?" I asked.

"Because you don't love him."

"I care about him," I said, and he shrugged. "And it's not like I love you."

"Maybe not," he allowed. "But you will."

"You think so?" I asked.

"Mark my words, Princess," Loki said. "One day, you'll be madly in love with me."

"Okay." I laughed, because I didn't know how else to respond. "But I should go. If I've given you amnesty, that means I have to go about enacting it, and getting everyone to agree that it's not a suicidal decision."

"Thank you."

"You're welcome," I said and opened the door to go.

"It was worth it," Loki said suddenly.

"What was?" I turned back to him.

"Everything I went through," he said. "For you. It was worth it."

FOUR

fiancé

My relaxing birthday turned into a meeting frenzy because I'd granted Loki amnesty. Most people thought I was insane, and Loki had to be brought in for questioning. They had a big meeting in which Thomas asked him lots of questions, and Loki answered them the same way he had for me.

But truthfully, he didn't have to explain much after he lifted his shirt and showed them the scars. After that, they let him go lie down.

I did have a nice, quiet dinner with Willa and Matt, and that was something. My aunt Maggie called, and I talked to her for a while. She wanted to come see me, but I'd been stalling the best I could. I hadn't explained to her what I was yet, but she knew I was safe with Matt.

I'd wanted her to come out for Christmas, and I'd planned on telling her about everything then. But then the Vittra started going after the changelings, and I thought they might go after her to get to me, so I postponed seeing her again.

She'd been traveling a lot, which was good, but it didn't keep her from wondering what was going on with me. I couldn't wait until this all calmed down so I could finally have her in my life again. I missed her so much.

After dinner, I went back to my room and watched bad eighties movies with Duncan. He had to stay with me sixteen hours a day, then the night watchman took over. I'd wanted to study, since Tove was teaching me Tryllic, but Duncan wouldn't let me. He insisted I needed to shut off my mind and relax.

Duncan fell asleep in my room, which wasn't unusual. Nobody said anything, since he was my guard, and it was better that he was with me. He probably wouldn't be able to sleep in my room after Saturday, which made me a little sad. I slept sprawled out in my bed, and Duncan was curled up on the couch, a blanket draped over him.

"It's Thursday," I said when I woke up. I was still in bed, staring at the ceiling.

"It certainly is." Duncan yawned and stretched.

"I only have two days until I get married."

"I know." He got up and opened the shades, letting a wall of light into my room. "What are you doing today?"

"I need to stay busy." I sat up and squinted in the brightness. "And I don't care what anybody says about me needing to relax and take time off. I have to keep active. So I think I'll train with Tove today."

Duncan shrugged. "At least you're spending quality time with your fiancé."

Whenever I thought about the wedding I got a sick feeling in my stomach. Sometimes, if I thought about it too much, I actually threw up. I don't think I'd ever been so afraid to do anything in my life.

I showered and ate a quick breakfast, then I went down to Tove's room to see if he wanted to do any training. I'd mostly gotten the hang of my abilities, and they weren't something I wanted to lose, so I practiced often to keep them strong.

Tove had moved into the palace after the Vittra had kidnapped me, to help keep things safe. He was actually much stronger than any of the guards here, and he may have even been stronger than me. His room was down the hall from mine, and the door was open when I stopped by.

A few cardboard boxes were scattered around the room, some of them empty, one with books overflowing from it. Another sat on the bed, where Tove was putting a few pairs of jeans in it.

"Going somewhere?" I asked, leaning on the door frame.

"No, just getting ready for the move." He pointed down the hall toward Elora's room—our new room. "For Saturday."

"Oh," I said. "Right."

"Do you need help with anything?" Duncan asked. He'd followed me down to Tove's, since he followed me everywhere.

Tove shrugged. "Sure, if you want."

Duncan went in and pulled out some of Tove's clothes from the drawer. I stayed where I was, hating how awkward everything felt between us. When we were training or talking politics, everything was good with Tove and me. We were almost always on the same page, and we talked openly about anything having to do with the palace or work.

But when it came to our wedding and our actual relationship, neither of us could ever find the words.

This may have had something to do with what Finn had told me a few months ago—namely, that Tove was gay. I had yet to bring this up with Tove, so I couldn't say that it was true for certain, but I believed that it probably was.

"Did you want to train today?" I asked Tove.

"Yeah, that'd be great, actually." Tove sounded relieved.

Training helped him a lot too. The palace was so full of people, and Tove could sense their thoughts and emotions, creating loud static in his head. Training silenced that and focused him, making him more like a normal person.

"Outside?" I suggested.

"Yeah." Tove nodded.

"But it's so cold out," Duncan lamented.

"Why don't you stay in here?" I asked. "You can finish packing up some of Tove's stuff." Duncan looked uncertain for a second, so I went on, "I'll be with Tove. We can handle ourselves."

"Okay," Duncan said, sounding reluctant. "But I'll be here if you need me."

Tove and I headed out back to the secret garden behind the palace. It wasn't really secret, I guess, but it felt that way since it was hidden behind trees and a wall. Even though a strong January storm had been blowing the last few days, the garden was peaceful.

The garden was magic. All the flowers still bloomed, despite the snow, and they sparkled like diamonds from the frost. The thin waterfall that flowed down the bluff should've frozen over, but it still ran, babbling.

A drift of snow had blown over the path. Tove simply held out his hand, and the snow moved to the sides, parting like the Red Sea. He stopped in the orchard under the branches of a tree covered with frozen leaves and blue flowers.

"What shall we do today?" Tove asked.

"I don't know," I said. "What are you in the mood for?"

"How about a snowball fight?" he asked with a wicked grin.

Using only his mind, he threw four snowballs at me. I held up my hands, pushing them back with my own telekinesis, and they shattered into puffs of snow from the force. It was my turn to sling a few back at him, but he stopped them just as easily as I had.

He returned fire, this time with even more snowballs, and while I stopped most of them, one of them slipped by and nicked me in the leg. I ran back, hiding behind a tree to make my counterattack.

Tove and I played around, throwing snow at each other, but it became increasingly hard as it went on. It looked like a game, and it was fun, but it was more than that. Stopping a slew of snowballs helped me learn to quickly stop multiple attacks from different directions. I tried to return fire even before I stopped the snowball, and that helped me learn how to fight back while defending myself.

Those were two completely different tasks, and they were difficult to master. I'd been working on this for a while, but couldn't get it down. In my defense, neither could Tove, but he didn't really think it was possible. My mind would have to be able to hold something back and throw something at the same time, which it could do, but doing both things at the *exact* same time was impossible.

When we were both sufficiently frozen and exhausted, I collapsed back in the snow. I'd worn pants and a sweater today because I knew we were training, but all that exertion always left me overheated, so the snow felt good.

"Is that a truce, then?" Tove asked, panting as he lay down in the snow next to me.

"Truce," I said, laughing a little.

We both lay back, our arms spread out wide as if we meant to make snow angels, but neither of us did. Catching our breath, we stared up at the clouds moving above us.

"If this is what our marriage will be like, it won't be so bad, will it?" Tove asked, and it was an honest question.

"No, it won't be so bad," I agreed. "Snowball fights I can handle."

"Are you nervous?" he asked.

"A little." I turned my head to face him, pressing my cheek into the snow. "Are you?"

"Yeah, I am." He furrowed his brow, staring thoughtfully at the sky. "I think I'm most scared of the kiss. It will be our first time, and in front of all those people."

"Yeah," I said, and my stomach twisted at the thought. "But you can't really mess up a kiss."

"Do you think we should?" Tove asked, and he looked over at me.

"Kiss?" I asked. "You mean when we get married? I think we kind of have to."

"No, I mean, do you think we should *now*?" Tove sat up, propping himself up with his arms behind him. "Maybe it will make it a bit easier on Saturday."

"Do you think we should?" I asked, sitting too. "Do you want to?"

"I feel like we're in the third grade right now." He sighed and brushed snow off his pants. "But you're going to be my wife. We'll have to kiss."

"Yeah, we will."

"Okay. Let's do it." He smiled thinly at me. "Let's just kiss."

"Okay."

I swallowed hard and leaned forward. I closed my eyes, since it felt less embarrassing if I didn't have to see him. His lips were cold, and the kiss was chaste. It only lasted a moment, and my stomach swirled with nerves, but not the pleasurable kind.

"Well?" Tove asked, sitting up straighter.

"It was all right." I nodded, more to convince myself than him.

"Yeah, it was good." He licked his lips and looked away from me. "We can do this. Right?"

"Yeah," I said. "Of course we can. If anybody can, it's us. We're like the most powerful Trylle ever. And we're neat people. We can handle spending the rest of our lives with each other."

"Yeah," Tove said, sounding more encouraged by the prospect. "In fact, I'm looking forward to it. I like you. You like me. We have fun together. We agree on almost everything. We're going to be the best husband and wife ever."

"Yeah, totally," I chimed in. "Marriage is about friendship anyway."

"And it's not like people in our positions get to choose who they want to be with," Tove added, and I think I heard a hint of sadness in his voice. "But at least we get to be with someone we enjoy."

We both lapsed into silence after that, staring off at the snow, lost in our own thoughts. I wasn't sure exactly what Tove was thinking. I wasn't even sure what I was thinking.

I guess it didn't make much of a difference that Tove was gay. Even if he wasn't, it didn't change my feelings for him. We could still form a strong union and have a meaningful marriage in our own way. He deserved nothing less, and I could give that to him.

"Should we go in?" Tove asked abruptly. "I'm getting cold."

"Yeah, me too."

He got up and then took my hand, pulling me to my feet.

He didn't need to, but it was a nice gesture. We went into the palace together, neither of us saying anything, and I twisted at my engagement ring. The metal was icy from the snow, and it suddenly felt too large and heavy on my finger. I wanted to take it off and give it back, but I couldn't.

FIVE

plans

I snuck in a copy of the Tryllic workbook Tove had gotten for me so I had something to do while Aurora went over all the last-minute details. It was the day before the wedding, so I hoped everything was on track. We didn't have time for anything else.

I sat in a chair with the book open on my lap while Aurora and Willa went over a checklist with about twenty wedding planners. Aurora had even put Duncan to work counting table centerpieces to make sure we had enough.

Sometimes they asked for my help, and I gave it, but I think Aurora was happier when I didn't have input so she could run the show.

All my bridesmaids were there, and most of them I'd never even met. Willa was my maid of honor, and she'd chosen the rest of the wedding party because she knew them. Aurora insisted that this had to be huge, so I had ten bridesmaids.

"It's the wedding of the century, and you're studying," Willa said with a sigh as the day drew to a close. Aurora had checked everything twice, and the only people left in the room were me, Willa, Aurora, and Duncan.

"I need to know this." I gestured to the book. "This is essential to being able to decipher old treaties. I don't need to know about lavish party planning. You and Aurora have that covered."

"That we do." Willa smiled. "I think everything's all set. You're going to have a fantastic day tomorrow."

"Thank you," I said and closed the book. "I really do appreciate everything you've done."

"Oh, come on, I loved it." She laughed. "If I can't have a fairy-tale wedding, at least I can plan one, right?"

"Just because you're not a Princess doesn't mean you can't have a fairy-tale wedding," I said and stood up.

She gave me a pained smile, and I realized what I'd said. Willa was a Marksinna dating my brother Matt, a human, and if anybody found out, she'd be banished. She wasn't even supposed to date him, let alone marry him.

"Sorry," I said.

"Don't be." She waved it off. "You're doing the best you can, and we all know it."

She was referring to my efforts for more equality among the Trylle, trackers, and mänks. We were losing a lot of our population because they fell in love with humans and then they were exiled. Nobody was staying around.

From any standpoint, it made more sense to let people love

who they loved. They were going to anyway, so if we stopped making it illegal, they would stick around more often and contribute to society.

I hadn't done much to convince people of this yet, because I was too busy struggling with the Vittra problem. Once we got it fixed (*if* we ever got it fixed), I would make equal rights for everyone in Förening my top priority.

"Are we all done here, then?" I asked.

"Yep," Willa said. "You've got nothing left to do except get some rest, and get pretty tomorrow before the wedding. Then you just have to say 'I do.'"

"I think I can handle that," I said, but I wasn't sure I could.

"Are you all right by yourself, Aurora?" Willa asked as we headed to the door.

"I'm just finishing a few things up," Aurora said without looking up from the papers she was going over. "Thank you, though."

"Thanks," I said. "I'll see you tomorrow, then."

"Sleep well, Princess." Aurora glanced up to smile at me.

Duncan and I walked Willa out, and she kept trying to convince me tomorrow would be fun. At the front door, she hugged me tightly and promised that everything would work out the way it was meant to.

I didn't know why that was supposed to be comforting. What if everything was meant to be a disaster? Knowing that it was meant to be horrible wouldn't make it any better.

"Do you want me to go in with you?" Duncan asked when we got to my bedroom.

"Not tonight." I shook my head. "I think I need some time to myself."

"I understand." He smiled reassuringly at me. "I'll see you in the morning, then."

"Thank you."

I shut the door behind me and flicked on my light, and I stared down at the giant ring on my finger. It signified that I belonged to Tove, to somebody I didn't love. I went over to my dresser to take off my jewelry, but I kept staring at the ring.

I couldn't help myself, and I pulled it off. It was really beautiful, and when Tove gave it to me it had been so sweet. But I'd begun to hate the band.

When I took it off, I glanced in the mirror behind the dresser, and I nearly screamed when I saw the reflection. Finn was sitting behind me on the bed. His eyes, dark as night, met mine in the mirror, and I could hardly breathe.

"Finn!" I gasped and whirled around to look at him. "What are you doing here?"

"I missed your birthday," he said, as if that answered my question. He lowered his eyes, looking at a small box he had in his hands. "I got you something."

"You got me something?" I leaned back on the dresser behind me, gripping it.

"Yeah." He nodded, still staring down at the box. "I picked it up outside of Portland two weeks ago. I meant to get back in time to give it to you on your birthday." He chewed the inside of his cheek. "But now that I'm here, I'm not sure I should give it to you at all."

"What are you talking about?" I asked.

"It doesn't feel right." Finn rubbed his face. "I don't even know what I'm doing here."

"Neither do I," I said. "Don't get me wrong. I'm happy to see you. I just . . . I don't understand."

"I know." He sighed. "It's a ring. What I got you." His gaze moved from me to the engagement ring sitting on the dresser beside me. "And you already have one."

"Why did you get me a ring?" I asked tentatively, and my heart beat erratically in my chest. I didn't know what Finn was saying or doing.

"I'm not proposing to you, if that's what you're asking." He shook his head. "I saw it and thought of you. But now it seems like poor taste. And here I am, the night before your wedding, sneaking in to give you a ring."

"Why did you sneak in?" I asked.

"I don't know." He looked away and laughed darkly. "That's a lie. I know exactly what I'm doing, but I have no idea *why* I'm doing it."

"What are you doing?" I asked quietly.

"I . . ." Finn stared off for a moment, then turned back to me and stood up.

"Finn, I—" I began, but he held up his hand, stopping me.

"No, I know you're marrying Tove," he said. "You need to do this. We both know that. It's what's best for you, and it's what I want for you." He paused. "But I want you for myself too."

All I'd ever wanted from Finn was for him to admit how he

felt about me, and he'd waited until the day before my wedding. It was too late to change anything, to take anything back. Not that I could have, even if I wanted to.

"Why are you telling me this?" I asked with tears swimming in my eyes.

"Because." Finn stepped toward me, stopping right in front of me.

He looked down at me, his eyes mesmerizing me the way they always did. He reached up, brushing back a tear from my cheek.

"Why?" I asked, my voice trembling.

"I needed you to know," he said, as if he didn't truly understand it himself.

He set the box on the dresser beside me, and his hand went to my waist, pulling me to him. I let go of the dresser and let him. My breath came out shallow as I stared up at him.

"Tomorrow you will belong to someone else," Finn said. "But tonight, you're with me."

His mouth pressed against mine, kissing me with that same rugged fierceness I had come to know and love. I wrapped my arms around him, gripping him as tightly as I could. He lifted me up, still keeping his lips on mine as he carried me over to the bed.

Finn lowered me down, and he was on top of me within seconds. I loved the feel of his body on mine, the weight of it pushing against me. His stubble scraped my skin as he covered my face and neck with kisses.

His hands went to the straps of my dress, pulling them

down, and I realized with some surprise how far things might actually go tonight. He'd always put the brakes on things before they got too heated, but his hands were cupping my breasts as he kissed me.

I reached up, unbuttoning his shirt so fast, one of the buttons snapped off. I ran my hands over his chest, delighting in the smooth contours of his muscles and the pounding of his heart. He leaned down, kissing me hungrily again, and his bare skin pressed to mine.

His skin smoldered against me, his mouth searched mine, and his arm was around me, holding me tighter still.

As we kissed, my heart swelled with happiness, and a surge of relief washed over me when I realized my first time would be with Finn. But that thought was immediately darkened when I realized something else.

My very first time might be with Finn, but it would also be my last time with him.

I still had to marry Tove tomorrow. And even if I didn't marry him, I could never be with Finn.

The last time I had really seen Finn was the night before my engagement party, nearly three months ago, when we kissed in the library. He'd been horrified by what he'd done, that he'd let himself choose a moment with me over duty, even for a second. He'd left the palace as soon as he had a chance.

He'd volunteered for the mission to track down the other changelings, and part of me knew it was to get away from me. We'd barely said a word to each other in months. I had been taking over the palace, making the most difficult decisions of my life, and I'd done it all without him.

If I slept with Finn now, that was exactly what would happen again, the same thing that always happened whenever we got close. He would vanish immediately afterward. He'd hide away in disgrace and avoid me.

And I couldn't bear that this time. He was asking me to give myself to him completely, and he'd never be willing to do the same. He would only disappear from my life again. I needed him to be here with me, by my side, instead of leaving in shame. I needed Finn to choose me over honor, and the best he could offer me was one night.

Even if I spent the night with him, it wouldn't mean anything. He would be gone tomorrow, I would marry Tove just as Finn would want me to, and I'd be even more heartbroken than before.

"What's wrong?" Finn asked, noticing a change in me.

"I can't," I whispered. "I'm sorry, but I can't do this."

"You're right. I'm sorry." Finn looked ashamed, and he scrambled to get off me. "I don't know what I was thinking. I'm sorry." He stood and hurriedly buttoned his shirt.

"No, Finn." I sat up, adjusting my dress. "You don't have to be sorry, but . . . I can't do this anymore."

"I understand." He smoothed out his hair and looked away from me.

"No, Finn, I mean . . ." I swallowed hard and let out a shaky breath. "I can't love you anymore."

He looked up at me, his eyes startled and hurt, but he said nothing. He only stood there for a moment.

"You said that I belong to somebody else tomorrow but you tonight, and that's not how it works, Finn." Tears slid down my cheeks, and I wiped them away. "I don't belong to anyone, and you don't get to just have a part of me when you can't help yourself.

"And I know that's never what you meant to do," I said. "Neither of us meant for things to end up this way. We were together when we could be. Hidden moments and stolen kisses. I get that. And I don't blame you or anything, but . . . I can't do it anymore."

"I hadn't . . ." Finn trailed off. "I never wanted this for you. I mean, this thing we've had going on, whatever it's been. You deserve more than I would ever be able to give you, more than I would ever be allowed to love you."

"I'm trying to change things," I said. "And I'll admit that part of it has been selfish. I wanted to repeal the laws so maybe someday we could have a chance to be together. But . . . I can't count on that. And even if I could, I am marrying somebody else tomorrow."

"I wouldn't expect any less of you, Princess," he said quietly. "I'm sorry to have disturbed you." He walked to the door and paused before leaving, but he didn't look back at me. "I wish you all the best for your marriage. I hope the two of you find nothing but happiness."

After Finn left, I tried not to cry. Willa would be so upset with me if my face was red and puffy tomorrow. I went into my closet, fighting back tears as I changed out of my gown and put on pajamas. On my way back to my bed, I noticed the small box on my dresser, the present from Finn.

Slowly, I opened the box. It was a thin silver band with my birthstone, a garnet, in the center of a heart. And for some reason, the sight of it broke me down. I lay down on my bed and sobbed, mourning a relationship I'd never even really been able to have.

SIX

altar

I wanted Matt to walk me down the aisle. He'd been the closest thing I had to a real parent for most of my life, but the other Trylle officials would have had a field day if he did. Marksinna Laris would probably get me overthrown on the grounds of insanity.

But at least Marksinna Laris and the other Trylle had no control over who I allowed in my dressing room. Duncan had been waiting outside my bedroom all morning, shooing anybody away who wasn't Willa or Matt. Everybody else could wait to see me until I was in the ballroom, with Willa's father Garrett giving me away.

I'd been ready for hours. After ending things with Finn, I hadn't really been able to sleep, and the sun hadn't even risen by the time I got up and started getting ready. Willa had come over early to help me, but I'd learned how to do my hair and makeup on my own. She really only helped button up my wedding gown, and she tried to comfort me, but that was all I needed.

"You're so pale," Willa said, almost sadly. "You're almost as white as your wedding dress."

She sat next to me on the chest at the foot of my bed. The long satin train of my gown swirled around us, and Willa continuously rearranged it to make sure it wouldn't get wrinkled or dirty. Her dress was lovely too, but it should be, since she picked it out. It was dark emerald with black embellishments.

"Stop fussing over her," Matt said when Willa once again tried to smooth out my dress. He'd been pacing the room, fiddling with his cuff links or pulling at the collar of his shirt.

"I'm not fussing." Willa gave him the evil eye but left my dress alone. "This is her wedding day. I want her to look perfect."

"You're making her nervous." Matt gestured to me, since I'd been staring off into space.

"If anyone's making her nervous, it's you," she countered. "You've been pacing around this room all morning."

"Sorry." He stopped moving but didn't look any less agitated. "My kid sister's getting married. And it's a lot sooner than I expected." He ruffled his short blond hair again and sighed. "You don't have to do this, Wendy. You know that, right? If you don't want to marry him, you don't have to. I mean, you shouldn't. You're too young to make a life decision like this anyway."

"Matt, she knows," Willa said. "You've only told her that exact same thing a thousand times today."

"Sorry," Matt repeated.

"Princess?" Duncan cautiously opened the door and poked his head inside the room. "You asked me to get you at a quarter to one, and it's a quarter to one now."

"Thank you, Duncan," I said.

"Well?" Willa looked at me, smiling. "Are you ready?"

"I think I'm going to throw up," I told her honestly.

"You won't throw up. It's just nerves, and you'll do fine," Willa said.

"Maybe it's not nerves," Matt said. "Maybe she doesn't want to go through with this."

"Matt!" Willa snapped, and she looked back at me. Her brown eyes were warm and concerned. "Wendy, do you want to do this?"

"Yes," I said firmly and nodded once. "I want to do this."

"Okay." She stood up. Smiling, she held her hand out to me. "Let's get you married, then."

I took her hand, and she squeezed it reassuringly when I got up. Duncan stood by the door, waiting for us, and when I started walking, he came over to gather the train so it wouldn't drag on the ground.

"Wait," Matt said. "This is the last moment I'll have to talk to you before this, so, um, I just wanted to say . . ." He fumbled for a minute and pulled at his sleeve. "There's so much I wanted to say, actually. I've watched you grow up so much, Wendy. And you were a brat." He laughed nervously at that, and I smiled.

"And you've blossomed right in front of me," he said. "You're strong and smart and compassionate and beautiful. I couldn't be more proud of the woman you've become."

"Matt." I wiped quickly at my eyes.

"Matt, don't make her cry," Willa said, and she sniffled a little.

"I'm sorry," Matt said. "I didn't mean to make you cry, and I know you've got to get down there. But I wanted to say that no matter what happens, today, tomorrow, whenever, you'll always be my little sister, and I'll always be on your side. I love you."

"I love you too," I said, and I hugged him.

"That was really sweet," Willa said when he let me go. She gave him a quick kiss on the lips before ushering me out of the room. "But I wish you'd said that sometime in the past hour when we were doing nothing. Now we really have to book."

Fortunately, we never wore shoes, which made it easier to jog down to the ballroom. Before we even reached it, I could hear the music playing. Aurora had a live orchestra playing "Moonlight Sonata," and I heard the murmurs of the guests accompanying it.

The bridesmaids and groomsmen were lined up outside the doors, waiting until I arrived to enter. Garrett smiled when he saw me. He'd always been kind to me, so I'd chosen him to walk me down the aisle.

"Be gentle with her, Dad," Willa said as she handed me off to him. "She's nervous."

"Don't worry." Garrett grinned, looping his arm through mine. "I promise I won't let you fall or stumble all the way down the aisle."

"Thank you." I forced a smile at him.

One of my bridesmaids handed me my bouquet of lilies. I felt a bit better gripping on to something, as if it kept me anchored.

As the wedding party walked down the aisle, I kept swallowing, trying desperately to fight back the nausea that overwhelmed me. It was only Tove. There was nothing to be afraid of. He was one of the few people in the world I actually trusted. I could do this. I could marry him.

Willa gave me a small wave before she turned down the aisle. Duncan was behind me, straightening my train out the best he could, but the music hit a crescendo, and it was my turn to go. Duncan stepped back from my dress, and he and Matt gave me encouraging smiles. They didn't want to sneak into the service now, so they'd have to wait outside the ballroom, watching from the back.

I stepped out on the green velvet carpet running down the aisle, littered with white rose petals from a flower girl, and I thought I might faint. It didn't help that the carpet seemed to go on for miles. The ballroom was packed with people, and they all stood and turned to face me when I entered.

Rhys and Rhiannon were in the very back row, and Rhiannon waved madly when she saw me. I'd met many of these people while running the palace, but I had so few friends here. Tove stood at the altar, looking almost as nervous as I felt, and that made me feel better somehow. We were both scared, but we were in this together.

Elora sat near the front, the only person in attendance not standing, but she was probably too weak to stand. I was just happy that she'd been able to make it here, and she smiled at me as I walked past. It was a genuine smile, and it pulled at my heart.

I walked the two steps up the altar, away from Garrett, and Tove took my hand. He squeezed it and offered me a subtle smile as I stood next to him. Willa moved around behind me, smoothing out my dress again.

"Hey," Tove said.

"Hey," I said.

"You may be seated," Markis Bain said. On top of being in charge of changeling placement, he was certified to perform Trylle weddings. He stood in front of us, dressed in a white suit, smiling nervously, and his blue eyes seemed to linger on Tove for a moment.

The guests sat down behind us, but I tried not to think of them. I tried not to think about how I had scanned the crowd, but I'd been unable to see Finn in their numbers. His father was here, standing guard near the door, but Finn had probably left again. He had work to do, and things were over between us.

"Dearly beloved," Markis Bain said, interrupting my thoughts. "We are gathered here to join this Princess and this Markis in holy matrimony, which is commended to be honorable among all Trylle. Therefore it is not to be entered into unadvisedly or lightly—but reverently, discreetly, and solemnly."

He opened his mouth to say more, but a loud banging sound shook the palace. I jumped and looked back at the door, the same way everyone did. Matt was standing just outside the open doors, but Duncan had run down the hall.

"What was that?" Willa asked, echoing the thoughts of everybody in the room.

"Princess!" Duncan yelled, and he appeared in the doorway. "They're coming for you."

"What?" I asked.

I tossed my bouquet aside, gathered my skirt, and raced from the altar. Willa called my name, but I ignored her. I'd only made it halfway down the aisle when I heard the gravelly boom of Oren's voice.

"We're not coming for anyone," Oren said. "If this were dirty work, I wouldn't be here."

I stopped in the aisle, unsure of what to do next, and Oren stepped into view. Duncan and Matt rushed at him, but the two Vittra guards Oren had with him grabbed them both. As soon as the guards touched Matt, I raised my hand and, using my abilities, I sent them flying backward. They slammed into the back wall, and I kept my hand up, holding them in place.

Oren smiled. "Impressive, Princess."

He clapped his hands at that, the sound muffled by his black leather gloves. His long, dark hair shimmered the way Elora's once had, but his eyes were black as coal.

I hadn't meant to leave him standing. I'd wanted to send

him falling back, so he could feel the force of what I could do, but he hadn't. The Vittra were stronger than the Trylle, Oren especially, and Tove had warned me that my abilities might be useless on him.

Matt and Duncan stood up, dazed by the immediacy of my response. Sara, Oren's wife, stood to his side but a bit behind him. She lowered her eyes and kept still. Both she and Oren wore all black, an odd choice for a wedding.

"What do you want?" I asked.

"What do I want?" Oren laughed and held his arms out to the side. "It's my only daughter's wedding." He took a step forward, and I let the guards go, so they fell to the floor. I wanted to be able to focus all my energy on Oren if need be.

"Stop," I commanded, holding my hand palm-out to him. "If you take another step, I will send you soaring through the ceiling."

The ballroom ceiling was made entirely of glass, so that wasn't as remarkable as it sounded, especially since I wasn't even sure I could do it. I could feel Tove standing a few feet behind me, though, and that gave me more confidence.

"Now, Princess." Oren made a *tsk* sound. "Is that any way to greet your father?"

"Considering you've kidnapped me and tried to kill me, yes, I think this is the only appropriate greeting," I said.

"*I* never did anything." Oren put his hands to his chest. "But look at me now. I've come without an army. Just my wife and two guards to help me travel. Nothing else. I assure you, Princess, I plan to uphold our treaty as long as you do.

I will refrain from attacking you or any of your people on the Förening grounds. Provided, of course, that you do the same."

His eyes sparkled at that. He was taunting me. He wanted me to launch an attack, to hurt him, so they could fight back. If I did this, I would start an all-out war between the Vittra and Trylle, and we weren't ready.

I might be able to defend myself and a few of the people, but most of our guards and trackers were gone. If Oren had any other Vittra waiting in the wings outside of Förening, the Trylle would be slaughtered. My wedding would turn into a bloodbath.

"In standing with our treaty, I ask that you leave the grounds," I said. "This is a private affair, and you were not invited."

"But I came to give you away," Oren said, pretending to be hurt. "I traveled all this way just for you."

"You're too late," I said. "And I was never yours in the first place, so you have no right to give me away."

"So who here has possessed you so much that they have a right to give you away?" Oren asked.

"Oren!" Elora shouted, and everyone in the room turned to look at her. "Leave her alone." She stood at the other end of the aisle, near the altar, and Garrett stood behind her. I'm sure it was to catch her in case she collapsed, but it looked like he was merely being supportive.

"Ah, my Queen." Oren smiled wickedly at her. "There you are."

"You've had your fun," Elora said. "Now be on your way. We've tolerated you enough."

"Look at you." He chuckled to himself. "You really let yourself go, didn't you? Now you look like the old hag I always knew you were."

"Enough!" I snapped at him. "I've asked you kindly to leave. I will not ask you again."

He sized me up, gauging my sincerity, and I kept my expression as hard as I could. Finally, he shrugged, as if it were nothing to him.

"Suit yourself, Princess," he said. "But by the looks of your mother, it won't be much longer until you're Queen. So I will be seeing you soon."

He turned to leave, and I lowered my hand, then he stopped.

"One more thing, Princess." Oren looked back at me. "I believe a piece of my trash has washed up here. He's been a horrible pain, but he does belong to me, so I would like him returned."

"I'm certain I don't know what you're talking about," I said, knowing that I would never turn Loki over to him. I'd seen what he'd done to Loki, and I wouldn't let it happen again.

"If he should turn up," Oren said, and I couldn't tell if he believed me or not, "send him my way."

"Of course," I lied.

Oren turned and stalked out, not even waiting for Sara. She gave me an ashamed smile before chasing after him. His guards finally picked themselves up off the floor and hurried to catch up. I heard him say something as they disappeared, but I couldn't understand him.

Duncan stayed in the doorway, and using my mind-speak I told him to make sure that Oren and Sara were really gone.

Everyone else was looking to me, waiting to see my reaction. I wanted to wilt, to let out a sigh of relief, but I couldn't do that. I couldn't let them know how rattled I was, that I'd been terrified that my father would kill us, and I would be unable to do anything to stop him.

"Sorry about the interruption," I said, my voice astonishingly even, and I gave all my guests my most polite smile. "But with that over, I believe we have a wedding to get on with." I turned to Tove, still smiling. "Assuming you'll still have me."

He returned my smile. "Of course."

He held out his arm, and I took it. As we walked back down the aisle, the orchestra began playing "Moonlight Sonata" again.

"How are you holding up?" Tove asked quietly as we climbed the altar stairs.

"Good," I whispered. "Getting married doesn't seem all that scary anymore."

We stood in front of Markis Bain, and I glanced back over my shoulder. Duncan stood in the doorway, and he mouthed the words *All clear.* I smiled appreciatively at him and turned back to the Markis.

"Shall we start with the vows, then?" Markis Bain asked. "Princess, Markis, turn and face each other."

I turned to Tove, forcing a smile and hoping he couldn't hear the pounding of my heart. With a few simple words and an exchange of rings, I vowed to take him as my husband until death. We sealed it with a quick kiss, and the guests erupted in applause.

SEVEN

interlude

Thankfully, between the wedding and the reception there was a brief interlude in which they cleared out the chairs and set up the tables and the dance floor. I wasn't sure where new brides were supposed to spend that time, but I spent mine locked in the nearest bathroom with Willa.

I splashed cold water on my face, and that helped clear my head, even if it did drive Willa nuts. I dried off my face with a paper towel once I felt better, and she frantically reapplied my makeup.

We left the bathroom in time for Tove and me to make our grand entrance as husband and wife. When we walked in, Garrett stood up and introduced us as Prince Tove and Princess Wendy Kroner, and everyone applauded again.

I wasn't sure how they'd done it in such a short time, but the ballroom looked amazing. If I'd been the kind of girl to imagine a fairy-tale wedding, this was exactly how I would've pictured it. The chandeliers that were lit during the ceremony had been shut off, so the room twinkled with fairy lights strung everywhere. Candles glowed on the tables. The whole room smelled of lilies from all the flowers.

While everyone watched, Tove and I danced our first dance to "At Last" by Etta James. I'd let him choose it, and he was an Etta James fan. We did dance well together, thanks to the countless lessons Willa made us go through to be sure we were perfect, but we didn't twirl around the room like magic.

When we finished the dance, the orchestra resumed, playing something by Bach. I would've been happy to spend the night dancing with Tove, but as soon as the song ended, everyone gathered on the floor. I would have to dance with anyone who asked.

Garrett stole the next dance with me, and Aurora danced with Tove. My own mother probably wouldn't dance with him, but she was still here for the reception. I imagined she would stay all night, no matter how weak or tired she got. After that comment Oren had made, she had to prove that she still had it, even if she really didn't.

Willa cut in to dance with me once, which was nice. She made me laugh, and that felt really good. I carried all my tension in my shoulders, and I knew they would ache like mad by the end of the night.

I caught sight of Matt, Rhys, Rhiannon, and Duncan sitting at a table in the back when a Markis was spinning me about. I wanted to escape from the dance to spend a few moments with them, but if I stopped dancing, it only meant I'd have to go table to table and talk to people. That was the only thing I could think of that would be worse than dancing.

I was annoyed and surprised to find out how many people used this opportunity to talk to me about some bill they wanted to pass, what family they wanted their child placed with, or to complain about taxes. Even though everything in my life had become politically motivated, it would've been nice to have a few dances where I could pretend that it wasn't.

The Chancellor cut in to dance with me, naturally, and I did my best to stay at arm's length, but he kept trying to press me to him. It was hard to stay away from his sweaty torso anyway, because his belly was so rotund. His massive hand would probably leave a sweat stain on my back from trying to hold me to him.

"You look very, very lovely tonight, Princess," the Chancellor said, and I hated the hungry way he looked at me. It made my skin crawl.

"Thank you." I smiled only because I had to, but it was difficult.

"I do wish you would've taken me up on my offer, though." He licked his lips, which were already damp with perspiration. "Remember? The last time we danced together, I suggested that you and I—"

"Excuse me," Tove said, appearing at my side. "I'd like to dance with my wife, if you don't mind."

"Yes, of course." The Chancellor bowed and stepped away, but he didn't bother to mask the irritation on his blubbery face.

"Thank you," I said as Tove took my hand in his.

"Do not dance with him anymore," Tove said, sounding exasperated. "I beg of you. Stay as far away from him as you can."

"With pleasure," I said and gave him an odd look. "Why?"

"That man is insufferable." He grimaced and glanced back at the Chancellor, who was already shoving another piece of wedding cake in his mouth. "He has the most perverse, vile thoughts I've ever heard. And he gets so much louder when he's close to you. The disgusting things he would do to you . . ." Tove actually shivered at that.

"What?" I asked. "How do you know? I thought you couldn't read thoughts."

"I can't," Tove said. "I can only hear when people are projecting, and he projects when he's excited, apparently. What makes it worse is that I spent all day moving things so my abilities would be weak. I can barely hear anything. But I hear him loud and clear."

"He's that bad?" I asked, feeling grossed out that I had let the Chancellor touch me.

Tove nodded. "He's horrible. As soon as we get a chance, we have got to get him out of office. Out of Förening, if possible. I don't want him anywhere near our people."

"Yes, definitely," I agreed. "I've already been working on a plan to get rid of him."

"Good," Tove said, then smiled at me. "We're already working together."

A murmur ran through the crowd, and I looked around to see what all the fuss was about. Then I saw him, walking past table after table as if everybody weren't stopping to stare at him.

Loki had ventured down from where he'd been hiding in the servants' quarters. Since I'd granted him amnesty, he was no longer being guarded and was free to roam as he pleased, but I hadn't exactly invited him to the wedding.

As Tove and I danced, I didn't take my eyes off Loki. He walked around the dance floor toward the refreshments, but he kept watching me. He got a glass of champagne from the table, and even as he drank his eyes never left me.

Another Markis came over and cut in to dance with me, but I barely noticed when I switched partners. I tried to focus on the person I was dancing with. But there was something about the way Loki looked at me, and I couldn't shake it.

The song had switched to something contemporary, probably the sheet music that Willa had slipped the orchestra. She'd insisted the whole thing would be far too dull if they only played classical.

The murmur died down, and people returned to dancing and talking. Loki took another swig of his champagne, then set the glass down and walked across the dance floor. Everyone parted around him, and I wasn't sure if it was out of fear or respect.

He wore all black, even his shirt. I had no idea where he'd gotten the clothes, but he did look debonair.

"May I have this dance?" Loki asked my dance partner, but his eyes were on me.

"Um, I don't know if you should," the Markis fumbled, but I was already moving away from him.

"No, it's all right," I said.

Uncertainly, the Markis stepped back, and Loki took my hand. When he placed his hand on my back, a shiver ran up my spine, but I tried to hide it and put my hand on his shoulder.

"You know, you weren't invited to this," I told him, but he merely smirked as we began dancing.

"So throw me out."

"I might." I raised my head defiantly, and that only made him laugh.

"If it's as the Princess wishes," he said, but he made no move to step away, and for some odd reason, I felt relieved.

"You didn't hear about the ceremony, then?" I asked, hoping to keep him from running off. "Oren came to wish me well."

"I heard one of the guards talking about it," Loki said, his caramel eyes growing serious. "They said you did well and that you stood up for yourself."

"I tried to anyway." I shrugged. "He's looking for you."

"The King?" Loki asked, and I nodded. "Are you going to hand me over to him?"

"I haven't decided yet," I teased, and he smiled again, erasing his momentary seriousness. "So, where'd you get the suit?"

"Believe it or not, that lovely friend of yours, Willa," Loki said. "She brought me a whole slew of clothes last night. When I asked her why she was being so generous, she said it was out of fear that I would run around naked."

I smiled. "That does sound like something you would do. Why are you wearing all black, though? Didn't you know you were going to a wedding?"

"On the contrary," he said, doing his best to look unhappy. "I'm in mourning over the wedding."

"Oh, because it's too late?" I asked.

"No, Wendy, it's never too late." His voice was light, but his eyes were solemn.

"May I cut in?" the best man asked.

"No, you may not," Loki said. I'd started to move away from him, but he held fast.

"Loki," I said, and my eyes widened.

"I'm still dancing with her," Loki said, turning to look at him. "You can have her when I'm done."

"Loki," I said again, but he was already twirling me away. "You can't do that."

"I just did." He grinned. "Oh, Wendy, don't look so appalled. I'm already the rebel Prince of thine enemy. I can't do much more to tarnish my image."

"You can certainly tarnish mine," I pointed out.

"Never," Loki said, and it was his turn to look appalled. "I'm merely showing them how it's done."

He began spinning me around the dance floor in grand arcs, my gown swirling around me. He was a brilliant dancer, moving with grace and speed. Everyone had stopped to watch us, but I didn't care. This was the way a Princess was supposed to dance on her wedding day.

The song ended, switching to something by Mozart, and he slowed, almost to a stop, but he kept me in his arms.

"Thank you." I smiled. My skin felt flushed from dancing, and I was a little out of breath. "That was a wonderful dance."

"You're welcome," he said, staring intently at me. "You are so beautiful."

"Stop," I said, looking away as my cheeks reddened.

"How can you blush?" Loki asked, laughing gently. "People must tell you how beautiful you are a thousand times a day."

"It's not the same," I said.

"It's not the same?" Loki echoed. "Why? Because you know they don't mean it like I do?"

We did stop dancing then, and neither of us said anything. Garrett came up to us. He smiled, but his eyes didn't appear happy.

"Can I cut in?" Garrett asked.

"Yes," Loki said, shaking off the intensity he'd had a moment ago, and grinned broadly at Garrett. "She's all yours, good sir. Take care of her."

He patted Garrett on the arm once for good measure and gave me a quick smile before heading back over to the refreshment table.

"Was he bothering you?" Garrett asked me as we began to dance.

"Um, no." I shook my head. "He's just . . ." I trailed off because I didn't know what he was.

I watched Loki as he drained another glass of champagne, and then he left the ballroom just as abruptly as he'd entered.

"Are you sure?" Garrett asked.

"Yes, everything is fine." I smiled reassuringly at him. "Why? Am I in trouble for dancing with him?"

"I don't think so," he said. "It's your wedding. You're

supposed to have a little fun. It would've been nice if it was with the groom, but . . ." He shrugged.

"Elora's not mad, is she?" I asked.

"Elora doesn't have the strength to be mad anymore," Garrett said, almost sadly. "Don't worry about her. You've got enough to deal with."

"Thank you," I said.

I looked around the dance floor. Willa was dancing with Tove again, and when she caught my eyes, she gave me a what-the-hell look. I assumed it was in reference to my dance with Loki, but Tove didn't seem upset. That was something, at least.

EIGHT

morning after

Even though I wore a wedding gown that had to weigh at least twenty pounds, I'd never felt so naked in my life.

I stood at the foot of my new bed in my new bedroom. These had been Elora's chambers, but they were mine now, mine to share with my husband. Tove was next to me, and we both just stared at the bed.

When the reception started winding down, Tove's parents, my mother, Willa, Garrett, and a few other ranking officials, including that disgusting Chancellor, had ushered us up to the room. They were all laughing, talking about how magical this would be, then they shut the door behind us.

"On wedding nights, when a Prince or a King were married, they used to close the curtains around the four-poster bed," Tove said. "Then the family and officials would sit around all night, so they could be sure that they were having sex."

"That is really disturbing," I said. "Why on earth would they do that?"

He shrugged. "To ensure they would produce offspring. That is the only reason why they arranged marriages."

"I guess I should be happy they're not doing that with us."

"Do you think they're listening outside the door?"

"I really, really hope not."

We kept staring at the bed, refusing to look at each other. I don't think either of us knew what to do. I had planned to wait long enough until I was certain everyone had grown bored and left, but past that, I had no idea how this night would go.

Tove and I would never have a normal marital relationship, but for some reason, I did assume we would consummate our union on our wedding night. We would have to eventually, because we would be expected to produce an heir to the throne, regardless of whether we were attracted to each other. Or in Tove's case, even attracted to my gender.

"This dress is really heavy," I said finally.

"It looks like it." Tove glanced at my dress and the piles of train that had been tacked up on the back so I could dance. "The train itself has to weigh like ten pounds."

"At least," I agreed. "So . . . I'd like to get out of it."

"Oh, right." He paused. "Go ahead. I guess."

"Well . . . I need your help." I gestured to the back of it. "There's like a thousand buttons and snaps to undo, and I can't reach them."

"Oh, right, of course." Tove shook his head. "I should've known."

I turned my back to him and stood patiently while he undid all the buttons and snaps. It seemed ridiculous when I thought about it. This dress was meant to come off, but it took him at least fifteen minutes to get them all undone. And the whole time, neither of us said anything.

"There you go," he said. "All done."

"Thank you." I held the dress in the front to keep it from falling off, and I turned to face him. "Should I . . . do I need to put pajamas on?"

"Oh." He rubbed his hands on his pants. "Um, if you want to."

"Are you going to?" I asked.

"I . . . yeah." He bit the inside of his cheek and lowered his eyes. "We don't have to. I mean, you know, have sex. We can if you want to. I guess. But we don't have to."

"Oh," I said, because that seemed like the only thing to say.

"Do you want to?" Tove asked, looking at me.

"Uh . . . not really, no," I admitted. "But we could try kissing, maybe."

"No, that's okay." He scratched the back of his head and looked around the room. "We can take this slow. Tonight's only the first night. We have our whole lives to . . . figure out how to sleep with each other."

"Yeah," I said, and laughed nervously. "So, I'll go put on pajamas?"

"Yeah, me too."

Still holding my dress around me, I went into the closet only to find a problem. I had no clothes here. None of Elora's clothes were even in here. The closet was bare.

"Do you have any clothes?" Tove asked from the bedroom. "Because these dressers are empty."

"Oh, hell, I bet they did that on purpose." I sighed and walked back out.

"They didn't give us clothes because . . ." He trailed off and smiled thinly.

"So I have nothing to sleep in."

"You can wear my T-shirt," Tove offered. He undid the top buttons of his dress shirt, then pulled it over his head, revealing a plain white T-shirt. "Do you want to?"

"Yes, thank you," I said.

He took off his shirt, then handed it to me. I turned around, so my back was to him, and I pulled on his T-shirt. I stepped out of my dress, and it felt amazing to be free of it. Everything about me felt lighter.

When I'd finished, I saw that Tove had taken off his pants, so he was wearing only his boxers. I went around to my side of the bed and sat down on the edge. I peeled off the jewelry I'd been wearing, except for my new wedding ring with a giant diamond.

I climbed into bed, sliding underneath the mounds of covers. The bed was massive, so even after Tove got in it, there was still plenty of room between us. I waited until he was settled, then I leaned over and turned off my bedside lamp, submerging the room in darkness.

"Is it okay?" Tove asked.

"What?"

"That I don't love you."

"Uh, yeah," I said carefully. "I think it's okay."

"I wasn't sure if I should tell you. I didn't want to hurt your feelings, but I thought you should know." He moved in the bed, and I felt a subtle motion on my side.

"No, it's okay. I'm glad you told me." I paused for a minute. "I don't love you."

"And that's okay?"

"I think so."

"It was a nice wedding," Tove said, somewhat randomly. "Except for the part with your dad."

"Yeah. It was really nice," I agreed. "Willa and Aurora did a good job."

"They did."

The day had been exhausting, and I hadn't slept much the night before. So it didn't take long for sleep to overtake me. I fell asleep on my wedding night, still a virgin.

The doors burst open, startling me awake. I nearly jumped out of bed. Tove groaned next to me, since I did this weird mind-slap thing whenever I woke up scared, and it always hit him the worst. I'd forgotten about it because it had been a few months since the last time it happened.

"Good morning, good morning, good morning," Loki chirped, wheeling in a table covered with silver domes.

"What are you doing?" I asked, squinting at him. He'd pulled up the shades. I was tired as hell, and I was not happy.

"I thought you two lovebirds would like breakfast," Loki said. "So I had the chef whip you up something fantastic." As he set up the table in the sitting area, he looked over at us. "Although you two are sleeping awfully far apart for newlyweds."

"Oh, my god." I groaned and pulled the covers over my head.

"You know, I think you're being a dick," Tove told him as he got out of bed. "But I'm starving. So I'm willing to overlook it. This time."

"A dick?" Loki pretended to be offended. "I'm merely worried about your health. If your bodies aren't used to strenuous activities, like a long night of lovemaking, you could waste away if you don't get plenty of protein and rehydrate. I'm concerned for you."

"Yes, we both believe *that's* why you're here," Tove said sarcastically and took a glass of orange juice that Loki had poured for him.

"What about you, Princess?" Loki's gaze cut to me as he filled another glass.

"I'm not hungry." I sighed and sat up.

"Oh, really?" Loki arched an eyebrow. "Does that mean that last night—"

"It means that last night is none of your business," I snapped.

I got up and hobbled over to Elora's satin robe, which had been left on a nearby chair. My feet and ankles ached from all the dancing I'd done the night before.

"Don't cover up on my account," Loki said as I put on the robe. "You don't have anything I haven't seen."

"Oh, I have plenty you haven't seen," I said and pulled the robe around me.

"You should get married more often," Loki teased. "It makes you feisty."

I rolled my eyes and went over to the table. Loki had set it all up, complete with a flower in a vase in the center, and he'd pulled off the domed lids to reveal a plentiful breakfast. I took a seat across from Tove, only to realize that Loki had pulled up a third chair for himself.

"What are you doing?" I asked.

"Well, I went to all the trouble of having someone prepare it, so I might as well eat it." Loki sat down and handed me a flute filled with orange liquid. "I made mimosas."

"Thanks," I said, and I exchanged a look with Tove to see if it was okay if Loki stayed.

"He's a dick," Tove said over a mouthful of food, and shrugged. "But I don't care."

In all honesty, I think we both preferred having Loki there. He was a buffer between the two of us so we didn't have to deal with any awkward morning-after conversations. And though I'd never admit it aloud, Loki made me laugh, and right now I needed a little levity in my life.

"So, how did everyone sleep last night?" Loki asked.

There was a quick knock at the bedroom doors, but they opened before I could answer. Finn strode inside, and my stomach dropped. He was the last person I'd expected to see. I didn't even think he would be here anymore. After the other night I assumed he'd left, especially when I didn't see him at the wedding.

"Princess, I'm sorry—" Finn started to say as he hurried in, but then he saw Loki and stopped abruptly.

"Finn?" I asked, stunned.

Finn looked appalled and pointed at Loki. "What are you doing here?"

"I'm drinking a mimosa." Loki leaned back in his chair. "What are you doing here?"

"What is he doing here?" Finn asked, turning his attention to me.

"Never mind him." I waved it off. "What's going on?"

"See, Finn, you should've told me when I asked," Loki said between sips of his drink.

"Hey, did you guys . . ." Duncan was saying when he walked into my room. Apparently, since Finn had left the door open, he thought he could waltz on in.

"Sure, everybody just walk on in. It's not like I'm a Princess or anything and this is my private chamber." I sighed.

When Duncan saw the bizarre scene, he stopped and motioned to Loki. "Wait. Why is he here? He didn't spend the night with you two, did he?"

"Wendy is into some very kinky things that you wouldn't understand," Loki told him with a wink.

"Why are you here?" Finn demanded, and his eyes blazed.

"Will somebody please tell us what the hell is going on?" Tove asked, exasperated.

"I would, but this is a private conversation." Finn kept his icy gaze locked on Loki, who looked completely unabashed.

"Come, now, Finn, there are no secrets between us." Loki grinned and gestured widely to Tove and me.

"Is it private as in Tove, Loki, and Duncan should leave?" I asked carefully. I didn't know if Finn's visit was about me. If it was, I wasn't sure if I should let him have a moment alone with me.

"No." Finn shook his head. "It's about the kingdom, and I don't trust the Markis Staad."

"I have amnesty, you know." Loki leaned forward, sounding irritated. "That means she trusts me. I'm an accepted member of your society."

"No one will ever accept you," Finn said coolly. "And I sincerely doubt that—"

"Just spit it out!" I snapped. "I'm very tired. I've had a very long weekend. So if there's something I need to know, you should hurry up and tell me."

"My apologies." Finn lowered his eyes. "I was in a security briefing this morning with my father. Apparently there's been a Vittra attack on Oslinna, and it was brutal."

"Oslinna?" I asked. "I have a meeting with their head Markis tomorrow morning."

"Not anymore," Finn said quietly. "He's dead."

"They killed him?" I gasped, and I heard Tove swear under his breath. "When did this happen? How many others were killed?"

"We're not certain of the total loss yet," Finn said. "It

happened sometime during the night, and we're still getting word on it. But so far, the death toll is high . . . and mounting."

"Oh, my god." I put my hand to my mouth, wanting to throw up or cry.

Scores of people had been killed while I was dancing. My people, who I was sworn to protect. And it might have been my father after he left the wedding. It was a ten-hour drive to Oslinna from here, but it would be possible for him to get there. He could have slaughtered them all because he was angry with me.

Or maybe not. This might have been his plan all along. He agreed to peace with Förening, and then went after our changelings, and now apparently was following it up by attacking other Trylle communities. This could be his first step toward total war.

I swallowed back any emotion I had, because that would only get in the way. I needed a clear head if I wanted to help what was left of the Oslinna people.

"We have to do something," I said numbly.

"My father is arranging a defense meeting now," Finn said.

"Is that why he didn't come to get me?" I asked. Finn's father, Thomas, was head of security, and he was the one who usually reported the problems to me.

"No." Finn gave me an apologetic look. "He didn't want to inform you. He thought we should wait until we knew more, since you'd just gotten married."

"I'm still the Princess!" I stood up. "This is still my duty. It doesn't stop because of a silly party."

"That's why I came to get you," Finn said, but he'd looked away, and I didn't think that had been his only motive for retrieving me this morning.

"Is this why you're here?" I asked Duncan.

He nodded. "Yeah. I was downstairs getting breakfast, and I heard a couple of guards talking about the Oslinna attack. I thought you'd want to know."

"Thank you," I said. I held my hand to my stomach, trying to ease my nerves. I had to be cool and calm. "Get the defense meeting set up. We need to get moving on this as fast as we can."

Finn nodded. "Of course."

"Duncan, can you run and get Willa?" I asked, and, using mind-speak, I said, *She's down in Matt's room.* She'd spent more nights with him than at her home lately.

"Yes, of course." Duncan made a quick bow and started walking out.

"Oh, and can you run to my room and grab some clothes?" I asked. "They didn't seem to make it in the move yesterday."

"Sorry about that." Duncan's cheeks reddened. "It was Willa's idea. She thought it would be—"

"Never mind that." I waved it off. "Just grab me something to wear. And make sure Willa comes. I want her at this meeting."

"Yes, Princess." He rushed out of the room, hurrying to complete his tasks, but Finn stayed where he was.

"What?" I asked.

"What about him?" Finn's eyes went to Loki.

"What about him?" I asked, annoyed.

"He's Vittra," Finn said.

"He's not—" I stopped and turned back to Loki. "Did you know about the attack on Oslinna?"

"No, of course not," Loki said, and he did seem genuinely distressed about it. His smirk was gone, his eyes were pained, and his skin was ashen. "The King would never tell me of his plans."

"See?" I turned to face Finn again. "He didn't know anything."

"Princess." Finn gave me a hard look.

"I don't have time to stand here and argue with you, Finn," I said. "You need to get down to the meeting and make sure nobody does anything stupid before I get there. Don't let the Chancellor decide *anything*. I'll be in the War Room in ten minutes, okay?"

"Yes, Princess." Finn didn't look happy, but he nodded and left the room.

"I need to get clothes too," Tove said and pushed back his chair. He got up and tossed his napkin on his half-eaten meal. "Do you have any idea how you want to handle this, Wendy?"

"Not yet." I shook my head. "But I don't entirely know what's happened."

"We'll figure this out." Tove walked over to me and touched my arm gently. "I'll meet you in the War Room."

"Okay." I nodded. "Hurry."

I ran a hand through my hair. My mind raced. An attack meant that people had been killed, but it also meant that many were injured and their homes might be destroyed. We had to help the survivors somehow, as well as figure out how to deal with the Vittra.

"I should probably let you get ready," Loki said, rising.

"What?" I turned back to face him. I'd forgotten he was there.

"I am truly sorry for what happened," Loki said solemnly. "Your people didn't deserve that."

"I know." I swallowed hard. He turned away to leave and I asked, "Would you have done it?"

"What?" Loki paused at the door.

"If you were with the Vittra still?" I asked, and I looked at him directly. He stood a few feet from me, his golden eyes looking dark and sad. "Would you have attacked Oslinna? Would you have killed them?"

"No," he said. "I have never killed anyone."

"But you fought with them."

He shook his head. "I never fought for my King. That's why I ended up in the dungeon."

"I see." I looked down at the floor, understanding dawning. "Stay out of sight. Nobody else will trust you."

"I will."

"Loki," I said just before he slipped out the door, and I turned to him, so he could see I was serious. "It seems to me that the King has wreaked as much destruction on your life as he has on mine. But if I find out you knew anything about the attack, I will bring you to the King myself."

"Yes, Your Highness." He bowed, then left my chambers.

NINE

repercussions

Duncan came in a few minutes later, and I dressed quickly. I smoothed out my hair the best I could, because I couldn't look a fright at this meeting, but I didn't have time to make sure I looked top-notch.

I practically ran down the hall with Duncan at my heels, and I reached the top of the stairs at the same time as Willa. Her dress was a bit askew, and her hair was tangled, so she'd obviously gotten dressed in a hurry too. I was happy to see that she'd listened.

"Duncan said you wanted me to come to the meeting?" Willa asked, sounding confused as we went down the stairs.

"Yes," I said. "I need you to start getting involved with this."

"Wendy, you know I'm not good at this kind of stuff," Willa said.

"I don't know why you say that. Public relations is your forte. And even if it wasn't, this is your job. You are one of the highest Marksinna we have. You should be helping shape the kingdom instead of letting others destroy it."

"I don't know." She shook her head, and when we reached the bottom of the steps, I stopped to face her.

"Look, Willa, I need you on my side," I said. "I'm going into a room full of people who think I'm an idiot and a liability. People are in trouble in Oslinna, *our* people. I don't have time to fight with them, and they are fond of you. I need you to help me. Okay?"

"Of course." Willa smiled nervously. "I will help you in any way I can."

Before we even reached the War Room, I could hear them arguing. There were too many voices to clearly understand what they were fighting about, but they were upset.

"We all need to calm down!" Finn was shouting to be heard over them when Willa, Duncan, and I arrived. Finn stood at the front of the crowded War Room, but nobody paid attention to him.

Tove leaned on the desk, watching them all. The Chancellor, his face beet-red, was yelling so much at poor Markis Bain that spittle flew from his mouth. Marksinna Laris was standing up and screaming at Garrett, who tried to keep his expression neutral, but I knew he wanted to smack her.

"Excuse me!" I shouted, but nobody even noticed me.

"I've been trying to get them to calm down." Finn looked at me apologetically. "But they're in a complete frenzy. They think we're next."

"I got this," Willa said.

She climbed up onto the desk behind Tove, carefully because she was wearing a short dress, and she put two fingers in her mouth and let out a loud whistle. So loud that Tove actually covered his ears.

Everybody stopped talking and looked up at her.

"Your Princess is here, and she'd like to talk to you, so you should give her your attention," Willa said with a smile.

Duncan walked over to the desk and gave Willa his hand to help her to the floor. She thanked him, then smoothed out her dress, and I walked over to stand between her and Tove.

"Thank you, Marksinna," I said, then turned my attention to the angry mob. "Who knows the most about the attack on Oslinna?"

"I do," Thomas said, stepping forward from behind Aurora Kroner.

"Tell me everything you know," I said.

"We've already gone over this," Marksinna Laris said before he could say anything. "We shouldn't be rehashing the same things. We should be plotting our attack."

"I am sorry to be wasting your time, but nobody is making any decisions until I know what's going on," I said. "This will all go much faster if you simply let Thomas tell me what happened."

Laris muttered something and looked away. When I was certain she was done, I turned back to Thomas and nodded for him to continue.

"Sometime late last night, the Vittra attacked Oslinna," Thomas said. "It's one of the Trylle's larger compounds located in northern Michigan. Reports vary, but we believe it started around ten-thirty P.M."

"Are we certain it was the Vittra?" I asked.

"Yes," Thomas said. "The King wasn't there, but a message was sent on his behalf."

"And the message was?" I prompted him.

" 'This is only the beginning,' " Thomas said.

Whispers filled the room, but I held up my hand to silence them.

"Do we know how many Vittra they had with them?" I asked.

Thomas shook his head. "It's hard to say concretely. They've begun using hobgoblins in their battles. In previous attacks on Trylle, they rarely used them, preferring to keep them hidden. So we are assuming the numbers of actual Vittra are running low."

"Ugly little creatures," Laris snorted at the mention of hobgoblins, and a few chuckled in response.

"So the hobgoblins comprise most of the Vittra army?" Tove asked dubiously. "How are they a threat? They're small and weak."

"They may be small, but they're still Vittra," Thomas said. "Physically, they have tremendous strength. They seem to be slow mentally and more susceptible to Trylle abilities than most trolls, but not that many of the Trylle in Oslinna even have abilities anymore."

"These hobgoblins caused real damage to Oslinna, then?" I asked.

"Yes," Thomas said. "The town is completely devastated. We don't have an exact figure of how many lives were lost, but we suspect the number to be at least two thousand, and they only had a population of three thousand to begin with."

Someone in the back gasped, and even Willa made a sound, but I kept my face blank. Here, compassion would be a sign of weakness.

"Do we know what kind of casualties we caused the Vittra army?" I asked.

"No, but I don't think it was substantial," Thomas said. "Possibly a hundred. Maybe more."

"So they killed thousands of our people, and we killed maybe a handful of them?" I asked. "How is this possible? How did this happen?"

"They were sleeping or getting ready for bed," Thomas said. "It was an ambush during the night. They might have underestimated the hobgoblins. We had no idea exactly how strong they were until this attack."

"What kind of strength are we talking about?" I asked. "Stronger than me? Stronger than Finn? What?"

"Strong enough to lift a house from its foundation," Thomas said, and the room erupted in more nervous chatter.

"Quiet!" I snapped, but it took them longer to silence themselves.

"We're next," Laris said and stood up. "You heard the King's threat. They are coming for us, and we're completely exposed! We can't stand up to that."

"There's no need for hysteria." I shook my head. "We have

the most powerful Trylle in the world, the most powerful of any creature on earth. Marksinna, you can create fire. Tove and I can move anything. Willa can harness the wind. We have more than enough power here to defend ourselves."

"What about those of us who can't?" the Chancellor asked. "We're defenseless against little monsters that can throw our homes!"

"We are not defenseless," I said, and I looked over at Finn.

"We should call the trackers in," Finn said, understanding my gaze. "We need the guards at home."

As much as I hated to do it, we would have to. That left our changelings unprotected, and they were just kids. We had no idea what the Vittra did with them when they took them, but we had no choice. We couldn't waste manpower protecting individual children when we had a whole kingdom to worry about.

"Do it," I said, and he nodded. "Before they get here, we need to figure out what to do about Oslinna."

"Why would we do anything with Oslinna?" Laris looked confused.

"They were just attacked," I said, speaking as if I were talking to a small child. "We need to help them."

"Help them?" the Chancellor asked. "We can barely help ourselves."

"We don't have the resources," Aurora agreed.

"We have more resources than any other compound," Tove said. "How can you even say that?"

"We need our resources for us," Laris said. "This is what

I've been saying all along. We knew this day would come. Ever since that bastard Princess was born—" She gestured to me.

"Marksinna!" Willa snapped. "She is your Princess. Remember who you're speaking to."

"How can I forget?" Laris asked. "She's the one that will get us all killed!"

"Enough!" I held up both my hands before everyone joined her. "This is what we are going to do. First, Thomas will call back all trackers. Every last one of them. When they return, we can work on assembling an army to defend ourselves, but that also means defending the other compounds.

"Second, we will send a team to Oslinna to assess the damage and relocate refugees. While there, the team will help them clean up and also try to learn more about the Vittra so we can prevent further ambushes.

"Lastly, you will all learn to use whatever abilities you have. We are powerful. I am not going to waste a soldier or a guard defending people who can protect themselves."

"You can't expect us to fight in the war!" Laris said, appalled.

"I am not asking you to, although it would be nice if some of you who can fight would offer to," I said.

"This is obscene," Aurora said. "You can't seriously mean for us to fight."

"Yes, I can," I said. "And frankly, I don't give a damn if you don't like it. This is our best hope to protect the kingdom."

"Who do you propose goes on the team?" Garrett asked.

"People who can help," I said. "I will go."

"Princess, it's unwise of you to leave Förening," Finn said.

"The truce with the Vittra King states that he will not attack our people *here*. He says nothing for the ones outside of Förening."

"You shouldn't travel," Willa agreed. "Not during a time of war."

"Why not?" Laris asked. "Let her go and get herself killed! It would save us all the headache! Not that I think she would be killed. She's probably working with them."

"Marksinna Laris," Tove said, glaring at her. "The next time you speak out against the Princess I will have you banished from Förening on the grounds of treason, and we'll see how well you do against the Vittra."

"Treason?" Her eyes widened. "I've committed no such thing!"

"Under the Treason Act, Article Twelve, anyone who plots or imagines the death of our King or Queen or their eldest child and heir has committed treason," Tove said. "And in a room full of witnesses, you just wished for the Princess's death."

"I . . ." Laris began to defend herself, then gave up and simply stared down at her hands.

"Who will go on the team, then?" Aurora asked.

"I would like volunteers," I said. "A high-ranking official needs to go as my proxy, and I will order people if I must."

"I'll go," Finn said. "My father can stay here and get the army ready. I can help lead a team into Oslinna."

"I'll go," Markis Bain offered. "My sister lives there. I should help her."

"Anyone else?" I asked, but I was met with blank stares. "A healer would be particularly useful now."

"Marksinna Kroner?" Willa prompted when Aurora said nothing.

"I'm the Prince's mother." Aurora put her hand to her chest, aghast. "I can't possibly go." Tove gave her a hard look, so she floundered for an excuse. "The Chancellor! He has some healing powers."

"Not as great as yours," he said defensively. "I'm nothing compared to you."

"You're an elected official," Aurora said. "These people voted for you. They deserve your help."

"Why don't you go, Chancellor?" Tove asked. "You can work as my liaison."

"Do I have a choice?" the Chancellor asked, sounding defeated, and Tove answered him with a glare.

The meeting went on for a few minutes longer. Willa gave an impassioned speech about the importance of helping our brethren. A few people seemed moved by it, but nobody else volunteered until Willa pointed out that if we helped them, the people from Oslinna could come back here and fight for us. That got a couple more hands in the air.

In the end, we managed to assemble a team of ten, and that was about the most I could hope for. Everyone dispersed, resolving that the team would depart the palace in two hours. After everyone else had gone, Tove, Willa, Duncan, and I lingered in the War Room.

"I think that went well." Willa leaned back against the desk.

"What if the Vittra start attacking other towns?" I asked. "What are we going to do?"

"There's nothing more we can do," Tove said. "Not right now. We need to get the trackers back. I'm sure that's what the King's plan was. To get all the trackers out after the changelings and leave us exposed."

"And I had to send them out," I said with a sigh. "The Vittra were kidnapping children. I couldn't let them."

"You did the right thing," Willa said. "And you're doing the right thing now. You're bringing the trackers back. You're helping Oslinna."

"Not enough." I shook my head and stepped away from them. "I should be going there. I should be helping. If these hobgoblins are throwing houses, they'll need people like me to move the rubble."

"Princess, you're a leader now," Duncan said. "You need to stay here and give orders. Let other people do the work."

"But that's not how it should be!" I argued. "If I have the most power, I should do the most work."

"Wendy, you are doing work," Willa said. "They wanted to leave the people in Oslinna to die without help. You need to stay here and organize the rescue efforts, and our defense. And if things are safe, maybe you can go out there and help clean up later, okay? The team needs to go out and investigate first."

"I know." I rubbed the back of my neck. "I've been trying

so hard to avoid unnecessary bloodshed, but Oren is determined to bring it on no matter what I do."

"That's not your fault, though," Willa said. "You can't control what he does."

"None of us can control our parents," Tove said. "But at least I shut Laris up."

"That was nice." Willa laughed.

"That was really nice," Duncan agreed.

"Thank you for that," I said, smiling despite myself. "Were you really going to banish her?"

"I don't know." Tove shrugged. "I just got sick of her always bitching about everything."

"What are you going to do now?" Willa asked.

"Now?" I exhaled heavily when I realized what I had to do. "I have to go tell Elora about this."

TEN

aid

Elora wasn't mad at me, but I hadn't expected her to be. She'd already begun the process of entrusting me with the kingdom, which was overwhelming, but I'd never let on. I asked for advice as infrequently as possible. I had to know how to do things on my own, and she accepted my decisions most of the time.

The news of the attack had upset her, and that was what I had been afraid of. She wanted to get out of bed and go after Oren herself, but simply getting angry tired her out too much to sit up. She'd become so fragile, and it scared me to see her that way.

I left her in Garrett's care and went to find Finn before he left. I wasn't sure how I felt about him leading the team. I had no right to stop him, and I knew that. I wouldn't even ask it of him if I could.

But this might be dangerous. I didn't know what the Vittra's plans might be. I hadn't expected them to start attacking us, so I'd clearly underestimated Oren's determination to destroy us. Or, more specifically, me.

Even though Finn hadn't been home for the better part of a month, his residence was still technically the palace. What few earthly possessions he had were here in his room in the servants' quarters. As I went to his room, I passed Loki's, and I was pleased to see that the door was shut. He'd taken my advice to lay low.

Finn's bedroom door was open, and he was packing a few clothes to take with him. I wasn't sure how long he'd be gone, but it had to be at least a few days. It depended on how badly damaged Oslinna was.

"Are you about packed?" I asked. I stood in the hall just outside his door, too afraid to go any farther.

"Yeah." Finn glanced back at me. He shoved a pair of boxers in the duffel bag and zipped it up. "I think so."

"Good." I twisted the wedding band around my finger. "Are you sure you want to do this?"

"I don't have much of a choice." Finn picked up his bag and turned to face me. He kept his expression blank, and I hated that he did it so well. I hated that I never knew what he was really thinking or feeling.

"Of course you have a choice," I said. "I'm not forcing you to go."

"I know that. But they need somebody experienced, someone who isn't an idiot, to go along. My father has to stay here, and I'm the next logical choice."

"I could go," I offered. "I should. I can be of more help."

"No. What I said at the meeting is still true," Finn said. "You're needed here."

"I'm not doing anything here except waiting until you get back." I didn't like the way that sounded, so I lowered my eyes.

"We won't be gone that long," Finn said. "We'll probably bring the survivors back to Förening. They can have shelter here."

"I should ready the palace for extra guests, then," I said, and I hated that. He would be out at battle, and I would be at home, making sure the beds were made. "I should be going with you. This is ridiculous."

"Princess, this is the right place for you," he said, almost tiredly. "But it's time for me to go. I don't want to make them wait for me."

"Yes, sorry." I stepped aside so he could walk past me. His arm brushed against me, but he didn't even notice. As he walked by, I said, "Be careful."

"You say that as if you care," he muttered.

"I do care," I said defensively. "I never said that I didn't. That isn't fair."

He stopped with his back to me. "The other night, you made your intentions perfectly clear."

"So did you," I said, and he pivoted to face me. "And you made your choice." He'd chosen duty time and time again, and if he had to sacrifice something, it had been me.

"I never had a choice, Wendy," Finn said, sounding exasperated.

"You *always* did. Everybody does. And you chose."

"Well, so did you," he said finally.

"That I did," I agreed.

He stared at me for a moment longer before turning and walking away. I hadn't wanted that to be my last conversation with him before he left. Part of me still feared that something might happen, but at the same time, I knew Finn could handle himself.

There were going to be survivors coming, and I needed to get the palace ready. I had never considered myself domestic, but Willa and Matt would be good at that sort of thing.

I found them together in Matt's room, where Willa was trying to explain what had happened in Oslinna without freaking him out too much. That was our general approach to telling Matt stuff. We didn't want to keep him completely out of the loop, but he would have had an aneurysm if he understood exactly what we were up against.

"The Vittra killed people?" Matt asked. He sat on his bed watching Willa straighten her hair. We may have been in crisis mode, but that didn't mean her hair had to look like it. "They actually killed people like you?"

"Yes, Matt." Willa stood in front of the full-length mirror across from him, running the straightener through her long hair. "They're the bad guys."

"And they're doing this because they're after you?" Matt asked, turning to me.

"They're doing it because they're bad people," Willa answered for me.

"But that Loki guy, he's one of them?" Matt asked.

"Not exactly," I said carefully. I stood off to the side of the room, and I leaned back against the wall.

"He was, though," Matt said. "He kidnapped you before. So why are you always hanging out with him?"

"I'm not."

"Yeah, you are," Matt insisted. "And the way you danced with him at your wedding? That's not the way a married woman acts, Wendy."

"I danced with a hundred guys last night." I shifted my weight and stared down at the floor.

"Leave her alone, Matt," Willa said. "She was having some fun at her wedding. You can't blame her for that."

"I'm not blaming her for anything. I'm trying to understand." He scratched at the back of his head. "Where is your husband, by the way?"

"He's down talking to the team before they leave," I said. "Giving them instructions and words of encouragement."

"You didn't want to see them off yourself?" Willa asked, turning a bit to look at me.

"No." I thought back to my conversation with Finn and shook my head. "No. Tove's got it covered. He's the Prince now. He can share some of the responsibility."

"Wait." Matt furrowed his brow. "An entire town of trolls just got attacked by hobgoblins. How is this not all over the news? How don't people know about this?"

"Oslinna is secluded, hidden in a valley," Willa explained. "All the other Trylle towns are the same. We live off the map, just out of sight, and we keep to ourselves as much as possible."

"But a big fight like that, somebody had to have heard," Matt insisted. "We may be obtuse, but I think people would notice a war in their backyard."

"Occasionally, a human will stumble onto something and find out more than they should," Willa said. "But that's what persuasion's for. If any humans did see or hear what happened in Oslinna—which is unlikely because of its isolation—they were made to forget it."

Matt shook his head, as if he still didn't understand. "But why all the secrecy? Why go to all the trouble of being hidden?"

"Think back to everything you've ever been told about trolls." Willa leaned forward, inspecting her hair in the mirror, and then she turned around. "Humans believe us to be horrible little creatures. In the past, when we've been discovered, they've called us demons and witches. We've been locked up and burned at the stake. And as powerful as we are, the humans still outnumber us by the millions. If they found out about us, they could destroy us. So we stay hidden, keeping our battles private."

After a pause, Willa changed the subject.

"When do you think the refugees will get here?"

She set the straightener down on the nearby dresser, and I could see burn marks on it from her doing the same thing many times before. She must pretty much live here now.

"I'm not sure," I said. "Maybe in a day or two or six. But we should have the rooms ready, just to be safe."

"Well, we can definitely help you with that," Willa said. "Where are the extra blankets and cleaning supplies?"

Most of the second floor of the south wing were servants' quarters, along with the Queen's chamber, which was now Tove's and my room. I wasn't sure exactly why the Queen resided with the servants, except that the south wing was where the more formal business took place.

Since we had almost no live-in servants anymore, other than two maids, a chef, and a couple of trackers, most of the bedrooms were empty. They hadn't been used in ages, so they were musty and needed freshening, but they weren't exactly dirty.

Each room had extra bedding in it, so we just needed to dust and vacuum. We raided the supply closet at the top of the stairs, and Duncan came up to meet us. He'd been with Tove sending the team off.

Tove stayed with Thomas to work on calling all the trackers in. It was a long and arduous task, and I thought about helping them, but I felt better doing physical work. It felt more like I was accomplishing something.

Duncan helped carry supplies down to the rooms, and I decided to enlist Loki to help us. I wanted to keep him out of sight, but nobody would be checking the servants' quarters. And if he was staying here, he might as well be of some use.

While we cleaned the first room, I asked Loki again if he

knew anything about the Vittra plans. He insisted that he didn't know anything about it, other than that Oren wanted me all for himself. His only advice was to stay the hell out of Oren's way when he was pissed off.

Matt and Willa took a room of their own to clean, while Duncan, Loki, and I cleaned a different one.

"Are you sure I shouldn't have gone with them?" Duncan asked. He'd gathered up the dirty bedding to throw down the laundry chute, while Loki helped me smooth out the fresh blankets on the bed.

"Yes, Duncan, I need you here," I told him for the hundredth time. He felt guilty about not going with the others to Oslinna, but I refused to let him go.

"All right," Duncan said with a sigh, but he still didn't sound convinced. "I'm going to go throw this down. I'll meet you in the next room."

"Okay, thank you," I said, and he left.

"What do you need him for?" Loki asked quietly.

"Shh!" I fixed the corner of the sheet and glared at Loki.

"You just don't want him to go." Loki smirked. "You're protecting him."

"I'm not," I lied.

"Don't you trust him in battle?"

"No, not really," I admitted and picked up a dust rag and glass cleaner. "Grab the vacuum."

"But you sent off that Flounder fellow," Loki said, and I rolled my eyes.

"His name is Finn, and I know you know that," I said as I left the room. Loki grabbed the vacuum and followed me. "You called him by his name this morning."

"Fine, I know his name," Loki admitted. We went into the next room, and he set down the vacuum as I started peeling the dusty blankets off the bed. "But you were okay with Finn going off to Oslinna, but not Duncan?"

"Finn can handle himself," I said tersely. The bedding got stuck on a corner, and Loki came over to help me free it. Once he had, I smiled thinly at him. "Thank you."

"But I know you had a soft spot for Finn," Loki continued.

"My feelings for him have no bearing on his ability to do his job."

I tossed the dirty blankets at Loki. He caught them easily before setting them down by the door, presumably for Duncan to take to the laundry chute again.

"I've never understood exactly what your relationship with him was, anyway," Loki said. I'd started putting new sheets on the bed, and he went around to the other side to help me. "Were you two dating?"

"No." I shook my head. "We never dated. We were never anything."

I continued to pull on the sheets, but Loki stopped, watching me. "I don't know if that's a lie or not, but I do know that he was never good enough for you."

"But I suppose you think you are?" I asked with a sarcastic laugh.

"No, of course I'm not good enough for you," Loki said, and I lifted my head to look up at him, surprised by his response. "But I at least *try* to be good enough."

"You think Finn doesn't?" I asked, standing up straight.

"Every time I've seen him around you, he's telling you what to do, pushing you around." He shook his head and went back to making the bed. "He wants to love you, I think, but he can't. He won't let himself, or he's incapable. And he never will."

The truth of his words stung harder than I'd thought they would, and I swallowed hard.

"And obviously, you need someone that loves you," Loki continued. "You love fiercely, with all your being. And you need someone that loves you the same. More than duty or the monarchy or the kingdom. More than himself even."

He looked up at me then, his eyes meeting mine, darkly serious. My heart pounded in my chest, the fresh heartache replaced with something new, something warmer that made it hard for me to breathe.

"But you're wrong." I shook my head. "I don't deserve that much."

"On the contrary, Wendy." Loki smiled honestly, and it stirred something inside me. "You deserve all the love a man has to give."

I wanted to laugh or blush or look away, but I couldn't. I was frozen in a moment with Loki, finding myself feeling things for him I didn't think I could ever feel for anyone else.

"I don't know how much more laundry we can fit down the

chute," Duncan said as he came back in the room, interrupting the moment.

I looked away from Loki quickly and grabbed the vacuum cleaner.

"Just get as much down there as you can," I told Duncan.

"I'll try." He scooped up another load of bedding to send downstairs.

Once he'd gone, I glanced back at Loki, but, based on the grin on his face, I'd say his earlier seriousness was gone.

"You know, Princess, instead of making that bed, we could close the door and have a roll around in it." Loki wagged his eyebrows. "What do you say?"

Rolling my eyes, I turned on the vacuum cleaner to drown out the conversation.

"I'll take that as a maybe later!" Loki shouted over it.

We worked all afternoon, and by the end we were all tired and cranky. Somehow, that felt good. It meant we'd done something today, and while it hadn't helped anybody in Oslinna yet, it would.

When suppertime came around, I wasn't hungry, so I retired to my room. I was exhausted, and I should've slept, but I couldn't. Tove came in shortly after I got in bed, and we didn't say much. He just crawled in bed, and both of us lay awake for a long time.

I wasn't sure I'd even fallen asleep when Duncan burst through the door. He didn't knock, and I was about to yell at him when I saw how he looked. He wore pajamas and his hair was mussed from sleep, but he was positively panicked.

"What is it, Duncan?" I asked, already throwing my legs over the side of the bed so I could get up.

"It's Finn," Duncan panted. "They were ambushed on the way to Oslinna."

ELEVEN

defeat

I don't remember moving or running. It was all a blur of nothing until I was in the front hall with Finn. A small crowd had gathered around, including Thomas, but I pushed them out of the way to get to him.

Finn was sitting on the floor, and I fell to my knees next to him. He was alive, and I almost sobbed at the sight of him. Blood covered his temple, and his clothes were disheveled. His arm hung at a weird angle, and it took me a moment to realize it had to be broken.

"What happened?" I asked, and I touched his face with trembling hands, mostly to be sure he was real.

"We caught them off guard," Finn said. He stared off at nothing, and his eyes were moist. "They were going home, I think, and we happened to run into them. We thought we could get the best of them. But they were too strong." He swallowed hard. "They killed the Chancellor."

"Oh, shit," Tove said, and I turned to see him standing behind me. He'd been tending to Markis Bain, making sure that he'd made it through all right.

"Tove, go get your mother," I said. Tove nodded once and left, and I turned back to Finn. "Are you okay?"

"I'm alive," he said simply.

Finn was in shock, so I didn't push him for details. Markis Bain ended up filling in the blanks about what had happened. They were on their way to Oslinna when they saw the Vittra camped out. The way he described it, it sounded all very Rumpelstiltskin. The hobgoblins had a fire going, and they danced around it, singing songs and telling tales of how they had defeated Oslinna.

The Chancellor thought they should get the drop on the hobgoblins. They could end the fight right there in the woods. Finn was initially against the idea, but he soon decided that if they had a chance to stop the Vittra before they hurt anybody else, they had to take it.

The only reason any of the team had survived was because they had surprised the Vittra, but the Chancellor wasn't the only one who died. Another Markis had been killed, and a second tracker was severely injured.

All of them were battered and bruised. When Aurora came over to heal them, Bain kept saying it was amazing that any of them were alive. Aurora healed Finn's arm, but that was all she'd heal on him. She wouldn't waste her energy on a tracker, no matter what I said.

Duncan and I helped Finn up to his room to rest, and Tove

stayed behind. He wanted to make sure the others had gotten home okay, although he seemed particularly interested in making sure that Bain was fine. We'd have to plan another way to help Oslinna, but we couldn't do it now.

"I don't need to lie down," Finn insisted as Duncan and I helped him sit on his bed. "I'm fine." He winced when I bumped his arm, and I sighed.

"Finn, you are not fine," I said. "You need to rest."

"No, I need to figure out how to stop those damned hobgoblins," Finn said. "They're going to come after us all eventually. We need to find a way to beat them."

"We will," I said, even though I wasn't sure that was true. "But we aren't going to do anything right now. It can wait until the morning, when you've slept some."

"Wendy." He looked up at me, his eyes stormier than usual. "You didn't see them. You don't know what they're like."

"No, I don't," I admitted, and the tone of his voice made my stomach twist up. "But you can tell me all about it. Tomorrow."

"Let me at least talk to Loki," Finn said, almost desperately.

"Loki?" I asked. "Why would you want to talk to him?"

"He has to know how to handle these things," Finn said. "There's got to be some secret to defeating them, and if anyone knows it, it would be a Vittra Markis."

"He's probably sleeping—"

"Then wake him up, Wendy!" Finn yelled, and I flinched. "People are dying!"

I twisted my ring around my finger and relented. "Fine. If you promise to lie down, I'll let Loki talk to you. But once he's done, you have to rest until tomorrow. Is that clear?"

"Fine," Finn said, but I had a feeling he'd agree to anything to be sure I got Loki.

"Duncan?" I looked back to where he waited in the doorway. "Can you get Loki? Tell him I asked for him."

Duncan left me alone with Finn. I motioned for Finn to lie back. He sighed but did it anyway. I sat next to him, and he stared at the ceiling, looking annoyed. His shirt was torn and bloody, and tentatively I reached out to touch a cut on his arm.

"Don't," he said firmly.

"Sorry." I dropped my hand. "And I'm sorry about what happened. I should've gone with you."

"Don't be stupid. If you'd gone with us, you'd only have gotten yourself killed."

"I'm a stronger fighter than you are, Finn."

"I'm not going to argue with you," he said, his eyes still staring straight up. "You don't even need to be here. I'm fine. I can talk to Loki alone."

"No, I'm not leaving you alone with him." I shook my head. "Not when you're weak."

"You think he'd hurt me?" Finn asked.

"No, but I don't want you getting all riled up."

Finn scoffed. I hated how strained things had become between Finn and me, but I didn't know how to fix it. I wasn't even sure it could be fixed. We sat in silence until Duncan came back with Loki.

"This is not at all what I had in mind when the Princess summoned me in the middle of the night," Loki said with a sigh, standing in the doorway to Finn's room. His light hair stood up all over, and he had red marks on his face from sleeping.

"Thank you for getting up," I said. "Did Duncan tell you what happened?"

"Obviously not," Loki said.

"The team we sent out to help Oslinna was overwhelmed by hobgoblins," I said. "Some of our people were killed."

"You're lucky not all of them were killed," Loki said.

"Good men died tonight," Finn growled and tried to sit up in bed, but I put my hand on his chest and pushed him back. "They fought to protect the people here! To protect the Princess! I would think that was something that mattered to you!"

"That wasn't a slam against the lives you lost," Loki said, managing to sound apologetic and irritated at the same time. "The hobgoblins are hard to beat. And from what I heard about the damage to Oslinna, it's astonishing to me that anyone in your rescue team lived."

"We caught them by surprise." Finn settled back down in bed again.

"That does help," Loki said. "The hobgoblins may be strong, but they're stupid."

"How do we defeat them?" Finn asked.

"I honestly don't know. I've never tried defeating them."

"You must know how it's done," Finn insisted. "There must be a way."

"Maybe there is," Loki admitted. "But I've never even fought beside them. The King usually doesn't let hobgoblins leave the grounds. He's afraid that humans will catch on to what we are if they see them."

"Why is he letting them out now?" Finn asked.

"You know why he is." Loki sighed and sat down in a chair in the corner of Finn's room. "The King's fixated on Wendy. He'll do anything to get her."

"How do we stop that?" Finn looked over at him.

Loki stared thoughtfully at the floor, biting his lip, then shook his head sadly. "I don't know."

"What if we can't stop him?" I asked.

"We'll find a way," Finn assured me, but he wouldn't look at me when he said it.

"The hobgoblins aren't very bright," Loki added quickly. "And they're helpless against abilities. Any power you have works twice as well on them as it does on humans."

"What do you mean?" Finn asked.

"Like persuasion or any of Wendy's abilities." Loki gestured to me. "It works on them like that." He snapped his fingers. "That's why I was in charge of guarding her at the Vittra palace. She could've convinced the hobgoblins to do anything for her."

"So the Markis and Marksinna, they can defeat the hobgoblins?" Finn asked. "But I can't?"

Loki shook his head. "Not in hand-to-hand combat, I wouldn't think."

"We're not going to get a Markis or Marksinna to fight in

the war," I said. "Especially not when a Markis was killed tonight, along with the Chancellor. They'll be too afraid."

"We can convince them," Finn said. "If it's the only way we can stop the Vittra, they'll have to do it."

"It's not the only way," I said, but both Loki and Finn ignored me.

"Your people are spoiled," Loki said. "You can't convince them to do anything."

"*We're* spoiled?" Finn scoffed. "That would mean something if it weren't coming from a brat Prince."

"I don't know why you find my comment so offensive." Loki sat up straighter. "I've seen the way these people treat Wendy, and she's their Princess. They're insolent."

"They don't know her," Finn said. "It takes time, and it doesn't help that she spends so much of it with Vittra prisoners."

"I'm not a prisoner." Loki looked disgusted. "I'm here on my own."

"I do not understand that." Finn shook his head in disbelief.

"Finn, he asked for amnesty, and I granted it," I said.

"But your motivations completely baffle me," Finn said. "We're fighting with the Vittra, and you let him stay without consequence."

"It really pisses you off that much that she wants me around?" Loki asked, and Finn glared at him.

"I don't—" I stopped myself and shook my head. "It doesn't matter why Loki's here, but he is here now, and he's trustworthy—I assure you of that. Plus, his intimate knowledge of the Vittra is invaluable."

"I'll tell you as much as I know, but I don't know very much that can help you, Wendy," Loki said. "If you want information about policies and procedures, I can help. But if I knew a way to stop the King, I would've done it myself."

"Why?" Finn asked. "Why would you stop the King?"

"He's a bastard." Loki lowered his eyes and pulled at something on his shirt. "Beyond measure."

"But hasn't he always been one?" Finn asked. "Why did you defect now? Why here? There are other troll tribes and hundreds of cities that aren't at war with your King."

"But only the Trylle have Wendy." Loki's smile returned but his eyes were pained. "And how could I pass on that?"

"She is married, you know," Finn said. "So it might be a good idea if you stopped trying to flirt with her. She's not interested."

"It's up to her to decide who she's interested in," Loki said, with an edge to his voice. "And it's not exactly like you're following your own advice."

"I am her tracker." Finn sat up in bed, but this time I didn't try to stop him. His eyes were burning. "It's my job to protect her."

"No, Duncan is her tracker." Loki pointed to where Duncan stood in the doorway, staring wide-eyed at their confrontation. "And Wendy's stronger than the both of you combined. You're not protecting her. You're protecting *yourself* because you're a lovesick ex-boyfriend."

"You think you have everything figured out, but you don't know anything," Finn growled. "If it were up to me I'd have you sent back to the Vittra in a flash."

"But it's not up to you!" I snapped. "It's up to me. And this conversation is over. Finn needs to rest, and you are not helping anything, Loki."

"Sorry," Loki said and rubbed his hands on his pants.

"Why don't you go back to your room?" I asked Loki. "I'll be over to talk to you in a minute."

He nodded and got up. "Feel better," Loki said to Finn, and he actually did sound sincere.

Finn grunted in response, and Loki and Duncan left. I wanted to reach out and touch Finn, comfort him in some way, because I felt like he needed it. Maybe I needed it too.

"Get some sleep," I told Finn, since I could think of nothing better to say to him. I got up, but he reached out and grabbed my wrist.

"Wendy, I don't trust him," he said, referring to Loki.

"I know. But I do."

"Be careful," Finn said simply and let go of me.

It was well after midnight, and the rest of the palace had fallen silent. The morning would bring endless meetings, but for now, everyone had returned to their beds. The hall was dark, and I could see the warm glow of the lamp in Loki's room.

He didn't hear me in the hallway, so I stood outside, watching him. He was making his bed, and when he'd finished, he chewed his thumb and stared down at it. He shook his head and pulled back the blanket a bit, so it looked more unmade. Then he changed his mind and smoothed out the bedding again.

"What are you doing?" I asked.

"Nothing." He looked startled for a second, then smiled and ran a hand through his hair. "Nothing. You wanted to talk? Why don't you come in?"

"Were you just straightening up the room for me?" I asked.

"Well . . ." He ruffled his hair again. "Whenever I have a Princess stopping by, I try to make my room presentable."

"I see." I went into his room and shut the door behind me, which only delighted him.

"Why don't you have a seat?" Loki gestured to his bed. "Make yourself comfortable."

"I need to ask you a favor."

He smiled. "For you, anything,"

"I want you to take me to Ondarike," I said, and his smile fell away.

"Except that."

"I feel horrible asking, because I know what Oren did to you, and I wouldn't expect you to go inside or anything," I said quickly. "I don't know how to get there or how to get inside, but you could tell me and drop me at the door. I'd never put you in danger or risk your life."

"But you expect me to risk yours?" Loki smirked and shook his head. "No way, Wendy."

"I can promise you your safety," I said. "Once I am there, I doubt he'd even care about you. You don't have to go anywhere near the palace even. Just tell me how to get there."

"Wendy, you're not listening," he said. "I'm not worried about me. I won't let you do that."

"I'll be fine," I insisted. "He's my father, and I'm strong enough to handle myself."

"You have no idea what you're up against." Loki laughed darkly. "No. This is completely ludicrous. I'm not even going to entertain the idea."

"Loki, listen to me. Finn almost died tonight—"

"Your boyfriend gets hurt, and suicide becomes the only viable option?" Loki asked.

"He's not my boyfriend," I corrected him.

"Fine. *Ex*-boyfriend," he said. "That doesn't make this better. And as much as I hate to admit it, Finn was right. We can find a way around this. I know I didn't help very much tonight, but I'm sure, if given time, I can come up with something."

"But we don't have time, Loki!" I took a deep breath. "I'm not saying that I'll give myself to Oren as a peace offering, but I have to talk to him at least. I have to do something to postpone the war a little longer. We need more time to get an army ready. And he's out there killing our people *now*."

"So you want me to take you to the Vittra palace so you can have a little meeting with the King?" Loki asked. "While you're in there, I'll wait outside, and after the meeting is done, you'll come out, and we'll drive back here? Is that the plan?"

"Not exactly, but sorta," I said.

"Wendy!" Loki sounded exasperated. "Why would he let you go? He is doing all of this for *you*. Once he has you there in the palace, why would he ever let you leave?"

"He can't stop me, for one thing," I said. "I can defend myself against him and the hobgoblins and anything else he might have. I can't fight an entire war on my own and defend every person in the entire kingdom all at once. But if I'm alone, I can take care of myself."

"Even if that's true, it's still too great a risk," Loki said. "If you try to leave, he could kill you. Not just hold you hostage. Not just threaten you. Actually *murder* you. He would rather do that than see you return here."

"No, not yet." I shook my head. "Someday, yes, that's true. But he wants me to be Queen. That's why he agreed to the truce. He wanted to ensure that I would be the Trylle Queen."

"He wants both kingdoms," he said quietly. "You're going to give him what he wants?"

"Yes." I nodded. "I will agree to rule alongside him over both the Trylle and the Vittra if he stops the bloodshed until I am crowned Queen."

"He won't rule 'beside' you. He'll take it from you."

"I know, but I would never let him rule anyway," I said. "I don't plan to follow through with it."

Loki whistled and shook his head. "If you went back on your deal, he would destroy everything—and I do mean *everything*—that you have ever cared about."

"I won't go back on it," I said. "It will never get to that point. I'm only buying us time to build up the army, and then we'll attack the Vittra, take them down, and I will kill Oren."

"You'll kill him?" He raised an eyebrow. "Do you even know how to kill him?"

"No. Not yet," I admitted. "That's why I haven't killed him. But I will."

"I don't even know if he can be killed," Loki said.

"Everyone can be killed."

"Many, many people have tried," he said. "And they've all failed."

"Yes, but none of those people have his blood pumping through their veins," I said. "I think I'm the only one strong enough to do it."

Loki studied me a moment before asking, "What if you can't? What if you do all this, and you can't find a way to stop him?"

"I don't know," I said. "I will have to find a way. He's going to keep coming until he has me. I would gladly hand myself over to him if I thought that would be enough, but I'm not sure that it is anymore."

Loki stared down at the floor, his golden eyes wide as he thought it through. I didn't know what he was thinking, but he didn't look happy.

"So, will you take me?" I asked.

He licked his lips and let out a deep breath. "You don't know what you're asking."

"I know perfectly well what—"

Loki cut me off, sounding exasperated. "No, Wendy, you don't. You have no idea what it's really like to live in Ondarike, under the rule of a truly merciless King. You don't understand what he's capable of. He—"

He stopped abruptly and stepped closer to me, his expression solemn and his eyes dark.

"Oren killed my father when I was a child. He hung him

from the ceiling by his ankles and slit his neck, letting him bleed out like a pig." Loki's eyes never wavered from mine as he spoke. "And it takes much longer than one would think. Or maybe it just seemed that way to me, since I was only nine, and Oren made me watch. He told me that's what happens to people who betray him."

"I'm so sorry," I whispered, unable to think of anything else to say.

"I'm not telling you this so you'll feel sorry for me," he said. "I want you to know what you're up against. This man has no soul."

"I know he's a monster." I lowered my gaze, trying to break the intensity of the moment. "Why did you stay in Ondarike after the King did that?"

"I was a child, for one thing. I had nowhere else to go."

"What about when you weren't a child?" I lifted my head cautiously, all too aware of how close Loki was to me. "Why did you wait so long to leave?"

"I stayed for Sara," Loki said simply. "She's been like a sister to me, and she's the only family I have. The King was as cruel to her as he was to me, if not worse, and I didn't want her to go through that alone."

"But now you don't care if she does?" I asked.

"No, I still care. But I can't do anything to protect her anymore. I was trapped in a dungeon, unable to help her in any way."

"So that's why you left?"

"No." He smiled as he stared down into my eyes. "I left for

you." I didn't know what to say to that, but he spoke before I could anyway. "And you're asking me to go back."

"No." I shook my head. "I won't force you to go back if you don't want to. I'll find someone else to take me there."

"Who?" Loki asked. "Who else would possibly take you?"

"I don't know." I floundered for a minute. "I'll find the way on my own."

Tove and a few trackers probably knew how to get to the Vittra palace, but they didn't know the intricacies of it like Loki did. But if I had to, I could take a map from the War Room.

"You can't go by yourself," he said.

"I am sorry the King hurt you, I truly am. I know what a terrible man he is, but you telling me how horrible he is only emphasizes why I need to go. I have to stop him from doing to my people what he's done to his own. I have to go."

I turned to reach for the door handle, but Loki stopped me before I could. He grabbed my wrist and stood right in front of me.

"Loki." I sighed and looked up at him. "Let go of me."

"No, Wendy, I won't let you do this," Loki said.

"You can't stop me."

"I'm much stronger than you."

I tried to shove him out of my way, but it was like pushing on concrete. He pressed me back against his bedroom wall and put an arm on either side of me. His body didn't touch me, but it was so close I couldn't move away.

"You may be physically stronger than me, but I can have

you on the floor writhing in pain in minutes. I don't want to hurt you, but I will if I have to."

"You don't have to," Loki said emphatically. "You don't have to do this."

"Yes, I do. I will do whatever it takes to save lives," I said. "If you can't, that's fine. But get out of my way."

He bit his lip and shook his head, but he didn't move away from me.

"It's the middle of the night, and you want to run away with me," Loki said. "What will you tell your husband?"

"Nothing."

"Nothing?" Loki raised an eyebrow. "The Princess goes missing without a word? It would be total pandemonium."

"I'll have Duncan tell them in the morning where I've gone," I said. "That'll buy us a few hours to get there before somebody comes after us."

"If the King doesn't let you leave, he'll kill the rescue party that they send," Loki pointed out. "That would be Finn, Tove, Duncan, maybe even Willa. You're willing to risk them on this?"

"This might be my only chance to save them," I said thickly.

"I can't talk you out of this?" he whispered, his eyes searching mine.

"No."

He swallowed and brushed back a hair from my forehead. His hand lingered on my face, and I let it. His eyes were strangely sad, and I wanted to ask him why, but I didn't dare speak.

"I want you to remember this," he said, his voice low and husky.

"What?" I asked.

"You want me to kiss you."

"I don't," I lied.

"You do. And I want you to remember that."

"Why?"

"Because." Without further explanation, he turned away from me. "If you want to do this, hurry and put some clothes on. You don't want to see the King in your pajamas."

TWELVE

rendezvous

Loki liked alternative country, and the satellite radio in the Cadillac had been playing Neil Young, Ryan Adams, the Raconteurs, and Bob Dylan since we left Förening. He sang along with it sometimes, in an off-key way that was strangely endearing.

It was still dark out, and snow was falling around us, but Loki didn't seem to mind. The car slid in a few places, but he always corrected it. I'd put my makeup on in the car, and he'd managed to keep it steady enough so I didn't poke myself in the eye with liner.

Loki had teased me about the makeup and my choice of clothing. It was a long, dark violet gown, covered in lace and diamonds, with a black velvet cloak over it. I'd chosen it because I knew reverence would go a long way with Oren.

After they'd kidnapped me, Sara wouldn't let me see him without wearing a gown. Respect was important to him, and making sure I looked nice when I saw him would show him that I respected him.

I'd actually been lucky that I'd been able to find something this nice to wear. Most of my clothes had been moved from my old room into the Queen's chambers that I shared with Tove, but some had been left behind. I'd gone to my old room to get dressed because I didn't want to see Tove and tell him what I was doing.

After I had changed, I went to Duncan's room. He'd freaked out when I told him what my plans were, and I knew he'd run to tell Tove as soon as I'd gone, if he didn't *before* I left. I'd used persuasion to get him to hold off as long as possible, which I estimated to be until roughly eight A.M. Maybe longer if my persuasion lasted.

Since I was the Princess, I had access to everything. I'd gone to the garage and taken the keys to a black Cadillac. We'd left Förening without anybody else seeing us, except for the guard at the gates. I used persuasion on him to keep him from alerting anyone, and we were on the road.

"You can sleep," Loki said as I stared out the window at the snowflakes landing against the glass. "I will get us there."

"I know, but I'm fine." Even though I hadn't really slept last night, I wasn't tired. My nerves had me on edge.

"We can always turn back," he reminded me, not for the first time.

"I know."

"I thought I would offer," he said, sounding disappointed.

He sat in silence for a minute before singing along to the radio.

"Your father was Trylle, wasn't he?" I asked, cutting off his singing.

"My father was born in Förening," Loki answered carefully. "But he was more closely related to a snake than Trylle or Vittra."

"You're being metaphorical, right?" I asked. "Your father wasn't literally a reptile?"

"No." Loki laughed a little. "He wasn't an actual snake."

"How did he end up with the Vittra?" I asked. "Did he leave for your mom?"

"No." He shook his head. "He was the Chancellor in Förening, and he met your father when Oren came around courting your grandparents for Elora's hand in marriage."

"I didn't realize your father was a high-ranking official," I said.

"That he was." Loki nodded. "In arranging the marriage, my father had to work with Oren a lot, and Oren's lust for power appealed to him. Evil attracts evil, apparently."

"So he left to join the Vittra?" I asked.

"Not exactly," he said. "The plan at the time was to unite the kingdoms. Oren would rule both of them, once your mother was Queen. This was before she'd even come back to Förening, when she was still living with her host family, but they had already begun working on the deal. As Chancellor, my father was sent to the Vittra kingdom as the Trylle ambassador. That's how he met my mother."

"I thought you said he didn't leave for her," I said.

"He didn't. She was a means to an end. He married her so he'd have a reason to leave, not the other way around," Loki said.

"So he didn't love her?" I asked.

"No, he couldn't stand her. Though she was beautiful." He paused, thinking of her. "But I don't think he even cared. She was a powerful Marksinna. My father wanted power, and she had it.

"For a time, he was both the Trylle Chancellor and a Vittra Prince," he went on. "I'm not technically a Prince, and neither was he, but since we have the title as the highest-ranking Markis, they refer to us that way."

"Your father committed treason against the Trylle, didn't he?" I asked tentatively, remembering how he'd told me that Oren had executed his father.

"Do you know?" Loki glanced over at me. "Did they tell you what my father did?"

"Elora said that your father told Oren where my grandmother and she were hiding," I said. "Because of that, Oren found them and killed my grandmother."

"He did," Loki said. "He did more than that, actually. He tried to tell Oren where you were, but you were too well hidden, so my father was never able to find out.

"But because of his efforts, he became Oren's right-hand man," Loki continued with a bitter smile. "He got everything he ever wanted, and you'd think that would make him happy, but no."

"What happened?" I asked.

"When I was nine, Oren married Sara, and my father was furious," Loki said. "There was a chance they might produce a healthy child, and my father didn't want that. Without a child, I was the only viable heir to the throne."

"But Sara can't have kids?" I questioned.

"We didn't know that at the time," Loki explained. "She has some Trylle blood in her, two generations back, and that's how she has the ability to heal. But the Vittra blood must have thinned out the Trylle in her too much, because she's been unable to have kids."

"But when she married Oren, your dad thought they might have a child?" I asked.

"Right." He nodded. "My father wanted nothing more than for me to be King. It didn't matter that I had no urge to be King, or that Oren might live forever and I would never be King anyway."

"Why did he want you to be King so badly?" I asked.

"He wanted power, more power," Loki said. "He thought if I became King, we could rule the world or something. He never got specific about his plans, but he just wanted more."

"So what happened?" I asked. "I heard he tried to defect back to Förening."

"Yes, that was after everything went to hell," Loki said. "My father came up with some plan to kill Sara. I don't know exactly what it was, but I think he meant to poison her. My mother found out about it, and she . . ." He stopped and shook his head.

"My mother was kind," Loki went on. "I'd been betrothed to Sara, so she'd become like a member of our family. My mother invited her for supper regularly and treated her as a daughter. Even after Sara married Oren, my mother remained close to her."

"And your father was going to kill her?" I asked.

"Yes, but my mother wouldn't let him." He chewed the inside of his cheek and stared straight ahead at the snow coming down. "So he killed her."

"What?" I asked, thinking I'd misunderstood. "Sara's alive."

"No, my father killed my mother," Loki said flatly. "He hit her in the head with a metal vase, over and over. I was hiding in the closet, and I saw the whole thing."

"Oh, my god," I gasped. "I'm so sorry."

"The King found out, and he didn't care that my father had murdered someone," he said. "But then I told the King *why* my father killed her, about his plan to assassinate Sara.

"My father tried to make it back to the Trylle," Loki continued. "He offered Elora trade secrets, anything she'd want to know. I've been told that she accepted, but he never made it there. Oren found him and executed him."

"I'm sorry," I said, unsure of what else to say.

"I'm not," Loki said. "But I am lucky that the King didn't kill me too. Sara took pity on me, and I moved into the palace with them."

"The King and Queen raised you," I said, realizing more what Loki had meant about Sara being his only family.

He nodded. "They did. Sara more so. The King's never

been that fond of me, although I don't think he's ever been that fond of anyone."

Silence settled over us, and Loki seemed morose. Bringing up the death of his mother would have that effect.

What had happened to him was horrible, not that I'd had a great childhood myself. I thought back to when he'd arrived in Förening, and I'd put my hand on the scar on his chest. I'd felt like he was a kindred spirit, and the more I thought about it, the more I realized how alike we really were.

We both had a parental figure who hated us, and we were left orphaned at a young age. His father wanted him to be King, even though Loki didn't want it, and my mother wanted me to be Queen, even though I didn't want it. And we both shared a mixed bloodline of Trylle and Vittra.

"Why aren't you like me?" I asked when I thought of it.

"Pardon?"

"Why aren't you as powerful as me?" I asked. "We're both Trylle and Vittra."

"Well, for one thing, you're the product of the most powerful Trylle and the most powerful Vittra," Loki said. "I'm the product of a very powerful Vittra and a fairly weak Trylle. My father was a low-ranking Markis. He had hardly anything. I did get his ability to render people unconscious, though, but mine is much stronger than his ever was."

"But you have more physical strength than I do," I pointed out.

"Your father isn't physically that strong," Loki said. "Don't get me wrong, he is very strong, especially by Trylle standards. But mostly he's just . . . immortal."

"*Just* immortal," I said. "That's good. That'll make killing him so much easier."

"We can turn back," Loki offered again.

I shook my head. "No, we can't."

The car hit a patch of ice and jerked to the side. Loki reached out, putting his hand on my arm to make sure I was safe, before straightening out the car.

"Sorry about that," he said, keeping his hand on my arm.

"It's okay."

His hand felt warm on my bare skin, and I moved my arm so I could take his hand in mine. I don't know why I did it exactly, but I felt better. It helped quiet my nerves and ease the tightening of my stomach.

I stared out the window, almost embarrassed to look over at him, but he said nothing about it. He just held my hand, and eventually he started singing along with the radio again.

The snow had lessened by the time we reached the Vittra palace in Ondarike. I hadn't really had a chance to look at it the last time I was here. Now I saw how much it looked like an old castle. The brick towers and spirals loomed against the overcast sky. Tall trees without any leaves filled the surrounding forest, and I almost expected there to be a moat to cross.

Loki pulled up in front of the massive wooden doors and turned off the car. I gaped at the palace and tried not to let my nerves get the best of me. I could do this.

"How do I find him?" I asked. "Where's the King?"

"I'll show you." Loki opened his car door.

"What are you doing?" I asked as he got out.

"Taking you inside," he said and slammed the door shut.

"You can't go in there," I said once I'd climbed out of the car. "The King could do something to you."

"What kind of tour guide would I be if I didn't show you all the sights myself?" He grinned at me, but it didn't meet his eyes.

"Loki, be serious." I wouldn't walk with him up the path, so he turned back to face me. "The King will throw you in the dungeon again."

"Maybe," Loki agreed. "But I don't think he will if you succeed in making a deal with him, and we're both counting on you to make a deal."

"I don't like the idea of you going in there," I said.

"Yeah, well, I don't like you going in there either." He shrugged. "So we're even."

Reluctantly, I nodded. I didn't want to put him in danger, but he had a point. If Oren agreed with me, which was what I was counting on, I could get amnesty for Loki thrown in along with it.

Loki walked beside me up the pathway to the doors. I tried to open one, but it wouldn't budge. Loki laughed a little and reached around me. He pulled it open like it was nothing, and then we stepped inside the Vittra palace.

THIRTEEN

the truth

I'd forgotten how cavelike it was inside the King's chamber. The room was windowless, and the walls were dark mahogany. The ceilings were high, and candelabras cast a pale glow over us.

We sat in elegant red chairs, the only furniture in the room aside from a bookcase and large desk. Loki, Sara, and I sat, saying nothing, and waited for the King. Loki chewed his thumbnail, and his leg bounced nervously. Sara had her hands in her lap, and she stared off with a blank expression on her face.

As soon as we'd come inside the castle, Sara's little Pomeranian had charged at us, barking. He growled at me, but he was thrilled to see Loki and peppered him with kisses. Sara came right after, responding to the sound of his barking.

When she saw us, she blanched. She only stopped and stared, and Loki asked if she was happy to see him. Instead of answering him, she sent a nearby hobgoblin to get the King, and she led us to his chamber to wait for him.

She handed the dog off to Ludlow, one of the hobgoblins, and motioned for us to sit down. We waited in silence for what felt like a long time but may have been only minutes.

"You shouldn't have come here," Sara said finally.

"I know that," Loki said.

"You shouldn't have brought her," Sara said.

"I know that," he repeated.

"Why did you come back?" she asked.

"I don't know," Loki said, growing irritated.

"*That* you don't know?" Sara snorted. "He's going to kill you."

"I know," he said quietly.

"I won't let him," I said firmly, and Loki turned to look at me.

"Forgive me, Princess, but you are so naive," Sara said.

"I have a plan," I said, sounding more convincing than I felt. "I will make it work."

"He will never let you go," Sara said as if to warn me.

"He will," I insisted. "As long as I offer him something larger than myself in return."

"What do you have that's more than that?" Sara asked.

"My kingdom."

Loki tried to change the subject by pointing out two swords that hung on the wall. He explained that while most metal swords could probably kill the Vittra, Oren had a special set made with platinum and diamonds. He used them for all his executions, to be certain to get the job done.

I wasn't sure how that was supposed to ease the tension in

the room, but it no longer mattered because the double doors to the chamber were thrown open and the King walked in.

Loki's leg immediately stopped bobbing, and he dropped his hand to his lap. Oren smiled at us, and it made my skin crawl. Sara stood when he entered, so I did the same, but Loki was slow to follow.

"So you finally brought her?" Oren asked, giving him a discerning glare.

"I didn't bring her, sire," Loki said. "She brought me."

"Oh?" Oren looked surprised but he nodded approvingly at me. "You found the trash, and decided to return it, like I asked."

"No," I said. "He's coming with me when I leave."

"When you leave?" Oren asked, and his laugh echoed off the walls. "Oh, my dear sweet Princess, you're not leaving."

"You haven't heard what I am going to offer you," I said.

"I already have everything I want in this room." Oren had begun slowly walking around us in a large circle. Loki turned with him, to keep his eyes on him, but I didn't.

"You don't have Förening or any of the Trylle kingdom," I said. "You don't even have the remains of Oslinna. You may have devastated it, but it's still ours."

"I will get your kingdom," Oren said, his voice right behind me.

"Perhaps," I said. "But how long will it take you? Simply possessing the Princess doesn't ensure a victory over the Trylle. In fact, they will only fight you harder."

"What are you proposing?" Oren asked, and he walked around so he was in front of me.

"Time," I said. "Give me time to get the people behind the idea so you can avoid the uprising that happened when you married my mother."

"I quashed that uprising." Oren smiled slyly, probably fondly remembering all the women and children he'd killed.

"But you lost the kingdom, didn't you?" I asked, and his smile faltered.

"What could you possibly do to guarantee me the kingdom?" Oren asked.

"I will be Queen soon," I said. "You saw Elora. You know it won't be much longer."

"And our truce will end," Oren said, his words threatening.

"If you let me have the time from now until I'm Queen to get the people in order and prepared for the transition, we could do it," I said. "I could get them on your side. If I convinced them I was ruling *with* you, not under you, they would go along with me."

"You would not rule with me," he growled.

"I know," I said hastily. "I just need to get them on my side. Get them behind you. Once everything is in place, and you are King of all the Vittra and Trylle, they would bow before you without complaint. They would serve you as you desire."

"Why?" Oren raised a skeptical eyebrow and stepped back. "Why would you do this?"

"Because I know that you're going to keep fighting, and eventually you will win, but at the cost of thousands and thousands of my people's lives," I said. "I would rather work with you to ensure a bloodless takeover now than a brutal one later."

"Hmm." Oren seemed to think it over and nodded. "Smart. Very smart. What do you want in return?"

"No more attacks on any of our towns," I said. "Stop all fighting against us. If you keep slaughtering my people, it will be hard to convince them to trust you. And besides that, if it's all going to be your kingdom, you're destroying your own property."

"Those are valid points," Oren said. He'd taken to walking again, away from us this time, his back to me. "How does Loki play into all of this?"

"He's Vittra," I said. "By being kind to the Trylle, he will help convince them that you're not bad. That this has been a misunderstanding. He'll help gain the trust of the people on your behalf."

"Are you sure you want *him*, though?" Oren turned back to face us. "I could send Sara in his place."

"They already know Loki," I said. "They're beginning to trust him."

"You mean *you* trust him." Oren smiled wider at that. "He didn't tell you, did he?"

"That's too vague," I said. "I can't possibly know what you're referring to."

"Marvelous!" Oren laughed. "You don't know!"

I licked my lips. "Know what?" I asked.

Oren laughed again. "It's a lie."

"It's not all a lie," Loki said quickly. From the corner of my eye I saw the way his skin paled, and I heard the tremor in his voice. "The scars on my back are not a lie."

"Yes, well, you earned those." Oren stopped laughing and gave him a hard look. "You failed me one too many times."

"I didn't fail you," Loki said carefully. "I refused you."

"No, you failed." Oren stepped closer to him, and Loki struggled to keep eye contact with him. "She didn't run away with you. She chose someone else over you. So you failed."

"What?" I asked, and a sick feeling grew inside my stomach.

"I wouldn't have brought her back here," Loki insisted.

"You say that now," Oren said and stepped away from him. "But that's not what you said when you got back."

"I was in the dungeon, and you were beating me!" Loki shouted. "I would've agreed to anything."

"You did agree to anything," Oren said. "You agreed to seduce the Princess, to trick her into falling in love with you so you could bring her back here to me. Isn't that right?"

"That's right, but—" Loki began, but Oren cut him off.

"You went to her palace and got caught on purpose so you could stay with her, spend time with her, manipulate her," Oren said.

"That's not exactly how—" Loki said.

"And when Sara brought you back, you told me you almost had her." Oren smiled, as if telling a funny anecdote. "You told me how she'd nearly kissed you, and the way she blushed when you suggested that she marry you instead of that idiot she's with now."

Loki said nothing. He stared at the floor and bit his lip. A horrible pain grew inside my chest, because I knew it was true.

"Didn't you?" Oren yelled. Loki jumped at the sound, but he kept looking down.

"I had no choice," Loki said quietly.

"That's okay, then, isn't it?" Oren smiled when he looked at me. "Everything that has ever transpired between the two of you is a lie. But he did it because I asked him to, so that makes it okay. Doesn't it? It's okay knowing every word he ever said is a *lie*?"

"That's not true," Loki said and lifted his head. "I didn't lie. I *never* lied."

"How can you trust anything he says?" Oren shrugged.

"Why are you telling me this?" I asked, surprised by how even my voice sounded.

"Because I was hoping you would reconsider," Oren said. "You can go back to your palace, go back to your husband and your kingdom, but leave Loki here with me. You don't want or need him. He's useless. He's trash."

"No," I said, meeting Oren's eyes. "He goes with me. If you want the deal, if you want me and my kingdom as soon as I become Queen, then he goes with me now. Or the deal is off."

"He means that much to you?" Oren asked. He walked up to me, stopping in front of me so close I could feel his breath on my face. "Even knowing how he's betrayed you, you still want him back?"

"I promised I would take him back with me, and I will," I answered deliberately.

"You keep your promises," Oren said. "Good. Because if you don't keep this one, if you don't give me your kingdom as soon as you are Queen, Loki will be the first one I kill. I will do it right in front of you. Do you understand me?"

"Yes," I said.

"Good." He smiled. "Then we have a deal. All of Trylle will be mine."

"And until then, you won't lay a hand on any of the Trylle people or towns," I said. "You will leave us all in peace."

"Agreed," Oren said and held out his hand.

I shook it and I couldn't help but feel like I'd made a deal with the devil.

Sara walked us to the door, and I didn't say anything the entire way. She said very little, but at the door she told us both to be careful. She hugged Loki, and it looked like she wanted to hug me, but I wouldn't have let her.

Loki and I went out to the car, and I refused to even look at him. When we got in the car, I stared out the window.

"Wendy, I know you're upset, but you *must* listen to me. Some of what the King said is true, but he twisted it all up."

"I don't want to talk about it."

"Wendy."

"Just drive," I snapped.

He sighed but said nothing more, and the car pulled away from the Vittra palace.

I should've felt more relief. I'd gone to talk to Oren, and I'd gotten what I wanted. Oren hadn't killed either of us, which had actually been a very real possibility, and I'd bought more time for my people.

I didn't even realize how much I'd cared about Loki until I

found out it had all been a lie. Loki had just been following orders, and in a weird way I didn't blame him for that. But I still felt like a foolish idiot, and I didn't know why he'd continued to play games with me even after he'd left the Vittra.

What hurt the most was that I had been tempted. The night that Loki had come for me in the garden, I had been tempted to run off with him. I'd even felt bad for turning him down. I'd been afraid that I'd hurt his feelings.

But it had all been a lie.

I kept twisting my wedding ring and refusing to cry. I supposed this was what I deserved for cheating on my fiancé, for wanting to cheat on my husband. Regardless of what kind of marriage Tove and I had, that didn't justify whatever I had been feeling for Loki.

This could serve as a wake-up call. I should be concentrating on honoring my wedding vows and my kingdom. Not some stupid boy.

"I know you must think the worst of me right now," Loki said after we'd been driving for an hour or more. I didn't respond, so he went on, "Oren is a master manipulator. He's trying to poison your mind against me, to torture me, to torture us both."

I stared out the window. I hadn't even looked at him since we'd left.

"Wendy." He sighed. "Please. You have to listen to me."

"I don't have to do anything," I said. "I got you out of there alive. I did my part."

"Wendy!" Loki yelled. "I *never* had any intention of bringing you back to Oren. The King is many things, but he is not a stupid man, and he knows full well that I let you, Matt, and Rhys escape. He would have killed me, but he allowed me to go free to retrieve you. I told you that."

I laughed darkly. "You never told me he let you go so you could *seduce* me into coming back."

"Because I never had any intention of doing that. I swear to you, Wendy."

"I don't believe you," I said and wiped at my eyes. "I can never trust anything you say again."

"This is such bullshit." He shook his head, and abruptly he pulled the car over and put it in park.

"How is this bullshit?" I yelled. "You're the one that lied to me! You tricked me!"

"I never tricked you!" Loki shouted. "I never lied! Everything I have ever felt for you has been real! And I went through hell for you!"

"Stop, Loki! You can stop! I know the truth now!"

"No, you don't!"

"I can't do this." I shook my head. "I won't do this."

I had nowhere else to go, so I got out of the car. We'd traveled far enough so that we were in snow again, and I stepped barefoot into the cold. The stretch of highway was deserted, and empty cornfields went for miles.

"Where are you going?" Loki asked, jumping out of the car after me.

"Nowhere. I need fresh air." I pulled my cloak tighter around me. "I need to be away from you."

"Don't do this," Loki begged and walked after me. "You only heard it from him. You don't know what really happened. You have to listen to me."

"Why?" I asked, turning to face him. "Why should I listen to you?"

"He would've killed me. He executes everyone who doesn't follow orders. Surviving under Oren's rule requires saying and doing whatever the King wants to hear, truth be damned. You saw that tonight." He took a deep breath. "When you were first brought to the palace, he saw the way we interacted, and he thought he could use it against you. That you would fall in love with me."

"I will *never* love you," I said bitterly, and he winced.

"I'm only telling you what the King thought," Loki said carefully. "So he told me to get you to willingly come back with me, and I said I would. Because I didn't have a choice.

"But Wendy, I swear to you, I never would've brought you back to him. Otherwise I never would have tried to talk you out of going there tonight. If that were my plan, I would have encouraged you to place yourself in his hands."

"I understand that you had to appease Oren to survive," I said. "I really do. And I can even forgive that. But why didn't you tell me when you broke down my door begging for amnesty?"

He stared at the ground solemnly, then looked up and met my eyes. "Because I was ashamed that I'd ever agreed to it, even in pretense. And I didn't want to change the way you thought of me. I didn't want you to question all the real moments we'd shared together." He smiled sadly. "Like you do now."

"Why did you go back in the first place?" I asked thickly. "Why didn't you refuse to go back with Sara and stay in Förening?"

"Because if I stayed, it would break the truce, or the King could argue it did," Loki said. "He would come and take you. I didn't want to risk that."

"What about what you said in the garden?" I asked, looking down at my feet. For some reason, it was suddenly difficult to meet his gaze. "When you asked me to run away with you, you wouldn't have taken me back to him?"

"No," Loki said vehemently. "I never would have. Not to save my own life. Not for the fate of the entire kingdom. When I kissed you and asked you to marry me, I meant it. I wanted you to be with me."

I sniffled and stared out at the bleak whiteness around us, and the heaviness in my chest began to subside. I could see a car coming, far off down the road, but Loki put his hand on my chin, tilting it so I met his eyes.

"I made a choice between you and the King, and I chose you," Loki said. "In the garden, we were alone. I could've knocked you out and thrown you over my shoulder, then taken you back to the King. He would've spared me if I had.

"But I didn't." He stepped closer to me, and I could feel the heat radiating from his body. "He told me what he'd do to me if I didn't return you to him, but I couldn't do it."

He lifted his other hand, so he held my face in his hands. His skin was warm against mine, and even if he wasn't holding me, I wouldn't have looked away. There was something in his eyes, a longing and warmth, that took my breath away.

"Do you understand now?" Loki asked, his voice husky. "I would do it again for you, Wendy. I would go through hell and back for you. Even knowing how much you hate me right now."

I was so caught up in the moment I didn't even notice how close the passing SUV had gotten until it squealed to a stop next to us, nearly hitting our Cadillac. Loki moved toward me, and Tove jumped out of the driver's seat. Finn ran around the car and charged at Loki.

FOURTEEN

confrontation

Finn punched Loki in the face, and Loki raised his fist like he meant to strike back. That wouldn't have been so bad, except Loki was about fifty times stronger than Finn and would bust his face in.

"Loki!" I yelled. "Don't you dare hit him!"

"You are so lucky." Loki glared at Finn and wiped the blood from his nose.

"What the hell were you doing?" Finn shouted at him. "What's wrong with you? You had no right to take her anywhere!"

"Finn," Tove said. "Stop. Calm down. She's fine."

Duncan and Willa climbed out of the backseat of the SUV, and my heart sank. Loki had been right. They had been part of the rescue mission too, and if we'd left Ondarike an hour later, Duncan, Willa, Tove, and Finn would all be dead.

"Like this was my idea!" Loki yelled back at Finn. "She's the Princess. She commanded, and I obeyed!"

"You don't obey a suicide mission!" Finn shouted.

"It wasn't a suicide mission," I said, loud enough to be heard over their yelling.

They stood in front of the Cadillac, staring at each other, and, strangely, I was grateful that Loki was so much stronger than Finn. If they were equally matched, Loki probably wouldn't hold back, and there would be a hell of a fistfight.

"Are you okay?" Willa asked, walking over to me.

"Why are you on the side of the road?" Duncan asked.

"I needed fresh air," I said. "Everything's fine. I got the Vittra to back off until I'm Queen. They won't attack any of us, no matter where we are."

"What the hell did you agree to?" Finn asked, breaking his icy stare-down with Loki to look at me.

"It doesn't matter," I said. "We'll stop them before it comes to that."

"Wendy." Finn sighed and shook his head, then turned back to Loki. "And you, Markis, I lost any respect I had for you."

"She was going to go whether I went with her or not," Loki said. "I thought it would be better if she didn't go alone."

"She shouldn't have gone at all!" Finn yelled.

"Yes, I should have!" I shouted at him. "If I hadn't, the Vittra would still be killing our people. I bought us more time, and I saved lives. That is my job, Finn. I did what I had to do, and I would do it again."

"You didn't have to do it like this," Finn said.

"It doesn't matter," I said. "It's done. Now I've had a very long day, and I would just like to go home."

"Come on, Wendy." Willa put her arm around me.

"Duncan, would you mind riding with Loki?" Tove asked. "I'd like to talk to my wife."

Duncan nodded. "Yeah, sure."

Willa led me around the SUV, and I glanced back over my shoulder at Loki. He was still standing in the road, watching me walk away. Something in his eyes broke my heart, and I looked away from him.

I climbed into the SUV, and Willa got in the seat behind me. Finn stayed outside, and it looked like he wanted to say something to Loki, but Tove sent him to the car. When he climbed in back next to Willa, Finn was still seething and glared out the window.

Tove stayed outside a bit longer, talking to Loki, and I wished I could read lips.

"What were you thinking, Wendy?" Finn asked, barely restraining the anger in his voice.

"I did what was best for the kingdom," I said simply. "Isn't that what you always told me to do?"

"Not at your own peril," Finn said.

I looked in the rearview mirror so I could meet his eyes. "You've told me over and over again that I shouldn't make decisions because of you. That I should think of the greater good of the kingdom. You were right, but this isn't about me either."

"I'm glad you're safe," Willa said, breaking the tension.

"And I know that you're badass and all that, but you don't have to do this alone. You could've asked for help."

"I had help," I said, watching Loki out the car window. "Loki was with me."

Finn scoffed at that, but at least he didn't say anything.

Outside, I saw Loki nod and get in the driver's side of the car. Tove walked back to the SUV and got in. Loki's Cadillac sped off down the road, and Tove made a U-turn and drove behind him.

"You didn't tell me," Tove said at length.

"I'm sorry," I said. "But I did what—"

"Don't," Tove cut me off. "This isn't about what you did or why you did it or if it was the right thing to do."

"What is this about, then?" I asked.

"We're married, Wendy." Tove glanced over at me. "Do you know why I asked you to marry me?"

"No," I said, and I could feel Finn and Willa watching us from the backseat.

"So we could be a team," Tove said. "I thought you needed someone to support you and stand by your side, and I know I needed the same thing."

"We are a team," I said meekly.

"Then why did you go behind my back?" Tove asked.

"I didn't think you would understand," I said.

"When have I not understood?" Tove asked. "When have I not trusted you? When have I even tried to stop you from doing something?"

"You haven't," I admitted quietly. "I'm sorry."

"Don't be sorry," Tove said. "Just don't do it again. I want us to work. But to do that, you have to tell me what's going on. You can't risk your life or make major decisions about the kingdom without at least letting me know."

"I'm sorry," I repeated and stared down at my lap.

"Loki told me what you did," Tove said, and I lifted my head.

"What?"

"What you exchanged for the peace now," Tove said. "He told me the plan, and it's a good one. But we have our work cut out for us."

"What?" Willa leaned forward between the seats. "What's the plan?"

I didn't say anything, because I didn't want to talk anymore. I was exhausted, and I knew how much work we had ahead of us if we were going to stand a chance against the Vittra. But right now, all I wanted to do was sleep.

Thankfully, Loki had told Tove enough that he could explain it to Willa and Finn. I rested my head against the cold glass of the car window and listened to them talk about what we needed to do.

Some of the trackers had already made it back to Förening, and the rest would be there in the next few days. Thomas had already begun a boot camp for them.

Trackers had some combat training to help protect the changelings and other Trylle, but they weren't soldiers. Thomas was charged with turning them into an army, but they were going up against a powerful enemy they didn't know how to defeat.

Thanks to the extended peace agreement, we were now free to go to Oslinna. When we got back to Förening, we could set up another team and head out the next day. This time, Willa volunteered to go. I would go, whether anyone liked it or not, but I didn't say that during the car ride. I didn't have the strength to argue.

The hardest part would be convincing other Markis and Marksinna to join the fight. Loki thought the only thing stronger than the hobgoblins were Trylle abilities, so the ones best equipped to a fight them were the higher-ranking Trylle.

Willa said that we shouldn't tell the other Trylle what I had exchanged to get our new peace agreement. They would revolt if they thought I'd risked the kingdom. I would tell them that I had seen Oren and extended the agreement by offering to go with him voluntarily in six months.

The Trylle still wouldn't like that, but they would feel much better if they only lost me. In the meantime, we would rally them for a fight against the Vittra and hope that it worked when it came time for war.

We all had a mission when we got back to Förening. Willa was to start working on the Markis and Marksinna. They all seemed to like her, and she might be able to convince some of them to fight with us. She'd also been working on her own abilities, and she could train those who had let their abilities atrophy.

Finn would work with his father and the trackers to build up the army. He even grudgingly agreed to enlist Loki to help him. Loki was physically as strong as a hobgoblin, so at the very least, the trackers could practice fighting him to get an idea of what that kind of strength could do.

Tove had to figure out who to appoint as temporary Chancellor until an election could be held. He'd volunteered to fill the Chancellor position because he felt responsible for sending our old Chancellor to die. I assured him that it wasn't his fault, but he said he already had Markis Bain in mind for the role.

And I had what sounded like the easiest job but felt like the most impossible. I had to find a way to kill the King.

When we got back to the palace, there was a flurry of defense meetings going on. Tove had purposely not told anyone that I had left with Loki, out of fear of starting a panic, but I called a meeting as soon as we were back to let them all know.

Loki planned to head off to his room, but I asked him to go with us. I needed the Trylle to trust him. He had the most knowledge of the Vittra, so he would be the best-equipped to help us fight.

The meeting went about as well as I'd expected. Lots of yelling and disagreeing, although the Marksinna Laris was quiet since Tove had threatened to banish her. Once I got them calmed down and explained what I was going to do and what had to be done, they took it a bit better. A clear plan helped ease their fears.

I ended the meeting by telling them that we were going on a recovery and fact-finding mission to Oslinna. Without even asking them, I volunteered myself, Willa, Tove, Loki, and Aurora to go. I was trying to ease the Trylle population into the idea that Markis and Marksinna could do actual work, and hopefully they would when I called upon them.

Afterward, we all dispersed to complete our tasks. As desperately as I wanted to sleep, I didn't have time. I had to go to the library and find every book on the Vittra I could. There had to have been other immortals before Oren, and there had to be ways of killing them.

Of course, all the old texts were written in Tryllic in an attempt to disguise them from the Vittra. That was where the most useful information would be kept on how to stop them. My Tryllic had gotten better, but it wasn't fantastic. It took me ages to read a single page.

"Wendy," Tove said, and I looked up to see him standing in the doorway of the library. My vision was blurry, as I'd spent too long staring down at old texts.

I was sitting on the floor among a pile of books near the far wall. I'd started out carrying books over to the desk before deciding that was a waste of time, and I had no time to waste. We were leaving for Oslinna in the morning, and we would be gone for a few days, so I wouldn't be able to research then.

"Did you need something?" I asked.

"It's late," Tove said. "Very late."

"I have a few more documents to go through."

"When was the last time you slept?"

"I don't know." I shook my head. "It doesn't matter. I don't have time to sleep. There's so much to do, and I don't know how we can possibly do it. I don't know how we can be ready, unless I'm working every minute."

"You need sleep." He came into the room and walked over to me. "We need you to be strong, and that means you need to rest sometimes. It is a necessary evil."

"But what if I can't do this?" I asked, staring up at him with tears in my eyes. "What if I can't find a way to stop Oren?"

"You will," he assured me. "You're the Princess."

"Tove." I sighed.

"Come on." He held out his hand to me. "Sleep now. We can look more in the morning."

I let him take my hand and pull me to my feet. He was already in his pajamas, and his hair was even more disheveled than normal. I guessed he'd tried to sleep without me, but he'd gone looking for me when I hadn't come to bed.

My mind was racing, thinking of all the things I had to do. I didn't think I'd ever really be able to sleep, but as soon as my head hit the pillow, I was out.

FIFTEEN

oslinna

It looked like a bomb had gone off. Oslinna was a small town, even smaller than Förening. It was settled in a valley at the base of several low mountains. I'd never seen it before the attack, but by the looks of what was left of some of the buildings, it had been quite beautiful.

All of the trackers' homes were smashed. Trackers lived in small cottages, most of them nestled in trees or the mountains, and the floors were usually just dirt. They were very easily destroyed. But the nicer homes of the Markis and Marksinna were decimated too, with large sections of the roofs missing and entire walls collapsed.

The palace in the center was the only thing still standing. It was like a version of my own palace, except on a smaller scale and with fewer windows. While the back of my palace overlooked the river, this one was built into the mountain behind it.

Half of the palace had crumbled, and it was blackened, as if burned. The other half looked okay, at least from the outside. There had been some obvious damage, like broken windows and a destroyed fountain, but it looked much better than the rest of the town.

We'd driven slowly through the town, in awe of the carnage, and Tove had to swerve a few times to miss debris in the road. He stopped in front of the palace, parking next to an uprooted oak tree.

"This is too much for us to handle," Aurora said from the backseat. She'd been complaining about helping the entire way here, but we'd left her without a choice. She was the strongest healer, and the people of Oslinna had been hurt.

"We'll do all that we can," I said. "And if we can't do any more, then so be it."

I got out of the car before she could voice any more complaints, and Duncan pulled up in another Cadillac behind us. He had Willa, Matt, and Loki with him. Finn had wanted to come too, but he was still healing and Thomas needed him to help with the trackers. Matt had insisted on coming along, and at first I'd been against it, but we really could use all the hands we could get.

"This is even worse than I thought it would be," Willa said. She wrapped her arms around herself and shook her head.

"This is who you're fighting?" Matt asked, looking around. "The people who did this?"

"We're not fighting anyone right now," I said, cutting off his train of thought. "We're cleaning this up, helping the survivors, taking back refugees, and that's the only thing we need to worry about."

Loki lifted up a heavy branch and moved it off the path to the palace. The path had been cobblestone, but many of the stones were missing, tossed about on the lawn.

Tove and I approached the palace, trying to look both dignified and empathetic. The empathy part wasn't hard. Seeing that much damage was devastating.

Before we got to the palace, the door was thrown open. A girl not much older than me came out, her dark hair pulled up in a tangled mess, and smudges of dirt and ash covering her face and clothes. She was small, even shorter than I was, and she looked as though she might cry.

"Are you the Princess?" she asked.

"Yes, I'm the Princess from Förening," I said, then gestured to Tove. "This is the Prince. We are here to help you."

"Oh, thank god." She burst into tears and actually ran toward me and hugged me. "I didn't think anybody would come."

"We're here now." I patted her head because I wasn't sure what else to do and exchanged a look with Tove. "We'll do everything we can for you."

"Sorry." She pulled herself away from me and wiped at her eyes. "I didn't mean to do that. I've . . . There is much that needs to be done." She shook her head. "My father would be angry at me for behaving this way. I'm sorry."

"There's no need to apologize," I said. "You've been through so much."

"No, I'm in charge now," she said. "So I should act like it."

"Kenna Tomas?" I asked, hoping I remembered her name correctly. She'd once been a bridesmaid candidate and Willa had told me some about her. The only reason Kenna had not made it into my wedding party was because Aurora approved of her. Otherwise, she sounded like a nice girl.

She smiled. "Yes, I'm Kenna, and with my parents dead, I'm now the Marksinna of Oslinna."

"Do you have any survivors here?" I asked. "Any people who need medical treatment? We brought a healer."

"Oh, yes!" Kenna nodded. "Come with me."

As we followed her into the palace, Kenna explained what had happened. While the townspeople were sleeping, the hobgoblins had come in and started tearing the town apart. As far as she could tell, that was their main goal. People got hurt because the hobgoblins happened to be destroying homes with people in them, or throwing trees that would land on bystanders. It was like a tornado hitting a town in the middle of the night, without any sirens to give warning.

They had very few trackers here when the attack started, but the trackers hadn't lasted long. Kenna saw a tracker go up against a hobgoblin, and the hobgoblin snapped him in half. But the hobgoblins retreated pretty quickly after the Markis and Marksinna started defending themselves.

In the Oslinna palace, a small ballroom had been turned into a makeshift care unit. Some of the more injured Trylle had left to go to nearby hospitals, but most of them would rather die than be treated by humans.

It was horrifying to see. Cots were set up all over for survivors, and most of them were bloody and battered. Mänsklig children with broken arms and dirty faces were crying as their host parents held them.

Aurora immediately went to work without any prompting from me, which was nice. Willa and I went around talking to the people and giving them water, helping them if we could.

Kenna took Tove, Duncan, Loki, and Matt outside to show them where the most work needed to be done, and I wanted to go out with them. I would be much more useful lifting heavy objects than Matt or Duncan, because I could move them with my mind.

But I felt like I needed to be inside with the people, at least for a little while. Most of them I couldn't help, other than handing out bottled water, but I think some of them just wanted to talk, to know that somebody cared.

Their stories were heartbreaking. Wives had lost their husbands, children had lost their parents, and most trackers had lost everything. I wanted to cry, but I couldn't. It felt wrong and selfish. I needed to be calm and assure them that we would fix this, that *I* would make everything better.

I paused when I passed a young woman sitting on a cot. She couldn't have been more than a year or two older than me, if that, and even covered in dirt and bruises, she was still devastatingly beautiful. Her long brown hair had warm undertones, like a burnt umber.

It was her eyes, though, that caught me. They were an endless shade of brown, and stared vacantly at nothing. Tears fell from them without a sound.

In her arms she cradled a small child, less than a year old. The little girl had pudgy arms, and she clung to the young woman, reminding me of the way a monkey will cling to its mother. Based on the baby's appearance—her tanned skin, her dark wild curls—I'd say she was Trylle, meaning she was a tracker baby.

"How are you doing?" I asked. When she didn't look up at me, I knelt down in front of her. "Are you all right?"

"I'm okay," she said numbly, still staring off at the floor.

"What about the baby?" I touched the child tentatively. I'd never really interacted that much with babies, but I felt like I should do something.

"The baby?" She seemed confused at first, then looked down at the little girl in her arms. "Oh. Hanna is fine. She's sleepy, but she doesn't understand what's happened."

"That's probably for the best," I said.

Hanna stared up at me, her eyes seeming almost too large for her small face. Then she reached out and grabbed my finger, almost latching on to it, and smiled dazedly at me.

"Hanna's a beautiful little girl," I said. "Is she yours?"

"Yes." She nodded once. "Thank you." She swallowed hard and tried to force a smile at me. "My name is Mia."

"Where's her father?" I asked, hoping against hope that he'd been away when the attack happened.

"He . . ." Mia shook her head, and the silent tears fell faster. "He was trying to protect us, and he . . ."

"I shouldn't have asked." I put my hand on Mia's arm, hoping to comfort her.

"I just don't know what we'll do without him." She began sobbing.

I sat on the cot next to her and put my arm around her, because that was all I could think to do. There was something about her, something so sweet and helpless, and I wanted to fix her problems and ease her pain. But I couldn't.

She looked too young to be a wife, let alone a mother and a widow. I couldn't imagine what she was going through, but I would do anything I could to help her.

"You'll be all right," I tried to reassure Mia as she wept onto my shoulder. Hanna began to wail, most likely because she saw her mother crying. "It will take time, but you and Hanna will be fine."

Mia struggled to stop her tears and rocked her baby. Hanna stopped crying almost as soon as Mia did, and she let out a deep breath.

"I'm sorry to be like this, Princess," Mia said, looking at me. "I shouldn't be crying on you like this."

"No, don't worry about it." I waved it off. "But Mia, listen, when we leave Oslinna, I want you to come back to Förening with us. We'll have a nice place for you to stay, and we'll figure out what you'll do there. Okay? But you and Hanna will always have a place at the palace."

"Thank you." Her eyes were brimming with fresh tears, and I was afraid I would send her sobbing again, so I left her alone to cuddle her daughter.

Something about Mia lingered with me. Even as I went around the room, I couldn't shake the image of her heartbroken eyes. There was a warmth and kindness about her that I could see underneath the devastation, and I hoped that someday she would be happy again.

I stayed long enough to talk to every person in the room, but then I had to move on. I could be of more help to them outside than I could in here. Willa went with me for the same reasons, leaving Aurora alone to heal them as much as she could.

As we were leaving, Willa was tearing up. She had a small, dirty teddy bear clutched in her hands, and she wiped at her eyes.

"That was pretty rough in there," I said, holding back my own tears.

"A little tracker boy gave me this." She held up the bear. "His whole family died. His parents, his sister, even his dog. And he gave me this because I sang him a song." She shook her head. "I didn't want to take it. But he said it was his sister's, and she'd want another girl to have it."

I put my arm around her, giving her a half hug as we walked down the hall toward the palace door.

"We have to do more for these people," Willa said. "That little boy isn't hurt, but if he was, Aurora wouldn't heal him. She wouldn't want to waste her energy on a tracker."

"I know." I sighed. "It's insane."

"That's got to change." Willa stopped and pointed back to the ballroom. "Every one of those people in there has been through hell, and they all deserve help just as equally."

"I know, and I'm trying to make it better," I said. "When

I'm going to all those meetings, this is what I'm trying to do and why I want you to help me with them. I will change this, and I will make it better. But I need help."

"Good." She sniffled and played with the teddy bear. "I will start going to the meetings. I want to be a part of what it is you're doing."

"Thank you," I said, feeling some small bit of relief in that. "But right now, the best way to help these people is to get this place cleaned up so they can start rebuilding their homes."

Willa nodded and walked with me again. Outside, I could see some improvement. Half of a roof had been on the palace lawn, but it was gone now, as well as the uprooted oak by the cars. I could hear the men a few houses down arguing about what to do with the debris.

Matt suggested they make a pile in the road for now, and they could worry about moving it later. Loki started to argue against it, but Tove told him to just do it. They didn't have time to waste fighting.

Willa and I joined them, and we all went to work. Loki, Tove, and I did most of the lifting, while Matt, Duncan, and Willa tried to clean things and straighten up the houses. Just moving the garbage out of the way wouldn't solve the townspeople's problems, but it was the first step in being able to go back and fix it up.

As the day wore on, I started to feel exhausted, but I pushed through it. Loki had to move everything physically, so despite the chill, he ended up warm and sweaty. He took off his shirt, and the ordinarily pleasing sight pained me. The marks on his back looked better than they had before, but they were still there. Reminders of what he'd gone through, for me.

"What happened to him?" Willa asked me while we cleaned out one of the houses. A tree had gone through the window. I got it out, and she cleaned up the glass and branches.

"What?" I asked, but I saw her staring out the open window at Loki as he tossed a destroyed couch on the garbage pile in the road.

"Loki's back," she said. "Is that what the King did to him? That's why he has amnesty?"

"Yeah, it is."

Wind came up around me, blowing my hair in my eyes, as Willa created a small tornado in the middle of the living room. It circled around, sucking all the glass and little bits of tree into the funnel, so Willa could send it out to the garbage.

"So what's going on with you and him?" Willa asked.

"Who?" I said. I tried to pick up one of the couches that had been tipped over, and Willa came over to help me.

"You and Loki." She helped me flip the couch back on its feet. "Don't play dumb. There's something major there."

I shook my head. "There's nothing anywhere."

"Whatever you say." She rolled her eyes. "But I've been meaning to ask you, how's the marriage going?"

"The past three days have been fantastic," I said dryly.

"What about the wedding night?" Willa asked with a smile.

"Willa! This isn't the time to be talking about that."

"Of course it is! We need to lighten the mood," she insisted.

"And I haven't had a chance to talk to you about any of this yet. Your life has been all drama since the wedding."

"You're telling me," I muttered.

"Take five minutes." Willa sat down on the couch and patted the spot next to her. "You're visibly exhausted. You need a break. So take five and talk to me."

"Fine," I said, mostly because my head was beginning to throb from all the objects I'd moved. That last tree had been hard to get going. I sat down next to her, and a bit of dirt billowed up from the couch. "This is never going to be clean."

"Don't worry about that," Willa said. "We'll get this place picked up, and then we can send out all the maids in Förening to help them with the finishing touches. We're only focusing on getting them on the path to recovery right now. We can't do the entire recovery in one day, but eventually we'll get it all taken care of."

"I hope so."

"But Wendy, how was your wedding night?" Willa asked.

"You really wanna talk about this?" I groaned and leaned my head on the back of the couch.

"Right now there's nothing else I'd like to talk about."

"You're in for a real disappointment," I said. "Because there's nothing to tell."

"It was that bland?" she asked.

"No, it was nothing," I said. "And I mean literally nothing. We didn't do anything."

"Wait." She leaned back on the couch as if to look at me better. "You mean that you're married and still a virgin?"

"That is what I mean."

"Wendy!" Willa gasped.

"What? Our marriage is weird. Really weird. You know that."

"I know." She looked disappointed. "I was hoping you could have a happily-ever-after is all."

"Well, it's not ever after yet," I pointed out.

"Wendy!" Matt yelled from outside the house. "I need your help with something!"

"Duty calls." I stood up.

"That was barely even a minute," Willa said. "You do need to take a break, Wendy. You're running yourself ragged."

"I'm fine," I said as I walked out of the house. "I'll sleep when I'm dead."

We worked well into the night and ended up getting most of the big debris cleared out and piled up. I might have pressed on to do more work, but it was clear that everybody else couldn't.

"I think we need to call it a night, Wendy," Loki said. He rested his arms on an overturned refrigerator, leaning on it.

Matt and Willa were sitting on a log next to the pile, and Tove stood next to them, drinking a bottle of water. Only Duncan still helped me as we struggled to pull a shredded mattress from a tracker house. I had to stop using my powers, because it killed my head every time I did.

Only three streetlights in the entire town still worked, and Matt, Willa, Tove, and Loki had taken their break near one. They'd stopped working about fifteen minutes ago, but I insisted that I keep going.

"Wendy, come on," Matt said. "You've done as much as you can do."

"There's more stuff to do, so clearly I haven't," I said.

"Duncan needs a break," Willa said. "Let's quit. We can do more tomorrow."

"I'm fine," Duncan panted, but I stopped pulling on the mattress long enough to look up at him. He was filthy, his hair was a mess, and his face was red and sweaty. I'd actually never seen him look so terrible.

"Fine. We're done for the night," I relented.

We walked back over and sat down on the log next to Matt and Willa. She had a small cooler of water and handed a bottle to each of us. I opened mine and drank greedily. Tove paced in front of us, fidgeting with his bottle cap. I don't know how he had the energy to walk that much.

"We're getting this cleaned up, and that's good," Matt said. "But we're not doing anything to rebuild. We're not even qualified."

"I know." I nodded. "We'll have to send another team down that can rebuild and do more specialized cleaning. After we get back to Förening, we'll really have to get people down here."

"I could work on some blueprints, if you want," Matt offered. "I can design stuff that's quick and easy to build but doesn't look cheap."

"That would be fantastic," I said. "It'd be a great step in the right direction."

Matt was an architect, or at least he would've been if I hadn't dragged him to Förening with me. I wasn't entirely sure how he spent his days at the palace, but it would be good for him to work on something. Not to mention that it would be good for Oslinna.

"The good news is that the damage seems to support what Kenna was saying," Loki said. He stopped leaning on the fridge and walked over to sit next to me.

"What do you mean?" I asked.

"The hobgoblins aren't vicious or mean, not really," Loki said. "They're destructive and irritating, sure, but I've never known them to kill anybody."

"They have now." Willa gestured to the mess around us.

"I don't think murder was their ultimate goal, though," Loki said. "They were trying to destroy the town. And even when they fought with that team the other night, they didn't kill most of them."

"How does that help anything?" I asked.

"I don't know." Loki shrugged. "But I think they aren't as hard to defeat as we once thought. They're not fighters."

"I'm sure that will be real comforting to all the dead people here," Tove said.

"All right." Willa stood up. "That's enough for me. I'm ready to go inside and get cleaned up and get some sleep. What about you guys?"

"Do we have places to sleep?" Duncan asked.

"Yes." Willa nodded. "Kenna told me that most of the bedrooms in the palace weren't that damaged, and they have some running water if we want to wash up."

"Well, I definitely want those things." Loki got up.

We all walked back to the palace, but Tove lagged behind. I slowed down to walk with him, and he twitched a lot. He kept swatting at his ear, like there was a mosquito or a fly buzzing by, but I didn't see any. I asked if he was okay, but he just shook his head.

Kenna showed us to the extra rooms in the palace, and I felt bad taking them when there were so many people without homes. She pointed out that there were too many people for the bedrooms, so she didn't want to divvy them up among the survivors because it would only create discord and add misery to a difficult situation.

Besides that, the rooms she showed us weren't in such great shape. They were small, and while they didn't have major damage, they were in disarray. Our whole room seemed to slant slightly to the side, and books and furniture were tossed all over.

I straightened up the room and let Tove shower first down the hall. Something seemed off with him, and I thought it would be better if he had a chance to rest instead of doing more work.

"What are you doing?" Tove asked. He came back to the room after the shower, his hair all wet and a mess.

"I'm making the bed." I was smoothing out the sheets but I turned to face him. "How was your shower?"

"Why are you making the bed?" he snapped and rushed over to it. I moved out of the way and he pulled down the sheets.

"Sorry," I said. "I didn't know it would upset you. I thought it would be—"

"Why?" Tove whirled around to face me, his green eyes burning. "Why would you do that?"

"I just made the bed, Tove," I said carefully. "You can unmake it if you want. Why don't you get into bed? Okay? You're exhausted. I'll go shower, and you get some sleep."

"Fine! Whatever!"

He ripped the sheets off the bed and muttered to himself. He'd done too much today and overloaded his brain. My head was still buzzing, and I was stronger than him. I couldn't imagine how he felt.

I grabbed the duffel bag I'd packed in Förening and went to take a shower. Leaving him alone to rest would probably be the best thing I could do for him. I wanted to take a long hot shower, but by the time I got to it, the water was cold, so I showered quickly.

Even before I made it back to the room, I could hear Tove. His mutterings had gotten louder.

"Tove?" I said quietly and pushed open the bedroom door.

"Where have you been?" Tove shouted, his eyes wide and frantic. All the cleaning I had done in the room had been undone. Everything was strewn about, and he was pacing.

"I was in the shower," I said. "I told you."

"Did you hear that?" He froze and looked around.

"What?" I asked.

"You're not even listening!" Tove yelled.

"Tove, you're tired." I walked into the room. "You need to sleep."

"No, I can't sleep." He shook his head and looked away from

me. "No, Wendy." He ran his hands through his hair. "You don't understand."

"What don't I understand?" I asked.

"I can hear it all." He put both his hands to the sides of his head. "I can hear it all!" He kept repeating that, and he held his head tighter. His nose started to bleed, and he groaned.

"Tove!" I rushed over to him and I reached out, just to comfort him, but when I did, he slapped me hard in the face.

"Don't you dare!" Tove turned on me and threw me back on the bed. I was too startled to do anything. "I can't trust you! I can't trust any of you!"

"Tove, please calm down," I begged him. "This isn't you. You're just tired."

"Don't tell me who I am! You don't know who I am!"

"Tove." I slid to the edge of the bed, so that I was sitting, and he stood in front of me, glowering down at me. "Tove, please listen to me."

"I can't." He bit his lip. "I can't hear *you*!"

"You can hear me," I said. "I'm right here."

"You're lying!" Tove grabbed me by my shoulders and started shaking me.

"Hey!" Loki shouted, and Tove let go of me.

I'd left the bedroom door open when I came in, and Loki had been on his way back to his room from his own shower. He was still shirtless, and his light hair was dripping water onto his shoulders.

"Go away!" Tove yelled at him. "I can't have you here!"

"What the hell are you doing?" Loki asked.

"Loki, it's not him," I said. "He's used his abilities too much, and it's done something to him. He needs to sleep."

"Stop telling me what I need to do!" Tove growled. He raised his hand like he meant to slap me again, and I flinched.

"Tove!" Loki shouted and ran over to him.

"Loki!" I yelled, afraid that he would hit him, but he didn't.

Loki grabbed Tove by the shoulders, making Tove look at him. Tove tried to squirm away, but within seconds he was unconscious. His body slacked, and Loki caught him. I moved out of the way so Loki could lay him back down on the bed.

"Sorry," I said, unsure of what else to say.

"Don't be sorry. He was about to hit you."

"No, he wasn't." I shook my head. "I mean, he was. But that's not Tove. That's not who he is. He would never hurt anybody. He just . . ."

I trailed off. I wanted to cry. My face stung from where Tove had slapped me. But that wasn't even why I wanted to cry. He was sick, and he was only going to get sicker. Tomorrow he'd be better, but eventually his powers would eat away at his brain. Eventually, there wouldn't be any Tove left.

Loki leaned in, staring at my cheek with a pained expression. My cheek began to throb, and I realized there must be a red mark. I turned my face away, embarrassed.

"Thank you," I said, "but I'm fine."

"No, you're not," Loki said. "I don't care if he's your husband, and I don't care if he's lost his mind. There's no excuse for hitting you, and if he does it again . . ." The muscle in his jaw twitched, and his eyes flashed with a protective anger.

"He won't do it again," I assured him, even though I wasn't entirely sure if that was true.

"He better not," Loki said, but his anger seemed to lessen, and he touched my arm tenderly. "Now come on. You can't stay here with him tonight."

SIXTEEN

one night

I'd gotten Aurora and sent her in to stay with Tove for the night. I felt guilty for leaving him, but she would be better equipped to handle him if he got out of control again.

Since she was staying with Tove, I took her room. The four-poster bed sat in the corner, draped with red curtains and sheets. One of the walls was very crooked, practically leaning on top of the bed, and it made the room feel even smaller.

"Are you going to be all right now?" Loki asked. He'd walked me over here, and he waited just inside the doorway.

"Yeah, I'm great," I lied and sat down on the bed. "The entire kingdom is falling apart. People are dying. I have to kill my father. And my husband just went crazy."

"Wendy, none of that's your fault."

"Well, it feels like it's all my fault," I said, and a tear slid down my cheek. "I only make everything worse."

"That's not true at all." Loki walked over and sat on the bed next to me. "Wendy, don't cry."

"I'm not," I lied. I wiped at my eyes and looked at him. "Why are you even being nice to me?"

"Why wouldn't I be nice to you?" he asked, looking confused.

"Because." I pointed to the scars covering his back. "That's because of me."

"No, it isn't." Loki shook his head. "That's because the King is evil."

"But if I had gone with him in the first place, none of this would've happened," I said. "None of these people would've died. Even Tove would be better."

"And you would be dead," Loki said. "The King would still hate the Trylle, maybe even more so if he blamed them for brainwashing you. He would eventually attack them and take the kingdom for himself."

"Maybe." I shrugged. "Maybe not."

"Stop." He put his arm around me, and it felt safe and warm. "Not everything is your fault, and you can't fix everything. You're only one person."

"It never feels like enough." I swallowed and looked up at him. "Nothing I do is ever enough."

"Oh, believe me, you do more than enough." He smiled and brushed a hair back from my face.

His eyes met mine, and I felt a familiar yearning inside of me, one that got stronger every time I was with him.

"Why did you want me to remember?" I asked.

"Remember what?"

"When we were in your room, you said you wanted me to remember that I wanted you to kiss me."

"So you admit you wanted me to kiss you?" Loki smirked.

"Loki."

"Wendy," he echoed, smiling at me.

"Why didn't you just kiss me?" I asked. "Wouldn't that have been a better thing to remember?"

"It wasn't the right time."

"Why not?"

"You were on a mission. If I kissed you, it would've only been for a second, because you were in a rush to go," he said. "And a second wouldn't be enough."

"So when is the right time?" I asked.

"I don't know," he whispered.

He had his hand on my cheek, wiping away a tear, and his eyes were searching my face. He leaned forward, and his lips brushed against mine. Delicately at first, almost testing to see if this was real. His kisses were soft and sweet, and so very different from Finn's.

As soon as I thought of Finn, I pushed him from my mind. I didn't want to think of anything else. I didn't want to feel anything except Loki. The exhaustion of the night was pushed away as something surged through, something warm and intense.

Loki kissed me more deeply and pushed me back on the bed. He wrapped an arm around my waist, lifting me up and pulling me farther onto the bed. I clung to him, my hands digging into his bare back. The scars felt like braille under my fingers, scars he'd gotten to protect me.

"Wendy," he murmured as he kissed my neck, his lips trailing all over my skin and making me tremble.

He stopped kissing me long enough to look at me. His light hair fell into his eyes. Something about the way he looked at me, his eyes the color of burnt honey, made my heart beat faster.

It was like I'd never truly seen him before. All his pretenses had fallen away; his smirk, his swagger, were all gone. It was just him, and I realized that this might be the first time I was really seeing him.

Loki was vulnerable and kind and more than a little frightened. But more than that, he was lonely, and he cared about me. He cared about me so much it terrified him, and as much as that should've scared me too, it didn't.

All I could think about was that I'd never seen anything more beautiful. It felt strange thinking of a guy that way, but that's what he was. Looking down at me, waiting for me to accept him or push him away, Loki was *beautiful*.

I reached for him and touched his face, almost astonished that he could be real. He closed his eyes and kissed the palm of my hand. One of his hands was on my side, and his grip tightened, sending hot shivers all through my body.

"I hate to even ask this, but . . ." Loki trailed off, his voice husky. "Are you sure you want to do this?"

"I want you, Loki," I said before I could let myself think about anything.

I wanted him, *needed* him, and for one night I refused to think about the consequences or the repercussions. I just wanted to be with him.

Loki smiled, relieved, and he almost seemed to glow. He bent down, kissing me again, only deeper and more fervently.

His hand slid under my nightgown, strong and sure on my thigh. I loved his strength and power, and the way I could feel it in even his smallest touches. He tried to hold back so he wouldn't hurt me, but when he tried to slide off my panties, he tore them in half.

I took off my nightgown, slipping it up over my head, because I didn't want him ripping that too. He tried to be gentle with me, and some part of me did want him to be, because that was the way I thought my first time should be. But we were both far too eager.

He started out slow, trying to ease himself in me, but I moaned in his ear, gripping tightly on to him, and any pretense of restraint was gone. It hurt, and I buried my face into his shoulder to keep from crying out. But he didn't slow, and very soon the heat grew inside me. I was glad he didn't slow. Even the pain felt like pleasure.

Afterward, he collapsed on the bed next to me, both of us gasping for breath. We'd knocked the bed off-kilter, and I vaguely remembered hearing the sound of a board cracking, so we might have broken it. The red curtains of the four-poster bed had been tied open, but they had come loose, so they fell around the bed and closed off the world around us.

A few candles lit the room, and we were shrouded in a warm

red glow as their light flickered through the curtains. I felt sheltered, like I was wrapped in a warm cocoon, and I didn't think I'd ever felt more content or safe in my life.

I lay on my back, and Loki moved next to me, almost encircling me. One arm was behind my neck, and the other one was draped over my belly. I wrapped my arms around his so I could hold him closer to me.

Because I was nestled in his arms this way, the scar on his chest was right next to me. I'd never seen it this close before. It looked so jagged and rough. It slashed at an angle, starting right above his heart, and stopping below his other nipple.

"Do you hate me?" I asked quietly.

"Why on earth would I hate you?" Loki asked, laughing.

"Because of this." I touched his scar, and his skin trembled around it. "Because of what my father did to you over me."

"No, I don't hate you." He kissed my temple. "I could never hate you. And it's not your fault what the King did."

"How did you get this?" I asked.

"Before he decided to punish me, the King considered execution," Loki said, almost wearily. "He used a sword before deciding that torture might be more fun."

"He almost killed you?" I looked at him, and the very thought of Loki dying made me want to cry.

"He didn't, though." He brushed back my hair, his fingers running through the tangles of it, and he smiled down at me. "The King couldn't, no matter how hard he tried. My heart refused to give up. It knew I had something to fight for."

"You shouldn't say things like that." I swallowed back tears and lowered my eyes. "Tonight was . . . beautiful and amazing, but it was only for tonight."

"Wendy." Loki groaned and rolled onto his back. "Why did you have to say something like that now?"

"Because." I sat up and pulled my knees to my chest. The sheets hung over my legs, but my back was bare to him. "I don't want you to . . ." I sighed. "I don't want to hurt you any more than I already have."

"It looks like I hurt you, actually." Loki sat up and touched my arm. "You have a bruise."

"What?" I looked down and saw a purplish blotch on my arm. "I don't remember you doing that." I'd probably have bruises on my thighs, but Loki didn't grab my arms. "Oh. This isn't from you. It's from Tove."

"Tove." Loki sighed. He didn't say anything for a minute, then looked over at me. "You're going back to him tomorrow, aren't you?"

"He is my husband."

"He hit you."

"He wasn't in his right mind. Once he's back to himself, he'll feel terrible. It won't happen again."

"It better not," he said firmly.

"Anyway, I married him for a reason, and that hasn't changed."

"What reason is that?" Loki asked. "I know you don't love him."

"The Trylle don't want me to be Queen," I said. "They don't trust me, because of who my father is, among other things. Tove's family is very influential and helps balance it out. If I wasn't married to him, his mother would be leading the campaign to get me overthrown. Without Tove, I'd never be Queen."

"Why is that a bad thing?" Loki asked. "These people don't trust you or like you, and you're sacrificing everything for them. How does that make sense?"

"Because they need me. I can help them. I can save them. I'm the only one who can stand up to my father, and I'm the only one that cares enough to fight for the rights of the trackers and the less powerful Trylle. I have to do this."

"I wish you didn't say that with such conviction." He put his arm around me and moved closer. He kissed my shoulder, then whispered, "I don't want you to go back to Tove tomorrow."

"I have to."

"I know," he said. "But I don't want you to."

"You can have me for tonight, though." I gave him a small smile, and he lifted his head so his eyes met mine. "That's all I can give you."

"I don't want only one night. I want *all* the nights. I want all of you, forever."

Tears swam in my eyes, and my heart yearned so badly it hurt. Sitting there with Loki, I didn't think I'd ever felt quite so heartbroken.

"Don't cry, Wendy." He smiled sadly at me, and I saw the heartbreak in his eyes mirroring my own. He pulled me to him and kissed my forehead, then my cheeks, then my mouth.

"So, if this is all you'll let me have, then I will take it all," Loki said. "No talking or even worrying about the kingdom or responsibility or anyone else. You're not the Princess. I'm not Vittra. We're only a boy and a girl crazy about each other, and we're naked in bed."

I nodded. "I can do that."

"Good, because I'm determined to make the most of it." He smiled and pushed me down on the bed. "I think we broke the bed a little bit last time. What do you say we see if we can destroy it?"

I laughed, and he kissed me. Tomorrow I might regret this. Tomorrow I might have hell to pay. But for one night, I refused to think or worry. I was with Loki, and he made me feel like the only thing in the world that truly mattered. And in that night, he was the only thing that truly mattered to me.

A knocking woke me in the morning, and I was surprised that I'd even slept at all. The night washed over me in a hazy, happy blur. Everything felt like a wonderful dream, and I'd never known that I could feel that close to another person or that . . . *happy.* Loki's arms were strong around me, and I snuggled deeper into them. I wanted to stay curled up next to him forever.

"Princess?" Aurora called from outside my bedroom, and it was like a cold slap pulling me from my dream. "Are you up? I need to get my clothes." Loki's arms tensed around me, and before I could answer, the bedroom door creaked open and Aurora walked into the room.

SEVENTEEN

consequence

The curtains were still drawn around the bed, but if Aurora pulled them back, she would find me naked in bed with a guy who was not her son. I heard her moving about the room, and I was too scared to speak or even breathe.

My mind raced to remember what had become of our clothes. Were Loki's pajama pants on the bedroom floor? And what became of the panties he'd torn off me?

"Princess?" Aurora said again, and I could see her silhouette through the curtain. She was right outside. "Are you in here?"

"Yeah," I said, afraid that she would open the curtain if I didn't answer. I tried to quiet the panic in my voice. "Uh, yeah. Sorry. I'm really . . . out of it. Yesterday was . . . exhausting."

"I understand," Aurora said. "I'll take my bag so I can get ready and give you time to wake up."

"Okay. Thank you."

"Of course." Aurora's footsteps went toward the door, then she stopped. "Tove feels terrible about what happened last night. He never meant to hurt you."

"I know that." I winced at the mention of Tove. The warm memories of last night turned into cold truths. I'd cheated on my husband.

"He'll want to apologize for himself, but I wanted to be sure you knew," Aurora said. "He'd never hurt you on purpose."

That was like a knife to my heart, and it cut so deep I could barely breathe for a second. I knew that Tove didn't love me, but I doubted he'd be happy about me having sex with another guy. And he deserved so much better than that.

"I will see you downstairs for breakfast," Aurora said.

"Yes," I said, my voice tight to keep back tears.

The bedroom door shut behind her, and I let out a long shaky breath. I pulled away from Loki and sat up. I'd never felt so conflicted in my life. I wanted nothing more than to lay with him forever, but being with him made me feel guilty and horrible.

"Hey." Loki put his arm around my waist, trying to pull me back to him. "You don't have to rush away. She left."

"We have a lot to do today." I pushed his arm off me, hating that I had to reject him, and grabbed my nightgown from where it lay crumpled at the end of the bed.

"I know," Loki said, sounding a little hurt. He sat up as I pulled the nightgown on. "I'd never try to keep you from your work, but can't you spend five more minutes in bed with me?"

"No, I can't." I shook my head and refused to look back at him. I didn't want to see the look on his face or think about what we'd done. I could still taste him on my lips and feel him inside me, and I wanted to sob.

"So . . . that's it, then?" Loki asked.

"I told you that last night was all we could have," I said.

"That you did." He breathed deeply. "I guess I was hoping that I could change your mind."

I got out of bed and found my torn panties sticking out from under the dust ruffle. The bed creaked as Loki got out after me. I turned back to face him. He'd pulled on his pants, but he hadn't worn a shirt here.

"You'll have to sneak back to your room," I told him. "Nobody can see you."

"I know. I'll be careful."

We stood there, staring at each other and not saying anything. There were only a few feet between us, but the distance felt like miles. There was so much that I wanted to say but couldn't. Any words would only make it worse.

If I said aloud how much last night had meant to me, it would make it too real.

Loki walked toward the door but stopped next to me. His hands were balled up into fists, and I could see him struggling with something. Without saying anything, he grabbed me suddenly and pulled me toward him.

He kissed me so passionately, my knees felt weak. I wasn't sure I would be able to stand when he let go, but I did.

"That was the last time," I breathed when we stopped kissing.

"I know," he said simply. Then he let go of me and walked out of the room.

As soon as he was gone, I folded my arms across my chest, hugging myself. My stomach lurched, and I was certain I would throw up for a moment, but it passed. *Don't cry, don't cry, don't cry.* I repeated it over and over in my head, but I couldn't use my own persuasion on myself. I reached behind me and grabbed the bedpost, afraid that my legs would give out.

What had I done? To Loki? To Tove? To myself?

"Princess?" Duncan knocked on the door, but I couldn't form the words to answer him. The lump in my throat was too great. "Princess?" He opened the door, and I did my best to compose myself. "Wendy, are you okay?"

"Yes." I nodded and swallowed back tears. "I'm tired. Yesterday was too much."

"Yeah, I know," Duncan said. "I slept like the dead, but I had all these weird dreams about banging noises. Did you hear anything last night? My room was right next to yours."

"No." I shook my head. "Sorry."

"I just wanted to check on you," Duncan said. "Are you sure you're okay?"

"I'm fine," I lied.

"I talked to Kenna this morning, and she'd like to send those whose homes are unlivable to Förening for now," Duncan said. "Willa suggested that we all return today and get the survivors settled in at the palace. Then we can send back people that actually know how to rebuild Oslinna, since none of us really know how to build a house."

"Um, yes, I think that sounds good," I said. "I'll have to speak with Kenna first." I realized something and looked back at him. "Is everyone up, then?"

"Yeah, everyone but you, Tove, and Loki," Duncan said. "But I just saw Loki in the bathroom, so I guess he's up now. What happened with Tove last night? Aurora said that he was sick or something?"

"Yes," I said quickly. "He's . . . sick." I rubbed the bruise on my arm, trying to cover it up. "I need to talk to him. Is he in his room?"

"As far as I know," Duncan said.

"Thank you," I said. "I'll go talk to him and get dressed, and then I will meet everyone downstairs. Does that sound all right?"

"Yeah, that sounds great," Duncan said. "And, Princess, you should really take it easy today. You look like you're coming down with something."

I waved him off, and he left. As I walked down to Tove's room, I kept trying to think of what I wanted to say. Should I tell him about Loki?

Not here. Not now. We had too much to do for the people here. I didn't want to waste time on a fight.

Timidly, I knocked on the door. I still hadn't come up with what I was going to say to Tove. He opened the door, and the sight of him made it worse. He looked like hell. His hair was always disheveled, but not this bad. I knew he'd slept, but he still had bags under his eyes. His normally mossy-tan skin had paled, and worst of all, he appeared to have aged a few years overnight.

"Wendy, I am so sorry" were the first words out of his mouth, and for a second I didn't understand what he had to be sorry for. "I never meant to hit you. I'd *never* do that. Not if I was thinking clearly."

"No, it's okay," I said numbly. "I know. Yesterday took a lot out of everybody."

"That's no excuse." Tove shook his head. "I should've . . . done something."

"You couldn't have," I said. "And I understand."

"No, you don't. What I did, it wasn't okay. It's never okay to hit a woman, let alone my wife."

The word *wife* made me flinch, but I didn't think he noticed. I didn't want to have this conversation anyway. I couldn't handle listening to him apologize to me after what I'd done. I didn't condone hitting women either, but that wasn't Tove. He hadn't been in his right mind.

And I'd done something just as bad by sleeping with Loki. I hadn't exactly been clearheaded myself when it happened, but if I was being honest, I *wanted* to, even when I wasn't drained from my powers. Yesterday's overload of work had only weakened my inhibitions, so I was more willing to give in to something I wanted.

I still wanted to be with Loki, and that was why my crime far outweighed Tove's.

I brushed past Tove and went over to my suitcase to get a change of clothes. He tried apologizing again, and I reiterated that he had nothing to be sorry for. Before he could bring up last night again, I changed the subject to talk about all the things we had to get done today.

We had gotten all of the major cleaning done, so there was nothing more we personally could do for Oslinna.

I got dressed and went down to start figuring out how to get people out of here. Some vehicles were still in working order, but not enough for everyone. We'd have to send out more cars once we got back to the palace.

As we helped organize the transport, deciding who would go and who would stay, Willa commented on how strange I seemed. I was acting as close to normal as I could, except anytime Loki came near me, I left in a hurry. It was hard to even be around him.

Once everyone was loaded up, we drove home. Kenna stayed behind to run what was left of Oslinna, but I promised her that more help would be on the way soon. Rebuilding the town would be my top priority. Well, right after protecting the kingdom from Vittra domination.

Willa and Matt rode with Tove and me to Förening, and I was grateful. I didn't think I would've been able to handle a long car ride with just Aurora and Tove. Matt sat in the backseat, sketching architectural designs and talking about all the things we could do for Oslinna.

When we got back, we helped get the refugees set up in the

spare rooms of the palace. It would be weird having so many people living here, but it might be good too. I personally helped Mia and her daughter Hanna get settled in a room, and they both seemed to be a bit happier.

I tasked Willa with getting the resources together to rebuild Oslinna, and Matt was more than happy to take over the reconstruction plans.

As soon as the people from Oslinna were taken care of, I went down to the library to continue my research. I still had to find a way to kill Oren and stop the hobgoblins. Eventually we would be up against the Vittra, and I needed to know how to defeat them.

Besides that, it would do me good to immerse myself in work. I didn't want to think about the mess I'd made of my personal relationships.

I spent most of the evening searching through old Tryllic texts to no avail. None of them mentioned anything about immortal trolls, or at least not that I could understand. I went back over to search for a different book. When I looked up, I saw Finn standing in the doorway to the library.

I didn't think my guilt could get any deeper until I saw him. Despite the fact that Finn and I had never even really been together, not to mention that whatever we had was officially over, I knew how disappointed he would be in me if he knew that I'd slept with Loki.

"Are you all right, Princess?" Finn narrowed his eyes in concern and came into the library.

"Um, yeah, I'm great." I lowered my eyes and walked back

to the desk I'd been studying at. I wanted space between us, and a huge wooden desk would definitely help out.

"You look so pale," Finn said. "The trip must've taken a lot out of you."

"Yeah, we all worked really hard there," I said and flipped open a book so I would look busy. Anything to keep me distracted from Finn and his dark eyes.

"That's what I heard." He leaned on the desk in front of me. "Loki came to see me today."

"What?" My head jerked up, and my stomach dropped. "I mean, did he?"

"Yeah." Finn gave me an odd look. "Are you sure everything is okay?"

"Yeah, it's all great," I said. "What did Loki say?"

"He told me what he learned about the hobgoblins from your visit to Oslinna," Finn said. "All of the damage was focused on property, and any casualties were people who just happened to get in the way. He seems to think the hobgoblins aren't particularly bloodthirsty, but he's still coming down to help me train the trackers tomorrow."

"Oh." I fidgeted with my wedding ring and lowered my eyes again.

"I'm starting to think he might not be quite as bad as I thought he was," Finn said, almost grudgingly. "But you still spend too much time with him. You have to be careful about appearances."

"I know." My mouth suddenly felt very dry. "I'm working on it."

Finn stood on the other side of the desk, as if waiting for me to say something, but I had nothing to say. I stared down at the book, almost too nervous to breathe.

"I just came to see how the trip went," Finn said.

"It went well," I said quickly, nearly cutting him off.

"Wendy." He lowered his voice. "Is there something you're not telling me?"

"Oh, Princess, sorry to bother you," Mia said, and I'd never been so relieved to have an interruption.

She stood in the doorway, holding Hanna against her side. Since they'd been here at the palace, they'd both had time to get cleaned up, and Mia looked even lovelier than she had at Oslinna, and I hadn't thought that was possible.

"No, no, Mia, you're no bother," I said quickly.

"I was just trying to find the kitchen." She gave me an apologetic smile. "Hanna's hungry, and I've been wandering around this place, but I keep making wrong turns. It's so much bigger than the one in Oslinna."

"The palace does take some time to get used to," Finn said, returning her smile. "I could show you to the kitchen if you'd like."

"That would be great." Mia smiled wider, appearing relieved. "Thank you." Then her expression fell, and she looked worried. "I'm not taking him away from you, Princess, am I?"

"No, not at all." I shook my head. "Finn would be glad to help."

"Yes, of course I would," he said. "Mia, is it?"

"Yeah." Mia smiled at him again, then motioned to her baby. "This is Hanna."

"It will be my pleasure to show you both around the palace." He started to leave with them, but he turned back to me before he left, his lips pursed together, and nodded once.

After he left with Mia, I let out a shaky breath.

I buried myself in the books, although it didn't do much good. I still hadn't found anything useful yet.

It was getting late when Willa knocked on the open door.

"Wendy, I know you're really busy, but you need to come see this," Willa said. "The whole palace is talking."

"About what?" I asked.

"Elora's new painting." Willa pursed her lips. "It shows everyone dead."

EIGHTEEN

future

Elora had the "gift" of precognitive painting, although she'd be the first to tell anyone it was more of a curse. She would paint a scene from the future, from an event yet to happen, and that was it. No context, no preceding actions—just one solitary scene from the event.

Since she'd been so weak lately, she'd hardly painted anything. It drained her too much, but if Elora had a powerful vision, she couldn't hold it in. The precognition caused her terrible migraines until she painted these visions and got them out.

Also, Elora tried to keep her paintings as private as possible, unless she thought they had some value that everyone should see. And this one definitely did.

The painting sat on an easel at one end of the War Room. Elora had tried to keep the gathering small, so only the people who needed to know would see it, but as Willa said, word of the painting was spreading through the palace like wildfire.

Garrett stood by the door, keeping the riffraff from sneaking a peek. When Willa and I entered, Marksinna Laris, Markis Bain, Thomas, Tove, and Aurora were gathered around it. A few others were sitting at the table, too stunned to say anything.

I pushed Laris to the side so I could get a good look, and Tove stepped back. The painting was even more horrifying than Willa had let on.

Elora painted so well it looked like a photograph. Everything was done in exquisite detail. It showed the rotunda, its curved stairwell collapsed in the middle. The chandelier that normally hung in the center had crashed and lay destroyed on the floor. A small fire burned at the top of the stairs, and gold detailing was coming off the walls.

Bodies were everywhere. Some of them I didn't recognize, but others were startlingly clear. Willa was hanging off the destroyed stairs, her head twisted at an angle that she couldn't survive. Duncan was crushed underneath the chandelier, broken glass all over him. Tove lay in a pool of blood spilling out from him. Finn was crumpled in a mess of broken stairs, his bones sticking through his skin. Loki had a sword run straight through his chest, pinning him to the wall like an insect in an entomologist's display box.

I lay dead at a man's feet. A broken crown lay smashed near my head. I died after I'd been crowned. I was Queen.

In the painting, the man's back was to the viewer, but his long dark hair and black velvet jacket were unmistakable—it was Oren, my father. He had come to the palace and caused all this carnage. At least twenty or more bodies littered the scene Elora had painted, including my own.

We were all dead.

"When did you paint this?" I asked Elora when I found the strength to speak.

She sat in a chair to the side of the room, staring out the window at the snow falling on the pines. Her hands were folded in her lap, the skin gray and wrinkled. She was dying, and this painting had probably pushed her to the edge.

"Last night, while you were gone," Elora said. "I wasn't sure if I should tell anyone. I didn't want to start an unnecessary panic, but Garrett thought that you all should know."

"It might help change things," Garrett said, and I glanced back over at him. Worry tightened his expression. His daughter was dead in the picture too.

"How can you change things?" Laris asked, her voice shrill. "It is the future!"

"You can't prevent the future," Tove said. "But you can alter it." He turned to me for confirmation. "Can't you?"

"Yes." I nodded. "That's what Elora told me. She said the future is fluid, and just because she paints something, it doesn't mean it will happen."

"But it might happen," Aurora said. "The course we are on now is set so that this will be our future. That the King of the Vittra will destroy the palace and take over Förening."

"We don't know that he'll take over Förening," Willa said, futilely attempting to help. "We only see that some of us are dead."

"That is a great consolation, Marksinna," Laris said snidely, and Tove shot her a look.

"Aurora has something," I said. "All we have to do is change the course."

"How can we possibly know that we're changing the course the right way?" Laris asked. "Maybe whatever action we take to prevent this scene is the action that will cause it."

"We can't simply do nothing." I stepped back from the painting. I didn't want to see everyone I loved dead anymore.

I leaned back against the table and ran my hands through my hair. I had to think of something to stop this. Something to change it. I couldn't let this happen.

"We have to take out an element," I said, thinking aloud. "We have to change something in the painting. Make something in it go away. Then we'll know we've changed it."

"Like what?" Willa asked. "You mean like the staircase?"

"I can go get rid of that right now," Tove offered.

"We need the staircase," Aurora said. "It's the only way to the second floor."

"What we don't need is the Princess," Laris muttered under her breath.

"Marksinna, I told you that if you said—" Tove began but I stopped him.

"Wait." I stood up straighter. "She's right."

"She's right?" Willa was confused.

"If we get rid of the Princess, the whole scene changes," Aurora said as it occurred to her. "The King has been coming for her this whole time, and in the painting, he finally succeeds. If we give her to him, the painting goes away."

Nobody said anything, and by the confused, worried expressions on both Willa's and Tove's faces, I'd say that even they were considering it. It was hard not to. If it was only one of them dead, they probably would still fight to keep me here, but everyone was dead. My life was not more valuable than all of theirs.

"But even if we give the King the Princess, he still wants the Trylle kingdom," Bain pointed out. "He'll still keep coming after us even if he has her."

"Maybe," I agreed.

"More like certainly," Tove said, giving me a knowing look. "Getting you is just a means to an end for the King. He wants you so he can have the kingdom."

"I know you're right, but . . ." I trailed off. "I'm not saying that surrendering myself to the King will prevent a war between the Vittra and the Trylle, because it won't. What I am saying is that it will prevent that painting."

"So?" Tove shrugged. "We won't die that way, that day. But the King will still kill us."

"No," I insisted. "I can hand myself over and buy more time for you to fight back. I can prevent the painting, and you can prepare the Trylle army to conquer him."

"He's just going to kill you, Wendy," Tove said. "And you know it."

"Tove," Aurora said gently. "If she's with the King, then she won't be in that painting. She'll have changed the course, and it might be the only way to prevent all those deaths. That's something we need to consider."

"You're not giving him my daughter," Elora said firmly. She grabbed the back of the chair and pushed herself up. "That is not an option."

"If I'm going to end up dead anyway, at least I should spare the people," I said.

"You will find another way," she insisted. "I am not sacrificing you for this."

"You're not sacrificing anything," I said. "I am willingly doing this."

"No," Elora said. "That is a direct order. You will not go to him."

"Elora, I know the thought of losing your child is unbearable," Aurora said as gently as she could. "But you need to at least consider what's best for the kingdom."

"If you won't, then we'll have you overthrown," Laris said. "Everyone in the kingdom would stand behind me if you were going to lead us all into certain death."

"Death isn't certain!" Elora snapped. "Overthrow me if you want. Until then, I am your Queen, and the Princess isn't going anywhere."

"Elora, why don't you sit back down?" Garrett said gently and walked over to her.

"I will not sit down." She slapped his hands away when he reached out for her. "I am not some feeble old woman. I am the Queen, and I am her mother, and I have a say in what happens here! In fact, I have the *only* say!"

"Elora," I said. "You're not thinking this through. You always told me that the good of the kingdom came first."

"Maybe I made a mistake." Elora's once-dark eyes, looking almost silver now, darted around the room. I wasn't sure she could really see anything anymore. "I did everything for this kingdom. *Everything.* And look what's become of it."

She stepped forward, although I didn't know where she intended to go. Her legs gave out under her, and she fell to the floor. Garrett tried to catch her, but he moved too late. She was unconscious by the time she hit the floor.

I rushed over to her side, and Garrett was already pulling her from the floor into his lap. Her white hair flowed around her, and she lay still in his arms. A thin line of blood came from her nose, but I doubt it came from her hitting her face on the floor. Bloody noses seemed to be a result of abilities being overloaded.

"Is she all right?" I asked, kneeling beside her. I wanted to touch her, but I was too afraid to. She looked so frail.

"She's alive, if that's what you're asking," Garrett said. He pulled a tissue from his pocket and wiped at the blood. "But she hasn't been doing well since she painted that."

"Aurora," I said, looking back over my shoulder at her. "Come heal her."

"No, Princess." Garrett shook his head. "It's no use."

"What do you mean, it's no use?" I asked, incredulous. "She's sick!"

"There's nothing more that can be done for Elora." Garrett stared down at my mother, his dark eyes swimming with love.

"She's not sick, and she cannot be cured. Her life has been drained from her, and Aurora can't give that back to her."

"She can do something, though," I insisted. "Something to help."

"No," he said simply. Still holding Elora in his arms, he got to his feet. "I'm taking her to her room to make her comfortable. That's all we can do."

"I'll go with you." I stood up and looked back at the room. "We will continue this discussion tomorrow."

"Hasn't it already been decided?" Laris asked with a wicked smile.

"We'll discuss it tomorrow," Tove said firmly, and he draped a cloth over the picture to cover it.

I went with Garrett to my mother's room and pushed thoughts of the painting from my mind. I wanted to see Elora while I still had the chance. She didn't have much time left, not that I even knew what that meant. Her time could be a few hours, a few days, maybe even a few weeks. But the end was drawing near.

That meant I'd be Queen soon, but I couldn't think of that either. I only had a little time left to spend with my mother, and I wanted to make the most of it. I didn't want to be distracted by thoughts of what would become of the kingdom or my friends or even my marriage.

I sat in the chair beside her bed and waited for her to wake up. It took longer than I'd expected it to, and I ended up dozing off. Garrett actually alerted me when she woke up.

"Princess?" Elora asked weakly, sounding surprised that I was there.

"She's been waiting by your side," Garrett said. He stood at the end of the bed, staring down at her looking so small beneath her blankets.

"I'd like a moment alone with my daughter, if that's all right," Elora said.

"Yes, of course," Garrett said. "I'll be right outside if you need me."

"Thank you." She smiled at him, and he left the two of us alone.

"How are you feeling?" I asked and scooted my chair closer to the bed. Her voice was hardly more than a whisper.

"I've seen better days," she said.

"I'm sorry."

"I meant what I said before." Elora turned her head to face me, but I didn't know if she could see me. "You shouldn't give yourself to the Vittra. Not for anything."

"I can't let people die over me," I said gently. I didn't want to argue with her, not when she was like this, but it seemed like sacrilege to lie to her on her deathbed.

"There has to be another way," she insisted. "There has to be something more than sacrificing you to your father. I did everything right. I always thought about what was best for the kingdom. And all I asked for in return is that you would be safe."

"This can't be about my safety," I said. "You never cared this much about it before."

"Of course I cared." Elora sounded offended. "You are my

daughter. I have always cared about you." She paused, sighing. "I regret making you marry Tove."

"You didn't make me marry him. He asked. I said yes."

"I shouldn't have let you, then," Elora said. "I knew you didn't love him. But I thought if I did the right thing, I could protect you. You could end up happy, but now I don't think I've ever done anything that will help you be happy."

"I'm happy," I said, and that wasn't a complete lie. Many things in my life made me happy. I just hadn't been able to enjoy them much lately.

"Don't make the same mistakes I did," she said. "I married a man I didn't love because it was the right thing for the kingdom. I let the man I did love slip away because it was the right thing for the kingdom. And I gave away my only child because it was the right thing for my kingdom."

"You didn't give me away," I said. "You hid me from Oren."

"But I should've stayed with you," Elora said. "We could've hidden together. I could've protected you from all this. That is my biggest regret. That I didn't stay behind with you."

"How come you're talking like this now?" I asked. "How come you didn't say any of this to me sooner?"

"I didn't want you to love me," she said simply. "I knew we didn't have much time together, and I didn't want you to miss me. I thought it'd be better for you if you never even cared at all."

"But you changed your mind now?" I asked.

"I didn't want to die without you knowing how much I love

you." She held out her hand to me. I took it in mine, and her skin felt cool and soft as she squeezed my hand. "I have made so many mistakes. I only wanted you to be strong so you could protect yourself. I am so very sorry."

"Don't be sorry." I forced a smile at her. "You did everything you could, and I know that."

"I know you'll be a good Queen, a strong, noble leader, and that's more than these people deserve," she said. "But don't give too much. You need to keep some of yourself for you. And listen to your heart."

"I can't believe you're telling me to listen to my heart," I said. "I never thought I'd hear that from you."

"Don't act on everything your heart says, but make sure you listen to it." Elora smiled. "Sometimes your heart is right."

Elora and I stayed up talking for a while after that. She didn't tell me much that I didn't already know, but in a weird way, it felt like the first real conversation we'd had. She wasn't talking to me as a Queen talking to the Princess, but rather as a mother talking to her daughter.

Too soon, she grew tired and fell asleep. I sat with her for a while after that anyway. I didn't want to leave her. What little time I had left with her felt precious.

NINETEEN

relief

I don't know, Wendy." Tove shook his head. "I don't want you to die, but I don't know what else to tell you."

"I know." I sighed. "That's where I'm at too."

Tove sat on the chest at the end of our bed, and I stood in front of him, chewing on my thumbnail. We were both still in pajamas, and I wasn't sure how well either of us had slept the night before. I woke him early in the morning, when it was still dark out, and immediately began asking him what he thought I should do about Elora's painting.

"You still don't know how to kill the King," Tove pointed out. "And you did promise him our kingdom when you're Queen."

"I won't be Queen if I'm with him."

"But he won't let that slide," Tove said. "Even if you go to him, he might reject you simply because he wants the kingdom."

"I can tell him that you all booted me out when you found out my plan to combine with the Vittra," I said. "Then he'll have me."

"But he still wants the kingdom," Tove said. "He'll still come after it, even if he has you. At best, you're postponing the inevitable."

"Maybe so," I admitted. "But if that's the best I can do, then that's what I have to do."

"But what then?" Tove asked, staring up at me. "What happens after the King has you?"

"You'll become the Trylle King," I said. "You'll protect our people."

"So that's it?" Tove asked. "You'll go, and I'll stay?"

I nodded. "Yes."

Loki threw open the bedroom doors, making them bang against the walls. I jumped, and Tove got to his feet. Loki's eyes were fixed on me as he stormed in, ignoring my husband.

"What are you doing?" I asked, too startled to sound angry.

"I knew it!" Loki shouted, and his eyes never wavered from me. "As soon as Duncan told me, I knew you would immediately jump to suicide. Why are you so intent on being a martyr, Wendy?"

"I'm not a martyr." I straightened my shoulders for a fight. "What did Duncan tell you? And what are you doing bursting into my room at six in the morning?"

"I couldn't sleep, so I came down to see if you were awake," Loki said. "I heard the two of you talking, but I already knew that's what you would do. Duncan told me about the painting, and I knew you'd try to go back to the Vittra."

"You were eavesdropping?" I narrowed my eyes at him. "I'm in my personal chambers! You have no right to spy on me or come into my room without being invited!"

Loki rolled his eyes. "I wasn't spying on you. Don't be so dramatic, Princess. I paused outside your door to see if you were awake, and you clearly were, so I came in."

"You still can't just barge in." I crossed my arms over my chest.

"Would you like me to go back out and knock?" Loki gestured to the doors behind him. "Would that make you feel better?"

"I would like you to leave and go back to your room," I said.

I hadn't really talked to Loki since we'd slept together, and I could see Tove from the corner of my eye, watching us. Loki wouldn't look away from me, and I refused to look away first, putting us in some kind of staring contest that I was determined to win.

"I will," Loki said. "As soon as you admit that giving yourself to the King is completely preposterous."

I bristled. "It's not preposterous. I know it's not ideal, but it's the best we can come up with. I can't let that painting come true."

"How do you know that going with the King will change anything?" Loki countered.

"You didn't see the painting. You don't understand."

"The only way to truly stop the painting is to kill the

King," Loki said. "And you're the only one strong enough to do that."

"But I don't know how to," I said. "And you're strong. You can do it. I need to do something to divert the outcome of the painting until you can figure out how to stop him."

"Wendy, if I could kill him, I would've done it by now," Loki said. "You know that."

"It doesn't matter." I waved my hands and stepped away from him. "This isn't open for discussion. I've decided what I'm going to do."

"And you think I'll just let you go?" Loki asked.

"*Let* me?" I glared at him. "You don't 'let' me do anything."

"You know I can stop you." His eyes met mine evenly, and he stepped toward me. "I will do everything in my power to keep you from him."

"Loki, he will kill us all," I said emphatically. "The King will kill Tove and me and *you*. This is the only way I can protect us."

"I don't care," Loki said. "I would rather die fighting him. I would rather see *you* die fighting, than know that you surrendered to him. You can't give up."

I lowered my eyes and swallowed. Tove stood off to the side. I'd hoped he would jump in, say something, but he didn't.

"What do you propose I do?" I asked quietly, still staring at the floor.

"We've still got time until he comes for you," Loki said. "Learn how to kill him, and when he comes, fight him."

"What if we lose?" I asked. "What if I can't stop him?"

"If you can't stop him later, then you can't stop him now," Loki said. "Giving up now doesn't mean you can stand up to him later. It just means you're dead."

I glanced over at Tove, who still kept silent, and I thought about what Loki had said. I hated that I didn't know what the right thing was. All I wanted to do was keep everyone safe, and I was terrified that if I made the wrong decision I would get us all killed.

"Okay," I said finally and turned back to Loki. "I'll stay for now. But you need to work twice as hard with Finn. The trackers must be prepared for whatever happens."

"As you wish, Princess." Loki smiled slightly, a corner of his mouth turning up.

But something glowed behind the usual sparkle in his eyes, something deeper, burning. When he looked at me like that, my heart pounded so loudly I was certain he could hear it.

I became acutely aware of how close Loki was to me. He could reach out and touch me if he wanted, and I made sure to keep my arms firmly folded across my chest so I wouldn't be tempted to do the same.

With all the chaos in the palace, I hadn't had a chance to think about Loki, but with him standing here, I could think of nothing else but the night we'd spent together.

More than the things we'd done, the imprints burned into my skin from where he touched me, was the memory of what we'd actually shared. A moment when I'd never felt closer to anyone, as if the two of us had become one.

The painting flashed in my mind, the image of Loki skewered

at the hands of my father, and I knew that I would do whatever it took to save him, even if it went against Loki's wishes. I could not let him die.

"I trust you have much to do, Markis," I said numbly, and my cheeks flushed when I realized we'd been staring at each other for some time. With my husband watching.

"Of course." Loki gave a quick nod and turned to leave.

Tove walked after him, closing the double doors behind Loki. Tove stood in front of them for a moment, leaning his forehead against the wood. When he turned back around to face me, he didn't look at me. His mossy eyes flitted around the room, and he pushed up the sleeves on his pajama shirt.

"Is everything all right?" I asked carefully.

"Yes." He furrowed his brow and shook his head. "I don't know. I'm happy that you're not going off to die. I don't think I would like it if you died."

"I wouldn't like it if you died either," I said.

"But . . ." Tove trailed off, staring intently at a spot on the floor. "Are you in love with him?"

"What?" I asked, and my heart dropped to my stomach. "Why would you . . ." I wanted to argue, but the strength had gone out of my words.

"He's in love with you." He lifted his head and looked up at me. "Do you know that?"

"I—I don't know what you're talking about," I stammered. I walked over to the bed, needing to do something to busy myself, so I pulled up the sheets. "Loki is merely—"

"I see your auras," Tove interrupted me, his voice firm but

not angry. "His is silver, and yours is gold. And when you're around each other, you both get a pink halo. Just now you were both glowing bright pink, and your auras intertwined."

I stopped and didn't say anything. What could I say to that? Tove could physically see how we felt about each other. I couldn't deny it. I kept my back to him and waited for him to go on, for him to yell at me and accuse me of being a slut.

"I should be mad," he said at length. "Or jealous. Shouldn't I?"

"Tove, I'm sorry," I said and looked back at him. "I never meant for this to happen."

"I am jealous, but not the way I should be." He shook his head. "He loves you, and I . . . I don't." He ran a hand through his hair and sighed. "The other night, when I had the breakdown, and I hit you—"

"That wasn't your fault," I said quickly. "That never changed the way I felt about you."

"No, I know." He nodded. "But it got me thinking. I only have so much time before I completely lose it. These abilities, they're going to keep eating at my brain until nothing is left."

"No matter what happens, I'll be by your side." I stepped closer to him, trying to reassure him. "Even if I care for . . ." I paused, still not wanting to admit how I felt about Loki. "Other people don't matter. You are my husband, and I am with you in sickness and in health."

"You really would, wouldn't you?" Tove asked, almost sadly. "You would take care of me if I lost my mind."

"Of course I would." I nodded.

It had never occurred to me to leave Tove, at least not because of what had happened the other night, or if he became sick and frail like Elora. Tove was a good man, a kind man, and he deserved as much love and care as I could give him.

"That makes what I'm about to say so much harder." He sighed and sat down on the edge of the bed.

"What?" I sat next to him.

"I've realized how little time I have," he said, "before my mind completely goes. Maybe twenty years, if I'm lucky. And then it's gone.

"And I want to fall in love with somebody." Tove took a deep breath. "I want to share my life with somebody. And . . . that somebody isn't you."

"Oh," I said, and for a moment I felt nothing. I didn't know how to feel about what he was saying, so my body just went numb.

"I'm sorry," Tove said. "I know what you've given up to be with me, and I'm sorry that I'm not strong enough to do the same for you. I thought I was. I thought because we were friends and I believed in you as Queen that would be enough. But it's not."

"No, it isn't," I agreed quietly.

"Wendy, I'm . . ." He paused, staring down at the floor. "I'm gay."

I swallowed hard. "I thought you might be."

"Did you?" He lifted his head to look at me. "How?"

I shrugged. "It was just a feeling." That was a lie. Finn had pointed it out to me, but once he did, it seemed rather obvious.

"So . . . I guess I'm sorry for marrying you. I shouldn't have let you, not when I knew that this would never be happy for you."

"Well, I didn't exactly think it'd be happy for you either." He rubbed the back of his neck. "In my defense, I didn't realize how strongly you felt for Loki until the wedding. When you danced with him, you both glowed so brightly . . ."

"So you knew?" I asked. "You always knew?" He nodded. "Did you . . . did you know that I slept with him?"

"You did?" Something flashed in his eyes then, something that might have been hurt. "When?"

"In Oslinna, after . . . we fought," I said, choosing my words carefully.

"Oh." He stared off and didn't say anything else for a moment.

"Are you mad?" I asked.

"Not mad." He shook his head. "But . . . I can't say that I'm happy either." He furrowed his brow. "I don't know how to explain it. But I'm glad you told me."

"I am sorry for that. I never meant for it to happen, and I'd never want to hurt you." I smiled wanly at him. "And it won't happen again. I promise you that."

"I know. Because, Wendy, I think . . ." He paused, taking another deep breath. "I want a divorce."

And then it happened. I started to cry. I'm not sure why exactly. A combination of relief and sadness and confusion, and so much else that I'd been struggling to hold in. I was happy and relieved but sad and frightened, and a million other things all at once.

"Wendy, don't cry." Tove put his arm around me to comfort me, the first time he'd really touched me since we'd been married. "I didn't want to make you sad."

"No, I'm not sad, but . . ." I sniffled and looked up at him. "Is this because I slept with Loki?"

He laughed a little. "No. I'd made a decision before you told me that. It's because we don't love each other, and I think we should have a chance to spend time with the people we do love."

"Oh. Good." I shook my head and wiped at my eyes. "Sorry. I'm overwhelmed. And you're right. We should get an annulment." I nodded and stopped crying almost as soon as I had started. "Sorry. I don't know where that came from."

"Are you sure you're okay with this?" Tove asked, eyeing me carefully.

"Yes, I am." I smiled weakly at him. "It's probably the best thing for us both."

"Yeah, I hope so." Tove nodded. "We're friends, and I'll always have your back, but we don't need to be married for that."

"True," I agreed. "But I want to wait until after this is all over with the Vittra. In case something happens to me, I want you to be King."

"Are you sure you want me to be King?" Tove asked. "I'm going to go crazy someday."

"But until then, you're about the only person I trust that has any power," I said. "Willa would be a good ruler someday, but I don't think she's quite there yet. She can take over for you, if you need her to."

"You really think something's going to happen to you?" Tove asked.

"I don't know," I admitted. "But I need to know that the kingdom will be in good hands, no matter what."

"All right," he said. "You have my word. We'll stay married until after the Vittra are defeated, and if something happens to you, I will rule the kingdom to the best of my ability."

I smiled at him. "Thank you."

"Good." Tove dropped his arm and stared straight ahead. "Now that that's out of the way, I suppose we should get ready. We have the Chancellor's funeral at eleven."

"I haven't prepared my speech yet." I sighed and Tove stood up. "What should I say about him?"

"Well, if you plan to say anything nice, you're going to have to lie," Tove muttered as he walked over to his closet.

"You shouldn't speak ill of the dead."

"You didn't hear what he wanted to do to you," Tove said, talking loudly to be heard from the closet. "That man was a menace to our society."

I sat on the bed, listening to my husband gather his clothes before he went to shower, and despite everything that was still going on, I felt as if an immense weight had been lifted from my shoulders.

I still had no idea how to stop the Vittra and save everyone I cared about, and I had to write a eulogy for the Chancellor. But for the first time in a long time, I felt like there might be life after this. If I could defeat the King, if I could save us, there might really be something to live for.

TWENTY

orm

Willa wore all black, but the hem of her skirt only came to the middle of her thigh. At least she had classed it up a little for the funeral. My eulogy had gone over well, or about as well as a eulogy could go over. Nobody had cried for the Chancellor, and that seemed sad to me, but I couldn't bring myself to cry for him either.

His funeral had been held in one of the larger meeting rooms in the palace. Black flowers and black candles decorated the room. I wasn't sure who had planned the funeral, but it looked like a Goth kid at a Cure concert had thrown up here.

After they took the Chancellor away to bury him in the palace cemetery, most of us stayed behind. He didn't have any family or friends, and I wasn't entirely sure how he got elected in the first place.

The mood was decidedly somber, but I didn't think that actually had much to do with the funeral. All the guests in attendance were muttering, whispering, huddled in corners talking quietly, and they kept glancing at me. I heard the word "painting" floating through the air like a breeze.

I stood off to the side of the room, talking mostly with Willa and Tove. Ordinarily, any of the royals would be eager to make some kind of small talk with me, but today they all avoided me. Which was just as well. I didn't have much I wanted to say to any of them.

"When is it polite for us to leave?" Willa asked, swirling her champagne around in her glass. I think she'd already had a couple glasses more than she should have, and she hiccupped daintily before covering her mouth with her hand. "Excuse me."

"I think we've been here long enough." Tove scanned the room, which had already thinned out. His mother and father hadn't been able to make it at all, and my mother could barely move, so she was still on bed rest.

"Whenever is fine with me," I said.

"Good." Willa set her glass on a nearby table, some of the bubbly pink liquid sloshing over the top. She looped her arm through mine, more to steady herself, and we left the room.

"Well, that went great." I sighed, plucking a black flower from my hair as we went down the hall.

"Really?" Tove asked. "Because I thought it went horribly."

"I was being sarcastic."

"Oh." He shoved his hands in his pockets as he walked beside me. "It could've been worse, I guess."

"You should've drunk more," Willa said to me. "That's

how I made it through that thing. And you're lucky you're my best friend, or I wouldn't have gone at all."

"You need to start doing more stuff like this, Willa," I told her. "You're so good at handling people, and someday you might need to do it officially."

"Nope, that's your job." She smiled. "I lucked out. I'm free to be the naughty drunk friend."

I tried to argue with Willa about the merits of being a good Trylle citizen. She schmoozed much better than I ever could, and she was a great ally, when she put her mind to it. But right now she was too tipsy to see reason in anything.

She was giggling at something I'd said when we reached the rotunda. Garrett was coming down the stairs, but he stopped halfway when he saw us. His hair was a mess, his shirt was untucked, and his eyes were red-rimmed.

As soon as his eyes met mine, I knew.

"Elora," I breathed.

"Wendy, I'm sorry," Garrett said, his voice thick with tears, and he shook his head.

I knew he wasn't lying, but I had to see it for myself. I pulled my arm from Willa's and lifted my black gown so I could race up the stairs. Garrett tried to reach out for me, but I ran past him. I didn't slow at all, not until I got to my mother's room.

She lay utterly still in bed, her body little more than a skeleton. The sheets were pulled up to her chest, and her hands were folded neatly over her stomach. Even her hair had been brushed and smoothed, shimmering silver around her. Garrett had arranged her the way she would've wanted him to.

I knelt down next to her bed. I wasn't sure why, except I felt compelled to be near her. I took her hand, cold and stiff in my own, and that was when it hit me. Like a wave of despair I hadn't even known I was capable of, I began to sob, burying my face in the blankets beside her.

I hadn't expected to feel this much. Her death felt as if the ground had been pulled out from under me. Epic blackness stretched on forever to catch me.

There were things her death would signify, consequences I wasn't ready for, but I didn't even think about that. Not at first.

I clung to her, sobbing, because I was a daughter who had lost her mother. Despite our rocky relationship, she did love me, and I did love her. She was the only person who knew what it was like to be Queen, to give me advice, to shepherd me into this world, and she was gone.

I allowed myself an afternoon to really feel the loss, to feel the new hole that had been torn inside of me. That was all the time I had to mourn Elora, and then I had so much more I needed to do. But for that one afternoon, I let myself cry over everything we'd never been able to have, and the moments we'd shared that were worth treasuring.

Willa eventually pulled me away from Elora's body so Garrett could begin the funeral arrangements, and she took me to Matt's room. He hugged me and let me cry, and I'd never been more grateful for my brother. Without him, I'd feel like an orphan.

Tove stayed with me in Matt's room, not saying anything,

and eventually Duncan joined us. I sat on the floor with my back leaning against the bed, and Matt sat beside me. Willa had sobered up rather quickly, and she sat on the bed behind me, her long legs draped over the edge.

"I hate to leave you like this, but I think I should go help my father." Willa touched my head when she stood up. "He shouldn't be doing this alone."

"I can help him." I started to push myself up, but Matt put his hand on my arm.

"You can help tomorrow," Matt said. "You're going to have a lot to do. Today, you can be sad."

"Matt's right," Willa said. "I can handle this for now."

"All right." I settled back down and wiped my eyes. "We need to keep this to ourselves if we can. Keep her death quiet, and hold off on the funeral for as long as possible. I don't want the Vittra King to find out."

"He will eventually," Willa said gently.

"I know." I rested my elbows on my knees and turned to Tove. "How long do I have until I'm Queen?"

"Three days," Tove said. He leaned back against Matt's dresser, his legs crossed at the ankles. "Then somebody has to be coroneted."

"So we have three days." I let out a deep breath, my mind racing with all the things that had to be done.

"We'll keep this quiet," Duncan said. "You can arrange a private funeral."

"We can't keep the death of the Queen secret forever," I said. "We have to begin to prepare now."

"I'll be back as soon as I can." Willa offered me an apologetic smile. "Take care, okay?"

"Of course." I nodded absently.

She gave Matt a quick kiss before leaving. Duncan came over and crouched down in front of me. His dark eyes were sympathetic, but I saw a fierce determination in them too.

"What do you need me to do, Princess?" Duncan asked.

"Duncan, not now," Matt said sternly. "Wendy just lost her mother. She's not in the right frame of mind."

"I don't have time to get in the right frame of mind," I said. "We have three days before I'm Queen. If we're lucky, we have four or five days until Oren comes to claim his prize. I've already taken too much time crying over Elora's death. When this is all over with, I can mourn her. But now I need to work."

"I should tell Thomas," Tove said. "He needs to have the trackers ready."

I nodded. "When Willa gets back, she needs to talk to the refugees from Oslinna. I'm sure some of them will want to fight against the Vittra that killed their families and destroyed their town."

"What are you going to do?" Tove asked.

"I still have to find a way to stop the King," I said, and I looked up at Duncan. "And Duncan's going to help me."

Matt tried to protest. He thought I needed to process what was happening, and maybe he was right. But I didn't have the time. Duncan took my hand and helped me to my feet. Tove opened the bedroom door to leave, but then he stepped aside, letting Finn come into the room.

"Princess," Finn said, his dark eyes on me. "I came to see if you were all right."

"Yes." I smoothed out my black dress, wrinkled from sitting on the floor for so long.

"I'm going to talk to Thomas." Tove glanced back at me, checking to see if that was still okay, and I nodded.

"I'll wait outside for you," Duncan offered. He gave me a small smile before hurrying out after Tove.

Matt, however, stood next to me. His arms were crossed firmly over his chest, and his blue eyes were like ice as he stared at Finn. I was actually grateful for Matt's distrust. It used to be that I would kill to get a moment alone with Finn, but I had no idea what to say to him anymore.

"I'm sorry to hear about your mother," Finn said simply.

"Thank you." I wiped at my eyes again. I'd stopped crying a while ago, but my cheeks were still sticky and damp from tears.

"She was a great Queen," Finn said, his words carefully measured. "As you will be."

"We have yet to see what kind of Queen I will be." I ran a hand through my curls and gave him a thin smile. "I have much to do before I am to be Queen, and I'm sorry, but I really must get to it now."

"Yes, of course." Finn lowered his eyes, but not before I saw the hurt flash in them for a moment. He'd grown accustomed to me turning to him for comfort, but I didn't need him anymore. "I didn't mean to keep you."

"It's quite all right," I said and turned to Matt. "Will you accompany me?"

"What?" Matt sounded surprised, probably because I hardly asked him to do anything with me anymore. So much of what I did involved palace business, and I couldn't let a mänsklig tag along with me.

"I'm going down to the library," I clarified. "Would you come with me?"

"Yeah, sure." Matt nodded, almost eagerly. "I'd love to help you any way I can."

Matt and I left his room, but Finn walked with us because he was going in the same direction, presumably back to train our army. The trackers were doing most of their training in the first-floor ballroom, since it had the most space.

Tove had already left to find Thomas, but Duncan had waited for us, following a step behind as we went down the hall.

"How is the training coming?" I asked Finn, since he was beside me, and I needed to fill the space with something.

"It's going as well as can be expected," Finn said. "They are learning quickly, which is good."

"Is Loki being of any help?" I asked, and Finn stiffened at the mention of Loki's name.

"Yes, surprisingly." Finn scratched at his temple and seemed reluctant to say anything nice about Loki. "He is much stronger than our trackers, but he's done a fine job of teaching them how to maneuver. We will be unable to beat the Vittra hobgoblins with our strength, but we have the upper hand with our wits."

"Good." I nodded. "You know we only have a few days until the Vittra will come."

"Yes," Finn said. "We will work overtime until then."

"Don't overwork them," I said.

"I will try not to."

"And . . ." I paused, thinking of exactly how I wanted to phrase it. "If they can't do it, if you don't honestly believe they stand a chance against the Vittra, do not let them fight."

"They stand a chance," Finn said, slightly offended.

"No, Finn, listen to me." I stopped and touched his arm, so he would stop and face me. His dark eyes still smoldered with something, but I refused to acknowledge it. "If our Trylle army cannot win against the Vittra, do not send them to fight. I will not let them go on a suicide mission. Do you understand?"

"Some lives will be lost, Princess," Finn answered cautiously.

"I know," I admitted, hating that it was true. "But it is only worth losing some lives if we can win, otherwise lives will be lost for nothing."

"What do you propose we do, then?" Finn asked. "If the troops aren't ready to fight the Vittra, what will you have us do?"

"You will do nothing," I said. "I will take care of this."

"Wendy," Matt said. "What are you talking about?"

"Don't worry about it." I started walking again, and they followed more slowly behind me. "I will handle things if it comes to that, but until then, we will continue with the plan. We will ready ourselves for war."

I marched ahead, walking faster so I didn't have to argue with Matt or Finn. Both of them wanted to protect me, but they couldn't. Not anymore.

On the way to the library, we went past the ballroom. Finn

went inside to finish the training, and I glanced in. All the trackers were sitting on the floor in a semicircle around Tove and Loki. They were both talking, explaining what would need to be done.

"Should I go in with them?" Duncan asked, gesturing to the room of trackers.

"No." I shook my head. "You come with me."

"Are you sure?" Duncan asked, but he followed me down to the library. "Shouldn't I be learning how to fight with the rest of them?"

"You won't be fighting with the rest of them," I replied simply.

"Why not?" Duncan asked. "I'm a tracker."

"You're my tracker," I said. "I need you with me." Before he could argue, I turned my attention to my brother. "Matt, we're looking for books that have anything in them about the Vittra. We need to find their weaknesses."

"Okay." He looked around at the ceiling-high shelves filled with books. "Where do I start?"

"Pretty much anywhere," I said. "I've barely made a dent in these books."

Matt climbed one of the ladders to reach the books at the top, and Duncan dutifully went along to start collecting books for himself.

While the history of the Vittra was interesting at times, it was irritating how little we knew about stopping them. So much of the Trylle past had been about avoiding them and making concessions. We'd never actually stood up to them.

By all accounts, Oren was the cruelest King the Vittra had had in centuries, maybe ever. He slaughtered the Trylle for sport and executed his own people for simply disagreeing with him. Loki was lucky to even be alive.

"What's this say?" Matt asked. "It doesn't even look like words." He was sitting on one of the chairs on the far side of the room, and he pointed to the open book on his lap.

"Oh, that?" Duncan was nearest to him, so he got up and leaned over Matt, looking at the book. "That's Tryllic. It's our old language to keep secrets from the Vittra."

"A lot of the older stuff is written in Tryllic," I said, but I didn't get up. I'd found a passage about the Long Winter War, and I hoped it would give me something useful.

"What does it say?" Matt asked.

"Um, this one says . . . something about an 'orm,'" Duncan said, squinting as he read the text. He didn't know very much Tryllic, but since he spent so much time researching with me, he'd picked up more.

"What?" I lifted my head, thinking at first that he'd said Oren.

"Orm," Duncan repeated. "It's like a snake." He tapped the pages and straightened up. "I don't think this will be helpful. It's a book of old fairy tales."

"How do you know?" I asked.

"We grew up hearing these stories." Duncan shrugged and sat back down in his chair. "I've heard that one a hundred times."

"What is it?" I pressed. Something about that word, *orm*, stuck with me.

"It's supposed to explain how trolls came to be," Duncan said. "The reason we split up into different tribes. Each of the tribes is represented by a different animal. The Kanin are rabbits, the Omte are birds, the Skojare are fish, the Trylle are foxes, and the Vittra are tigers, or sometimes lions, depending on who tells the story."

The Kanin, Omte, and Skojare were the other three tribes of trolls, like the Trylle and Vittra. I'd never met any of them. From what I understood, only the Kanin were still doing reasonably well, but they hadn't thrived as much as the Trylle or even the Vittra. The Skojare were all but extinct.

I'd only heard of five tribes, and all of the tribes were accounted for, yet Duncan had mentioned the orm.

"What about the orm?" I asked. "What tribe does that represent?"

"It doesn't." He shook his head. "The orm is the villain of the story. It's all very Adam and Eve in the Garden of Eden."

"How so?" I asked.

"I can't tell it with the same flourish as my mom did before I went to bed," Duncan said, "but the basic idea is that all the animals lived together and worked together. It was peace and harmony. Orm, which was this big snakelike creature, had lived for thousands of years, and he was bored. He watched all the animals living together, and for fun, he decided to mess with them.

"He went to each of the animals, telling them that they had to watch out for their friends," Duncan went on. "He told the fish that the birds were plotting to eat them, the birds that the fox had set traps to ensnare them, and the rabbits that the birds were eating all their clover.

"Then the orm went to the tiger and told him that he was bigger and stronger than all the other animals, and he could eat them all if he wanted to," he said. "The tiger realized he was right, and he began hunting the other animals. None of the animals trusted one another anymore, and they scattered.

"The orm thinks this is all funny and great, especially when he sees all the other animals struggling without their friends," Duncan continued. "They had all been working together, and they couldn't make it on their own.

"One day, the orm comes across the tiger, who is starving and cold," Duncan said. "The orm begins to laugh at how pitiful the tiger is, and the tiger asks him why he's laughing. When the orm explains how he tricked the tiger into betraying his friends, the tiger becomes enraged, and using his sharpest claw, he cuts off the orm's head.

"Usually the ending is told more dramatically than that, but that's how it goes." Duncan shrugged.

"Wait." I leaned forward on my book. "The Vittra killed the orm?"

"Well, yeah, the tiger represents the Vittra," Duncan said. "Or at least that's what my mom told me. But the tiger is really the only animal capable of cutting off the snake's head. At best, a fox could just bite it and the birds could peck out its eyes."

"That's it, isn't it?" I asked, and it suddenly seemed so obvious to me. I pushed aside my book and jumped up.

"Wendy?" Matt asked, confused. "Where are you going?"

"I have an idea," I said and ran out of the room.

TWENTY-ONE

preparation

In the ballroom, all the trackers were busy practicing moves on each other. Loki stood near the front, teaching a young tracker how to block. I tried not to think about how young that kid looked or about how he'd fight in battle soon.

"Loki!" I yelled to get his attention.

He turned toward me, smiling already, and his attention dropped from the tracker. Seizing the opportunity, the tracker moved forward, punching Loki in the face. It wasn't hard enough to really hurt him, but the tracker looked both frightened and proud.

"Sorry," the tracker apologized. "I thought we were still training."

"It's fine." Loki rubbed his jaw and waved him off. "Just save the good stuff for the hobgoblins, all right?"

I smiled sheepishly at Loki as he made his way across the ballroom over to where I stood at the door. I couldn't see Finn or Thomas, but I knew they had to be somewhere in the room, working with the other trackers.

"I didn't mean to distract you like that and get you sucker-punched."

"I'm all right," Loki assured me with a grin and stepped out into the hall, so we could have some privacy from onlookers. "What can I do for you, Wendy?"

"Can I cut off your head?" I asked.

"Are you asking for my permission?" Loki tilted his head and cocked an eyebrow. "Because I'm going to have to say no to this one request, Princess."

"No, I mean, can I?" I asked. "As in, am I capable of it? Would you die if I did?"

"Of course I would die." Loki put one hand against the wall and leaned on it. "I'm not a bloody cockroach. What's all this about? What are you trying to find out?"

"If I cut off Oren's head, would that kill him?" I asked.

"Probably, but you'll never get close enough to him to do that." He put his other hand on his hip and stared down at me. "Is that your plan? To decapitate the King?"

"Do you have a better plan?" I countered.

"No, but . . ." He sighed. "I've tried that before, and it didn't work. You can't get close enough to him. He's strong and smart."

"No, *you* can't get close enough to him," I clarified. "You don't have the same abilities as I do."

"I know that, but I can't knock him out," Loki said. "His mind is impenetrable. Even your mother couldn't use her powers on him." His eyes softened when he mentioned my mother. "I'm sorry about that, by the way."

"No, don't be." I shook my head and lowered my eyes. "It's not your fault."

"I wanted to see you, but I knew you'd have your hands full," Loki said, his voice quiet. "I thought you'd rather I be here, helping the Trylle."

I nodded. "You're right."

"But I still feel like a dick," he said. I could feel him studying me, his eyes all over me, but I didn't lift my head. "How are you doing with all this?"

"I don't have time to think about it." I shook my head again, clearing it of any thoughts of Elora, and looked up at him. "I need to find out how to stop Oren."

"That's a noble goal," Loki said. "Cutting off his head may do it, or running him through with a sword. It's never been a matter of killing him. It's getting close enough to do it. He'd have you on the floor before you could even draw your weapon."

"Well, I can do it," I insisted. "I can find a way. I have tiger blood, so I'm strong."

"Tiger blood?" Loki arched an eyebrow. "What are you going on about, Wendy?"

"Nothing. Never mind." I smiled thinly at him. "I can stop Oren. And that's what matters, right?"

"How?" he asked.

"Don't worry about it." I took a step back, walking away from him. "You concentrate on getting them ready. I'll deal with Oren."

Loki sighed. "Wendy."

I hurried back to the library, where Duncan and Matt were still waiting. I didn't let Matt know of my idea, because he would only disapprove. The last few days felt epic and long, and I told Matt to get some rest. We could pick things up in the morning.

I did need to rest myself. One thing I had learned from Tove was that my powers weakened and got more uncontrollable if I was overly tired. I'd been so completely exhausted lately that I wouldn't stand a chance against Oren.

Everything was so simple it was almost infuriating. Everyone had made it sound so difficult to kill Oren, but it would be the same as killing any other Vittra. I thought I'd need a magic spell or something. But all I had to do was get close to him.

I knew Loki was right, and it was easier said than done. Physically, Oren was still much stronger than me, he healed quickly, and his mind was virtually immune to my abilities. When he had interrupted my wedding, I'd tried to throw him back against the wall, and I'd only ruffled his hair.

Stopping him would be difficult, but it would be possible.

But I'd need my abilities to be up to full strength, which meant that I needed to rest. It felt lazy going to bed when so much was happening in the palace, but I didn't have a choice.

I went upstairs to go to my room, and I heard Willa rallying the displaced Trylle from Oslinna. She'd gathered them in one of the larger bedrooms and told them how they could make a difference, how they could avenge their loved ones.

I paused outside the door, listening for a moment. Something in the way she spoke always sounded seductive. It was hard saying no to Willa.

Willa was doing well with them on her own, so I continued down to my room. A rustling sound came from inside my chambers, so I cautiously pushed open the door. I poked my head in, and by the dim light of the bedside lamp I saw Garrett rummaging through my nightstand drawer.

"Garrett?" I asked, stepping inside the room.

"Princess." He immediately stopped what he was doing and stepped away from my nightstand. His cheeks reddened, and he lowered his eyes. "I'm sorry. I didn't mean to go through your things. I was looking for a necklace I gave Elora. I couldn't find it in her new room, and I thought it might have gotten left in here."

"I can help you look," I offered. "I haven't seen any necklaces, but I haven't been searching for any either. What did it look like?"

"It was a black onyx stone with diamonds and silver wrapped around it." He gestured to his own chest at about the spot a necklace would hang. "She used to wear it all the time, and I thought it would be good for . . ." He stopped, choking up for a second. "I thought she'd like to be buried with it."

"I'm sure she would," I said.

He sniffled and shielded his eyes with his hand. I had no idea what to do. I stayed frozen in place, watching Garrett as he struggled not to cry.

"I'm sorry." He wiped his eyes and shook his head. "You don't need to deal with me being like this."

"No, it's okay," I said. I took a step closer to him, but I didn't know what to do, so I didn't move forward any farther. I twisted my wedding ring and tried to think of something comforting to say. "I know how much you cared for my mother."

"I did." He nodded and sniffled again, but he seemed to have stopped crying. "I really did care about her. Elora was a very complicated woman, but she was a good woman. She knew she had to be Queen first, and everything else came after."

"She told me she regretted that," I said quietly. "She said she wished she'd made different choices and put the people she cared about first."

"She meant you." Garrett smiled at me, and it was both sorrowful and loving. "She loved you so much, Wendy. Not a day went by that she didn't think about you or talk about you. Before you came back, when you were still a child, she'd sit in her parlor and paint you. She'd focus all her energy on you, just so she could see you."

"She used to paint me?" I asked, surprised.

"You didn't know?" Garrett asked.

I shook my head. "She never mentioned it."

"Come on. I'll show you."

Garrett headed down the hall, and I went with him. I'd seen the room where Elora kept her precognitive paintings locked away in the north wing, and I thought about telling Garrett that. But I hadn't seen any paintings of me as a child. She'd only had a few of me as a teenager.

He led me all the way down the hall. At the very end, across the hall from my old bedroom, Garrett pushed on a wall. I didn't understand what he was doing, and then the wall swung forward. It was a door built to blend in seamlessly with the walls.

"I didn't know that was there," I said in dismay.

"Once you're Queen, I'll show you all the secrets of the palace." Garrett held the door open for me. "And believe me, there are quite a few."

I stepped through the door to find a small room. Its only purpose was to house a narrow spiral staircase. I glanced back at Garrett, but he gestured for me to go ahead. He stayed a step behind me as I went up the creaking iron stairs.

Before we even reached the top, I could see the paintings. Skylights in the ceiling lit the room, and I stepped onto the hardwood floor. It was small, a hidden attic room with a peaked roof. But the walls were covered with paintings, all of them hung carefully a few inches apart. And all of the paintings were of me.

Elora's meticulous brushstrokes made them almost look like photographs. They showed me in all stages of my life. At a birthday party when I was young, with cake on my face. A scraped knee when I was three, with Maggie helping me put on a Band-Aid. At a failed dance recital when I was eight, pulling at my tutu. In my backyard, on the swings, with Matt pushing me. Curled up in my bed, reading *It* by flashlight when I was twelve. Caught in the rain when I was fifteen, trudging home from school.

"How?" I asked, staring in awe at all the paintings. "How did she do this? Elora told me she couldn't choose what she saw."

"She couldn't, not really," Garrett said. "She never picked *when* she saw you, and it took a lot of her energy to focus on you, to see you. But . . . it was worth it for her. It was the only way she could watch you grow up."

"It took a lot?" I turned back to him with tears in my eyes. "You mean it aged her a lot." I gestured to the walls. "This is the reason why she looked fifty when I met her? This is why she died of old age before she even turned forty?"

"Don't look at it like that, Wendy." Garrett shook his head. "She loved you, and she needed to see you. She needed to know you were all right. So she painted these. She knew how much it cost her, and she did it gladly."

For the first time, I truly realized what I had lost. I'd had a mother who loved me my entire life, and I hadn't been able to see her. Even after I met her, I didn't get to really know her, not until it was too late.

I began to sob, and Garrett came over to me. Somewhat awkwardly, he hugged me, letting me cry on his shoulder.

After I'd gotten it all out, he walked me back down to my room. He apologized for upsetting me, but I was glad he had. I needed to see that, to know about the paintings. I went to bed and tried not to cry myself to sleep.

In the morning, I knew I had much to do, so I rose early and went down to the kitchen to grab breakfast. I only made it as far as the stairs when I heard arguing in the main hall. I stopped and peered down over the railing to see what the fuss was about.

Thomas was talking to his wife, Annali, and their twelve-year-old daughter, Ember. They were Finn's mom and sister, his family, but Finn wasn't around. Thomas kept his voice hushed, but Annali was insistent. Ember kept trying to pull away, but Annali had a firm grip on her arm and wouldn't let her go.

"Thomas, if it's that dangerous, you and Finn should come with us," Annali said, staring up at him. "He is my son too, and I don't want him in harm's way because of some misplaced sense of duty."

"It's not misplaced, Annali." Thomas sighed. "This is to protect our kingdom."

"Our kingdom?" Annali scoffed. "What has this kingdom ever done for us? They barely pay you enough to feed our children! I have to raise goats to keep a roof over our head!"

"Annali, hush." Thomas held his hands up to her. "People will hear you."

"I don't care if they hear me!" Annali shouted. "Let them hear me! I hope they banish us! I want them to! Then finally we can be a family instead of being ruled by this awful monarchy!"

"Mom, don't say that." Ember squirmed and pulled away from her mother. "I don't want to be banished. All my friends are here."

"You'll make new friends, Ember, but you only have one family," Annali said.

"Which is exactly why you need to go away," Thomas said. "It's not safe here. The Vittra will be coming very soon, and you need to be hidden."

"I will not go away without you or my son," Annali said

firmly. "I have stood by you through much worse, and I will not lose you now."

"I will be safe," Thomas said. "I can fight. So can Finn. You need to protect our daughter. When this is all over, we can go away together, if that's what you want. I promise you I will leave with you. But right now you need to take Ember."

"I don't want to go!" Ember whined. "I want to help you fight! I'm as strong as Finn!"

"Please," Thomas begged. "I need you safe."

"Where do you expect us to go?" Annali asked.

"Your sister is married to a Kanin," Thomas said. "You can stay with them. Nobody will look for you there."

"How will I know when you're safe?" Annali asked.

"I'll come for you when it's over."

"What if you never come?"

"I will come for you," Thomas said firmly. "Now go. I don't want you traveling at the same time as the Vittra. They're not something you want to mess with."

"Where is Finn?" Annali asked. "I want to say good-bye to him."

"He's with the other trackers," Thomas said. "Go home. Pack your things. I'll send him down to talk to you."

"Fine," Annali said reluctantly. "But when you come for me, you better bring my son with you, alive and intact. If not, you might as well not come at all."

He nodded. "I know."

Annali stared up at her husband for a moment, not saying anything.

"Ember, say good-bye to your father," Annali said. Ember started to protest, and Annali pulled at her arm. "Now, Ember."

Ember did as she was told. She hugged Thomas, and he kissed her cheek. Annali cast one more look at Thomas over her shoulder, and then she and Ember left through the front door. Thomas stayed behind for a moment, his whole body sagging.

He'd sent his family away to protect them. He'd seen the painting the same as I had, and he knew the destruction that was set to befall the palace. It was no place for innocent bystanders.

But then something occurred to me. I had been trying to find a way to change the outcome of the painting, to do something that would alter the course of events and make it so we wouldn't all die, and I finally figured it out.

TWENTY-TWO

offense

"We take the fight to them," I said, and I was met with five blank stares.

Thomas, Tove, Willa, Finn, and Loki stood across from me, none of them looking pleased with what I proposed. I'd called them all into the War Room to discuss things, but so far I'd done most of the talking.

"That's your grand idea?" Loki asked, looking vaguely bemused, and that was the most positive response I'd gotten. "Get killed there instead of here?"

"The idea is not to get killed anywhere," I said and leaned back against the table behind me.

"Well, if this is what you want to do, Wendy, I'll support it," Willa said, sounding reluctant. "But I don't know how much it will help. The Vittra will have home-field advantage."

"Loki knows his way around the Vittra palace." I gestured to Loki, who grimaced when I volunteered him to lead the way.

"And we'll surprise them. That was how Finn survived the hobgoblin attack before."

"I barely survived that, Princess," Finn reminded me. "And we don't have much of an element of surprise. The Vittra are about to come here and take the kingdom. As soon as they get word of your ascension to the throne, they'll be on their way."

"That's why we need to move *now,*" I said.

"Now?" Finn and Willa said in unison, both shocked.

"Yes." I nodded. "I've arranged to have my coronation in two hours. Then I'm Queen, and my first order as the ruling monarch will be to declare war against the Vittra. We will go to them, we will attack, and we will win."

"You want to hit them tonight?" Tove asked.

"Yes, when they're sleeping," I said. "It's the best chance we have."

"Princess, I don't know if that's possible." Thomas shook his head. "We can't plan a full-scale attack in a few hours."

"As soon as the King finds out I'm Queen, he will be at our door with an army of hobgoblins." I pointed toward the door to emphasize my point. "We are talking a matter of days here. What more can we do in the next two days that will be superior to attacking the Vittra when they're unprepared?"

"I don't know," Thomas admitted. "But it doesn't mean we should embark on a suicide mission."

"You're talking suicide?" I asked. "You saw the painting. Your son is dead. Everyone in this room, except for you, is dead." I paused, letting that sink in. "We have to do something to change that."

"Attacking the Vittra palace will only change the location of where we die," Finn said.

"Maybe so," I agreed. "But so what? I have read book after book of Trylle history. And you know what it says? We concede. We wait. We avoid. We only defend. We never stand up and fight for ourselves.

"And now is the time to fight. This is our last chance. Not just ours, as in the people in this room, but our entire kingdom's last chance to stand up and fight against the Vittra. If we don't do this now, they will conquer us."

"That's a shame," Willa said, looking awed.

"What is?" I asked.

"That you used that speech now instead of saving it to help me convince the Markis and Marksinna to go fight with us tonight," Willa said.

"So it's agreed, then?" I asked.

"You know that I'll always have your back," Tove said. "No matter what."

Loki nodded grimly. "I almost hate to say it, but yes, I'm with you. I'll attack the Vittra tonight."

"I still think there's a better way," Thomas said. "But I don't know what it is. If this is the best we have, then this is what we must do."

"Is there nothing that can convince you to stay?" Finn asked.

I shook my head. "This is my fight as much as it is yours, if not more. I will be there."

"Fine." Finn sighed. "Then I'm in too."

I wanted to smile. I felt like I should, to seal the deal somehow, but I didn't. My stomach was twisted too much.

"We have a few hours until we leave, then?" Thomas asked.

"Yes," I said. "After my coronation."

"I suppose that I need to brief everyone on the layout of the Vittra palace," Loki said.

"That would be helpful, yes," I said.

Loki scratched the back of his neck and looked over at Finn. "Let's get to it, then."

Loki, Finn, and Thomas went to deal with the schematics of the attack, and Willa had the harder job of convincing the higher Trylle to fight today. Tove had to go with me, because he had to be crowned King.

We waited in our chambers, and we discussed the Vittra a bit, but mostly we said nothing. There was so much to do and so little to say.

Markis Bain came in to officiate the coronation. It was normally a large ceremony, a huge spectacle for the entire kingdom to attend, but we didn't have time for that. Duncan was on hand to witness, and Bain swore us in.

With a few simple words and a quick signature on a piece of paper, we were King and Queen.

Tove immediately left to talk to his mother. He needed to convince her to join the attack on the Vittra. Her healing powers would be invaluable in battle. Duncan went down to work with the trackers. I would follow him soon, but first I needed to take a moment to breathe.

I stared out the window. The snow had taken a break. It was

just above freezing, and the air was thick with winter fog. Heavy white frost covered all the branches, like they had been wrapped in it.

"My Queen," Loki said from behind me, and I turned around to see him smiling.

"You're the first one to call me that."

"How does it feel?" he asked, sauntering over. He touched a vase sitting on the table, then looked at me. "Do you feel like Your Royal Highness yet?"

"I'm not sure," I admitted. "But I don't know that I ever did."

"You'll have to get used to it," Loki said with a smirk. "I predict a long reign ahead of you. Years of being referred to as Your Majesty, Your Grace, Your Excellence, My Liege, My Queen, My Lovely."

"I don't think that last one is a formal title," I said.

"It should be." Loki stopped in front of me, his eyes sparkling. "You are a vision, especially with that crown."

"The crown." I blushed and took it off. "I forgot I was wearing it." It was truly stunning, but I felt ridiculous in it. "I had to wear it for the ceremony, but . . . that's over now."

"It is a beautiful crown." Loki took it from me, admiring its intricacies for a moment, before setting it aside. He stepped closer to me, so we were nearly touching, and I stared up at him.

"How are things going?" I asked. "Does our army understand the layout of the Vittra palace?"

"No."

"No?"

"No, I'm not going to do this," Loki said, his voice firm but low. His hand went to my waist, feeling warm even through the layers of fabric. "Everything is about to go to hell very quickly, so I want one moment where we don't talk about that. We pretend it doesn't exist. I want one last quiet moment with you."

"No, Loki." I shook my head, but I didn't pull away. "I told you that was one night and it could never happen again."

"And I told you that one night wasn't enough."

Loki leaned down, kissing me deeply and pressing me to him. I didn't even attempt to resist. I wrapped my arms around his neck. It wasn't the way we had kissed before, not as hungry or fevered. This was something different, nicer.

We were holding on to each other, knowing this might be the last time we could. It felt sweet and hopeful and tragic all at once.

When he stopped kissing me he rested his forehead against mine. He breathed as if struggling to catch his breath. I reached up and touched his face, his skin smooth and cool beneath my hand.

Loki lifted his head so he could look me in the eyes, and I saw something in them, something I'd never seen before. Something pure and unadulterated, and my heart seemed to grow with the warmth of my love for him.

I don't know how it happened or when it had, but I knew it with complete certainty. I had fallen in love with Loki, more intensely than anything I had felt for anyone before.

"Wendy!" Finn shouted, pulling me from my moment with Loki. "What are you doing? You're married! And not to him!"

"Nothing slips by you, does it?" Loki asked.

"Finn," I said and stepped away from Loki. "Calm down."

"No!" Finn yelled. "I will not calm down! What were you thinking? We're about to go to war, and you're cheating on your husband?"

"Everything's not exactly the way it seems," I said, but guilt and regret were gripping my stomach.

My marriage might be over, but I was still technically wed to another man. And I should be worrying about things more important than kissing Loki.

"It seemed like you had your tongue down his throat." Finn glared at us both.

"Well, then, everything is exactly as it seems," Loki said glibly.

"Loki, can you give us a moment alone?" I asked. He sighed and looked like he was about to protest. "Loki. Now."

"As you wish, my Queen," Loki muttered.

He walked past Finn as he left the room, giving him one more discerning glare, but they said nothing to each other. Loki shut the doors behind him, leaving Finn and me alone in my room.

"What were you thinking?" Finn asked, sounding at a loss for words.

"I was thinking that we're about to go to war, and my mother just died," I said. "Life is so very, very short, and I . . . I love him."

Finn winced. He looked away from me, and he chewed the inside of his cheek. It broke my heart to hurt him, but he needed to hear the truth.

"You barely know him," Finn said carefully.

"I know." I nodded. "I don't know how to explain it. But . . . it is what it is."

"It is what it is?" He laughed darkly and rolled his eyes. "Your love must not mean much, the way you throw it around. It wasn't that long ago you pledged it all to me, and here you are—"

"Here I am married to another man because you wouldn't fight for me," I said, cutting him off. "I did love you, Finn. And I still care about you. I always will. You are good and strong, and you did the best you could by me. But . . . you never really wanted to be with me."

"What are you talking about?" Finn asked. "I wanted nothing more than to be with you! But I couldn't!"

"That's it right there, Finn!" I gestured to him. "You couldn't. We can't. I mustn't. You always took everything at face value, and you never even tried."

"I never tried?" Finn asked. "How can you even say that?"

"Because you didn't." I ran my hands through my hair and shook my head. "You never fought for me. I fought *so* hard for you. I was willing to give up everything to be with you. But you gave up *nothing*. You wouldn't even let me give up anything."

"How is that a bad thing?" Finn asked. "I only wanted what was best for you."

"I know that, but you're not my father, Finn. You were supposed to be my . . ." I trailed off. "I don't know what. You were never my boyfriend. You refused to be anything more to me, unless you saw me interested in another guy."

"I was only trying to protect you!" Finn insisted.

"That doesn't change anything." I took a deep breath. "I have been fighting to change things around here, to make the kingdom better for trackers and all the Trylle. And you have been fighting to keep things the same. You are content to live in this ridiculous hierarchy."

"I am not *content*," he said fiercely.

"But you're not doing anything to change it! You're just taking it, and that I could live with. You're willing to simply accept your fate. But you expected me to do the same, and that I can't stomach, Finn. I want more. I *need* more."

"And you think Loki will give that to you?" Finn asked, and most of the sarcasm had fallen away from his voice. He actually wanted to know if I thought Loki was good for me.

"Yes, he will."

"And how does your husband feel about all of this?" Finn asked.

"I don't know exactly," I said, which was true. Tove seemed to actually know more about the way Loki and I felt about each other than we did, but I wasn't entirely sure how he felt about it. "But once everything is settled with the Vittra, Tove and I are getting our marriage annulled."

"You're leaving him for Loki?" Finn asked, his voice astonished.

"No, actually," I said. "Tove is leaving me. He wants to

share his life with someone he actually loves, and that's not me."

His whole body slacked, and he stared at the floor. Finn ran a hand through his hair, and I realized that I would never again run my fingers through his hair. Whatever had happened between Finn and me, it was over. He was no longer mine. And for the first time, I was okay with that.

"I'm sorry," Finn said quietly.

"Pardon?" I asked, thinking I'd heard him wrong.

"You're right, and I'm sorry." He looked up at me, his eyes stormy. "I never fought for you. If anything, I fought to uphold a system that kept me from you. And . . . I am sorry for that." He swallowed. "I will always regret that."

"I'm sorry too." I bit my lip to keep tears from falling.

"But . . ." Finn sighed and looked away from me again. "At least he does love you."

"What?" I asked.

"Loki." He said his name bitterly and shook his head. "At first I thought it was a trick, but I've been around him enough now and heard him talk about you." Finn shifted his weight, seeming uncomfortable with the conversation. "And he does love you."

He nodded his head, but I wasn't sure why. He let out a shaky breath, and I think he was trying not to cry.

"So . . . I guess I can live with that." He rubbed his forehead.

I stepped over to him and put my hand on his arm, attempting to comfort him in some way. We were so close to each other, but I didn't feel that pull the way I did before. When he lifted his head, I smiled weakly at him.

"This really is for the best," I said. "Me and you never would've worked out anyway. You need someone that you can protect and shelter. And I need someone to push me to take risks, so I can pull this kingdom forward."

"There is more truth in that than I'm ready to admit," he agreed.

I swallowed, realizing something I'd never realized before. "I never could've really made you happy. I would've fought you at everything, frustrated by your attempts to keep me safe and hold me back. We would've made each other miserable."

"Had we ever really had a chance to be together." He exhaled again.

"I'm sorry," I told him again.

Finn shook his head. "Don't be. You're right. This is the best for both of us. And . . ." He paused. "As long as you're happy."

"I am." I smiled. "And you'll be much happier without me than you ever would've been with me."

He nodded, but I wasn't sure if he really believed it or not. "But if you'll excuse me, I should go down to finish getting ready to leave."

"Right, of course. I have much to do myself."

Finn smiled at me once before he left, and as soon as he was gone, I let out a deep breath. I can't say I felt good about ending things with Finn. It was more bittersweet than that. But I did feel better knowing that he finally knew the truth. Things between us were truly over—for both of us—and I could move on with my life. Assuming I still had a life to move on with after tonight.

TWENTY-THREE

time

Throughout the long drive to Ondarike, we said hardly anything. I rode with Tove, Loki, Duncan, and Willa, and the fear was almost palpable. I had no idea if we were doing the right thing. I had sounded so confident when I talked to them, but that was because this was the best I could come up with.

Before we left, I'd gone over the plan of attack with the heads of the teams. Loki thought it would be best to break up our army into several smaller teams that would sneak into different places in the Vittra palace.

Around two hundred trackers had joined our army, and most of the Trylle from Oslinna. Mia had tried to come along, but Finn had convinced her it would be better for her to stay behind and care for her baby, which I was grateful for. I didn't want Hanna to end up an orphan.

Maybe two or three dozen Markis and Marksinna had come

along, including Marksinna Laris. I promised myself to be nicer to her when we got back to Förening. *If* we got back.

A few mänks had even volunteered. I'd sent Rhys and Rhiannon away this morning, and I tried to send Matt away, but he refused to leave Förening. Matt had even wanted to fight with us, but I'd convinced him that he would only distract Willa and me, and he agreed to stay behind.

Willa would be leading her own team of twenty trackers and two Markis. They would be going in a side door off the kitchen, and Loki thought there would be hobgoblins in there getting a midnight snack. But Willa could blow around the pots and pans, and Markis Bain could control water, so maybe he could flood the place.

Finn and Thomas led two different teams, but they would be doing about the same things. They were coming up through the dungeon. Loki had escaped through a section of the cellar that connected with the dungeon. The cellar sprawled beneath the whole palace like a long maze, and through its long tunnels, Finn, Thomas, and their teams would be able to sneak up and deflect a lot of hobgoblins.

Tove had volunteered for the most dangerous mission. Bain had tried to go along with him, but Tove had insisted Bain go on Willa's team. Tove would go through the front doors, leading a team of fifty trackers. His objective was to make noise and alert the hobgoblins that he was there. That way, the other teams could sneak up behind the hobgoblins while they were busy trying to ward off Tove and his team.

Duncan had wanted to be on Tove's team, but I reassigned

him to Willa's team. So far, hers sounded about the safest. Not that any of this was really safe.

Loki's job was to get me into the palace and lead me to Oren, and then he would go help Tove fight. He wasn't thrilled about the idea, but he knew that I had to do this, and I had to do it on my own.

In the long history of the Trylle, we had never attacked. No matter how provoked we might be. This was the one thing Oren would never expect, and it might give us enough of an advantage to stop him.

Loki knew the palace best, so he drove our SUV and led the rest of the Trylle. We had a caravan of Cadillacs that we drove to Ondarike. When we got near the palace, he cut the headlights, and the cars behind us did the same. He parked at the bottom of the hill, so we were hidden behind the forest of dead wood, and that was as close to the palace as he felt comfortable.

"Are you sure you want to do this?" Loki asked me quietly after we got out of the car.

"Yes," I said. "Are you?"

"Not as much as I'd like," he admitted.

"Just get me to Oren."

I looked back behind me, at all the other Trylle getting out of their cars. Finn was already directing a few of them up the hill, telling them how to get inside. Loki had gone over detailed maps with the team leaders before we left, but we hadn't had enough time to show all the Trylle.

"Everybody knows what to do?" I asked and looked over at Willa, Tove, and Duncan.

"Yeah, we'll be okay." Willa reached out and squeezed my arm. "Just stay safe."

"We got it," Duncan said, flashing a nervous smile.

"Don't be a hero," I told him sternly. "Protect yourself."

"Take care of her," Tove said to Loki.

"I'll do my best," Loki said.

Most everyone else had started up the hill, with Loki and me going in an entrance on the far side of the palace, away from them. We were going a different route, sneaking around the hobgoblins and going directly to the King.

We went through the trees, slipping through snow and branches cracking under our feet. When we reached the palace, Loki led me to a small wooden door almost completely buried under vines. The vines looked brown and dead, but they were covered with sharp thorns that cut Loki's hand when he pushed them back.

He opened the door, then slid inside, and I followed. We stepped into a narrow, dimly lit hall. The floors were covered with red velvet carpets, and they helped silence our footsteps. As he led me through the back halls of the palace, I heard banging and yelling from far away. The fighting had started.

I jumped when something slammed into the wall right next to us, leaving a large crack in the wood.

"What's on the other side of that wall?" I asked, pointing to the crack.

"The front hall." Loki took my hand and looked at me. "If you want to do this, we need to hurry. He's going to hear the fighting."

I nodded, and we walked faster. The back hallways turned and twisted a few times before we came across a very constricted stairway. I almost had to turn sideways to climb up, and the steps themselves were so thin I had to stand on my tiptoes.

At the top of the stairs was a door, and when Loki pushed it open, I knew exactly where we were. Right across from us were the doors to Oren's chamber. Vines, fairies, and trolls were carved into the oak, depicting a fantasy scene. The hall was deserted, and the cacophony of fighting sounded farther away.

I heard a scream that sounded too much like Tove, and the entire palace shook.

"Go," I told Loki.

"I don't want to leave you to face the King alone."

"No, I can do this." I put my hand on his chest and faced him. "They need you downstairs. I can handle the King myself."

He shook his head. "Wendy, no."

"Loki, please. You must help them. You're strong. They need you," I said, but I knew that wouldn't convince him. "I will send you flying down the hall myself, but that will drain my abilities. I don't want to do it, but I will if I have to."

His eyes searched mine, and I knew he didn't want to leave me. But I couldn't let him come with me. I wanted him safe, or at least safer than he would be around Oren. And more important, my friends needed him to help fight against the hobgoblins.

"I can do this," I repeated. "I was born for this."

He didn't want to, but he finally relented. He kissed me, quickly and fiercely on the mouth.

"I will help them, and then I will be back for you," he said.

"I know. Now go."

He nodded and dashed down the hall. Taking a deep breath, I turned around to face the doors. I went down the hall, prepared to kill my father.

TWENTY-FOUR

beginning of the end

I pushed open the doors, and I wasn't exactly sure what I expected, but it wasn't this. Oren was awake, sitting on his throne. He wore black satin pants, and his robe hung open, revealing his shirtless torso, so I assumed he had been sleeping recently.

He sat casually in the chair, turned slightly to the side so one of his legs hung over the arm. His fingers were bedazzled with heavy silver rings, and he held a glass of red wine in one hand, sipping it slowly.

I glanced around the room, searching for the swords Loki had told me about. The platinum ones that could cut through anything. We had our own swords back in Förening, but Loki didn't think any of them would be powerful enough to use on Oren. Even his flesh and bone were stronger than the average Trylle or Vittra. I'd have to use the King's own weapons on himself.

"My child." Oren smiled at me in that way that made the hair stand up on the back of my neck. "You've come home."

"This isn't my home," I said, my voice as strong and sure as I could make it.

I spotted the swords, their handles glistening with diamonds from where they were mounted on the wall, and that helped give me a bit more confidence.

Oren ignored my comment. "It sounds as though you've brought guests." He twirled his glass, watching the wine swirl about in it. "You're supposed to wait until your parents go out of town to throw a party."

I grew irritated with his attempts at humor. "I'm not throwing a party. You know why I've come."

"I know why you *think* you've come," he clarified. He stood up, and in one quick swallow drained his glass. When he'd finished, he tossed it to the side, making it shatter against the wall. "But if I were you, I would seriously reconsider."

"Reconsider what?" I asked.

"Your plan." Oren walked toward me in that same stealthy gait he always had. "There is still time to follow through on the terms we agreed to. There is still time to save yourself and your friends, but not much.

"I'm not a patient man," he said, walking around me in a large circle. "If you weren't my daughter, you would already be dead. I have given you more than I've given anyone else. And it's time you show me some gratitude."

"Gratitude?" I asked. "For what? Kidnapping me? Killing my people? Overtaking my kingdom?"

"For letting you live," he said, his gravelly voice behind me, right in my ear, and I didn't know how he got that close to me so fast.

"I can say the same thing about you," I said, surprised by how even my voice sounded. "I've let you live thus far, and I will let you continue to live. If you call this off. Let us go. Leave us alone. Forever."

"Why would I do that?" Oren laughed.

"If you don't, I will have no other choice," I said as he strolled back in front of me, facing me as I spoke. "I will kill you."

"Have you forgotten our deal?" Oren asked, a twisted smile on his lips and something dark sparkling in his eyes. "Have you forgotten what you agreed to when you gave me your kingdom?"

"No, I haven't forgotten."

"You've merely decided to back out on it?" he asked, smiling wider. "Knowing what it would cost you."

"It will cost me nothing," I said firmly. "I will defeat you."

"Maybe you will." Oren seemed to consider this for a moment. "But not until you lose everything."

"Is that your answer, then?" I asked.

"You mean will I give up, let you and all your friends live happily ever after?" he asked, his tone condescending, but that changed instantly. "*I* get the happily ever after, and I will not concede to a spoiled brat like you." His face was hard, and his words were filled with venom.

"Then you leave me no choice."

I summoned all my power, concentrating and focusing on

everything I had been practicing. I held my hands out toward him, palms out, and, using everything I had in me, I began to push. I knew I couldn't kill him this way, but I hoped to get him incapacitated enough that I could get close to him.

His hair ruffled, his robe even blew back, but nothing else happened. I used everything inside me, and a buzzing sound started in the back of my head, growing more painful as I strained to use all my energy.

But Oren never even moved. He only smiled wider.

"Is that all you've got?" He threw back his head and laughed, the sound reverberating through the room. "I have highly over-estimated you."

I pushed and pushed, refusing to give up, even when the pain in my skull became excruciating. Everything else in the room, the furniture, the books, began flying around like there was a tornado, but Oren remained unmoved.

I could feel something warm and wet on my lips, and I realized my nose had begun to bleed.

"Oh, Princess, darling," Oren said, as sweetly as he could. "You're exhausting yourself. I hate to see you in so much pain." He sighed, attempting to sound regretful. "So I'll put you out of your misery."

He stepped forward and raised his hand. He struck me across the face, backhanding me so hard I flew across the room and slammed into a wall. Everything that I had sent flying in the air collapsed to the floor around me.

Loki had tried to warn me about how strong Oren was, but

I hadn't understood until now. It was like being hit with a wrecking ball. My side ached terribly where I'd crashed into the wall, and some of my ribs must have been broken. My leg screamed in pain and I was lucky I hadn't broken my neck.

"I hate to do this to you," Oren said, and at least he wasn't smiling when he said it. "But I told you what would happen if you went against me."

I pushed myself up so I was sitting, still leaning back against the wall. He towered over me, and I steeled myself, waiting for him to hit me again. But instead, he went over to his chamber doors and opened them.

"Bring him to me!" Oren shouted out into the hall. He left the doors open and returned to me. He crouched, his black eyes meeting mine. "I warned you. I gave you every chance to join me. I wanted you with me, not against me."

"I would rather die than serve you," I said.

"I see that." He reached out, meaning to wipe the blood from my forehead, but I pulled away from him, even though it sent shooting pain through me. "Well, the good news is you won't die alone."

He rose and stepped back from me. At the same time, Kyra—the Vittra I'd tangled with before—and another Vittra came into the room, carrying Loki with him. I hadn't seen the other Vittra before, but he was huge, a barbarian of a man.

They were literally dragging Loki. They held him by each arm, and his legs trailed limply on the floor. His head hung down, and blood dripped from his temple.

"No!" I shouted, and Loki lifted his head at the sound of my voice. He looked over at me, and it was clear they had beaten the hell out of him.

"I'm sorry, Wendy," he said simply. "I tried."

"No," I repeated and struggled to my feet. My body didn't move the way I wanted it to, but I ignored the pain. "No, don't hurt him. I'll do whatever you ask."

"It's too late." Oren shook his head. "I promised you that I would make you watch him die. And I am a man of my word."

"No, please," I begged him. I stumbled over to a chair and leaned against it, holding myself up, because I couldn't stand on my own. "I will do anything. *Anything.*"

"I am sorry," Oren said again.

He walked over to the wall where the two long swords still hung, the only things still intact in the room after I had sent it into a flurry. He pulled one down, the diamond-encrusted bell guard covering his hand.

I tried to use my powers to stop him. I held out my hand, pushing out what energy I had left. Some of the lighter things in the room stirred, like papers and a curtain, and Kyra winced. But Oren was unruffled.

"Loki's met with this blade before," Oren said, admiring the sword. "And it's the same one I ended his father with. It seems fitting that it will be the one to finish him."

"Please." I let my hand fall to the side. "I will do your bidding. I will do anything."

"I've already told you." Oren walked back, stopping in front of Loki. "It's too late."

Kyra and the other Vittra held Loki higher, and Loki grunted. Tears streamed down my face, and I could think of nothing to do to stop Oren. My powers weren't working on him. I wasn't strong enough to fight him. I had nothing to barter.

Still staring at me, Oren lifted up his sword, and with one quick move, he stabbed Loki straight through the heart.

TWENTY-FIVE

mortality

Kyra and the other Vittra instantly let go of Loki, and he collapsed on the floor. They both held their heads, clutching at them, and at first I didn't understand.

I couldn't really think or feel anything, except that I had been ripped in two. It felt as if Oren had torn my heart from my chest. I had never felt such consuming pain or anger as I did then.

Blackness surged through me with an intense heat. I didn't even really know what was happening around me. Everything felt like a hazy blur.

Then I saw Oren, squinting and touching his own head, and I remembered.

I could do something with my mind when I was frightened or angry. I'd done it to Tove when he tried to wake me, and I'd even done it on a smaller scale when Elora had been torturing Loki.

That feeling—that intense fear or anger—unlocked a power inside me. I did something to people inside their heads, causing great agony. It usually only lasted a few seconds, but I had never been as pissed off before.

As soon as I realized what I was doing, I harnessed it and directed it at Oren. At first he looked confused and simply started backing up. He kept squinting and tilting his head, as if he were staring at a very bright light.

In the back of my mind, I knew my body should hurt, but I felt nothing. I'd blotted out any pain. I walked evenly toward Oren, and he began to hold his head. He fell to his knees. He was moaning and begging but I couldn't understand anything he was saying.

Both Kyra and the other Vittra were curled up on the floor, and Kyra was actually sobbing. I went over to Loki, refusing to let myself actually see him, to really believe he was dead, and I pulled the sword from his chest.

I walked over to where my father was slumped on his knees, bent forward. His hands were clamped to his ears. He was muttering at first, but when I raised the sword over my head, I heard him begin to shout.

"Make it stop!" Oren yelled. "Please! Make the pain stop!"

"I'll put you out of your misery," I said, and I swung the sword down, slicing through his neck.

I turned away so I didn't have to see it, but I heard his head fall to the floor.

I stood there, still holding the sword, and looked around the room. The haze had faded away, and pain returned to my body. My body screamed in agony, and my legs threatened to give out beneath me. Kyra and the other Vittra had stopped writhing and they both sat up.

"Go," I said, struggling to catch my breath. "Tell them the King is dead."

Kyra looked at Oren's corpse with widened eyes, and she didn't question my orders. She and the other Vittra scrambled to their feet and ran out of the room, leaving me alone with Loki.

I dropped the sword and rushed to his side as quickly as my body would allow. I knelt next to him, and pulled his head onto my lap, but it lolled to the side. Blood stained the front of his chest, and I put my hand over the wound, trying to press the life back into him.

"No, Loki, please," I said as tears streamed down my face. "Loki, stay with me. Please. I love you. You can't leave me like this."

But he didn't move. He didn't breathe. I bent down, kissing his forehead as I sobbed, and I didn't even have words for the pain I felt. With nothing else to do, I began to wail.

"My god, I'm too late," someone said, and I turned to see Sara standing in the doorway. She looked at the dead King, her husband.

Loki had saved her life once, and she was a healer. She would be the only chance I would have at saving him.

"Help me," I begged and tried to hold Loki up to her. "Please. You have to help him."

"I . . ." Sara didn't answer for a second, and then she ran

over to us, kneeling on the other side of Loki. "I don't know that I can. He might already be gone."

"Please," I cried. "You have to try." She took a deep breath and nodded.

"Do you have any energy left?" Sara asked.

"I don't know," I admitted. I felt weak and drained. Fighting Oren had taken everything out of me.

"Well, help me, if you can," she said. She put her hand on top of mine, the one that covered the hole in Loki's chest. "Give me any energy you have. I need all I can get."

I nodded and closed my eyes, focusing on her and Loki. A warm tingling went through my hand, a sensation I was familiar with from being healed before. But something else happened. I felt it in my veins, flowing through me, being pulled from me. Like hot liquid escaping out through my fingertips.

Then I heard it. Loki gasped loudly, and I opened my eyes.

He took deep breaths, and tears of relief slid down my cheeks. Sara's hand was still over mine, and her skin had become wrinkled and loose. Her hair suddenly had gray in it, and her face had aged noticeably. She'd given Loki a lot of her life force to save him.

"Loki," I said.

"Hey, Princess." He smiled dazedly as he looked up at me. "What's wrong?"

"Nothing." I smiled and shook my head. "Not anymore."

"What's this?" He took my hair and held it out so I could see. A curl near the front had gone completely silver. "I take a nap, and you go gray?"

"You didn't take a nap." I laughed. "Don't you remember what happened?"

He furrowed his brow, trying to remember, and understanding flashed in his eyes.

"I remember . . ." Loki touched my face. "I remember that I love you." I bent down, kissing him full on the mouth, and he held me to him.

TWENTY-SIX

home

Wendy!" Willa was nearly screaming, and I rushed to try to get to my feet. The panic in her voice made me forget about how weak I was, and I would've fallen to the floor if Loki hadn't caught me.

"Easy, Princess," Sara said, looking up at me from where she knelt on the floor. Loki had gotten to his feet and had an arm around my waist, holding me up. "You used much of your life force today."

I wanted to thank her for helping me and ask her exactly why she had. Loki'd already explained to me how close he'd been to Sara, but I had no idea how she might feel about the fact that I'd just killed her husband.

Before I had a chance to say anything to her, Willa appeared in the doorway to the King's chambers. Her clothes were wet, her hair was a mess, and she had blood on her cheek.

"Wendy!" Willa shouted again and ran to me, throwing her

arms around me. She would've knocked me over if Loki hadn't been there.

"Willa, settle down." Loki gently pushed her off me, so she wouldn't smother me.

"I'm so glad you're okay." She stepped back from me and scanned the room, her eyes landing on the King's head on the floor, his long hair lying over it like a blanket. "So it's true, then? The King is dead? The war's over?"

"The King is dead." I nodded and turned to Sara to see how she would respond. She was Queen of the Vittra, after all, and she could continue this war if she wanted to.

Loki followed my gaze and his eyes met hers. "The war is over," he said, but I wasn't sure if he was simply telling her or declaring it.

"The King's reign of terror has lasted long enough," Sara said. She got to her feet slowly and smiled wanly at us. "Our war is over, and I'll be happy if I never see another one again."

"Good." Willa smiled in relief. "When that tracker came down and said the King was dead, the hobgoblins started retreating. A lot of them ran outside."

"They're happier in the woods than living indoors anyway," Sara explained.

"So how did we do?" I asked Willa, my heart tightening at the thought of how our army had fared in the battle. "Did everyone survive?"

Willa's expression fell. She pursed her lips and shook her head. "I don't know for sure. As soon as I heard the King was dead, I went to find you. But . . . I know not everyone made it."

"Who?" I demanded.

She hesitated before answering. "A few trackers. I don't know for sure."

Since Willa wouldn't answer me, I had to see for myself. I started walking away, again forgetting that my legs barely worked. This time, when they gave out under me, Loki scooped me up, carrying me in his arms.

I wanted to protest and insist I could walk, but I couldn't really. So the best I could do was direct him to take me down to the main hall, where Willa had told me the worst of the carnage was.

Loki carried me out of the room, with Willa at our side and Sara following a few steps behind. The upstairs didn't look that bad, but I doubted the fighting had really made it this far. We did pass a small table with a hobgoblin hiding underneath it, and when he saw us, he took off running the opposite way, his little legs moving as fast as they could.

When we reached the top of the stairs, I asked Loki to stop and put me down. From here, I had the best vantage point to view the front hall. The top of the stairs were over twenty feet above it, and I could survey the entire scene.

"Wendy, I don't think—" Loki tried to hang on to me, but I squirmed away from him, and he reluctantly set me down.

I grabbed the banister to steady myself and stared down. The room itself had once been lovely—plush red rugs, paintings on the wall, and all the furnishings dark mahogany, matching the walls.

Everything had been destroyed, and I do mean everything.

The paintings were shredded, the chairs broken, the rugs burned. Even the walls were cracked. Most of the crystals on the chandelier had been shattered, but it still hung from the ceiling, casting the room in light.

Bodies littered the floor, most of them Trylle, but there were a few hobgoblins. Fortunately, they mostly appeared to be wounded, but not all of them had survived. I knew all of the dead—not well, but I knew them. They were mostly trackers and mänks, those least equipped to fight the hobgoblins, and I wondered if I had done the right thing by allowing them to come into this war.

Aurora was going around tending to the injured, and I was pleased to see her moving from Markis to tracker without appearing to care about their standing. She was going to whoever had the worst injuries and helping them first.

Laris had no visible wounds, so she was helping organize those who had been hurt and helping treat those with the least serious injuries, like wrapping an arm.

Bain was leaning against one of the walls. His clothes were drenched, and he had blood on his shirt, but he was talking to Tove, so he must've been all right. Tove was crouched in front of him. He'd torn off the sleeve of his shirt and was wrapping it around Bain's leg, but other than that, Tove appeared to be no worse for the wear.

As I scanned the room, accounting for everybody, taking in the losses with a pained heart, I realized that Finn was absent from the room—not among the living or the dead.

"Where is everyone else?" I asked Willa without taking my eyes off the front hall.

"Um, I'm not sure," Willa said. "We told everyone to meet in the front hall once the fighting had stopped."

"So what does that mean if they're not here?" I asked, already fearing the worst about Finn.

My heart had already begun to panic when the door to the dungeon swung open. Finn came up the stairs, walking into the hall, with his father's arm looped around his shoulders. Thomas didn't look so good, but he was supporting some of his own weight, so that was a good sign.

Finn's face was bloodied and bruised, but when he glanced up at me at the top of the stairs, I saw a mixture of pride and relief in his eyes. I smiled down at him, happy to see him alive. Just because I'd ended things with him didn't mean I could handle him being dead.

Finn and Thomas hobbled past a tipped-over buffet table on their way over to where Aurora was treating people. My eyes were following them, and that was when I saw legs sticking out from underneath the table. They were clad in skinny jeans, and I only knew one person ridiculous enough to wear skinny jeans into battle.

"Duncan!" I shouted and raced down the stairs. Fortunately, adrenaline had kicked in, propelling my legs to move despite the pain.

I tripped when I reached the bottom step anyway, but Loki was right there, pulling me back up to my feet. When I reached the table, I collapsed next to it and immediately tried lifting it up. Obviously, I didn't have the strength for it, but Loki lifted it easily.

And it was just as I feared. Duncan had been crushed underneath it. As Loki moved the buffet table away, I scrambled over to Duncan's head, kneeling next to him. His chest was bloodied, and I could actually see a bone sticking out of his side.

"Duncan," I breathed, with tears sliding down my cheeks. I brushed the hair back from his forehead and tried not to sob. I'd tried to protect him, and I'd made him promise that he would do everything he could to save himself. And all of that had been in vain.

Suddenly he coughed, blood coming out of his mouth.

"Aurora!" I shouted and looked back over my shoulder for her. "Aurora, I need you!"

"Princess?" Duncan opened his eyes and smiled dazedly at me. "Did we win?"

"Yes." I nodded fervently, cradling his head in my hands. "Yes, we won."

"Good." He closed his eyes again.

"Duncan, stay with me," I begged, trying not to cry so my tears wouldn't land on his face. "Duncan. That's an order. You have to stay with me."

"Aurora!" Loki was yelling for her now, since she wasn't coming fast enough.

Duncan coughed again, harder this time, and finally Aurora appeared at my side. Her hands were already covered in blood from helping the other Trylle, and she pressed them against the bone protruding through his skin.

He groaned loudly when she did that and tried to jerk away, but I held him still. Aurora pushed on his side, and once the bone was back in, with the skin healed over it, she pulled her hands away.

"I can't heal him completely," Aurora said as Duncan took a deep breath. "I need to save my energy to help the others."

"Thank you." I smiled at her. "I understand."

"Do you need my help?" Aurora asked, holding her hands out toward me, but I shook my head. "Are you sure?"

"I'll be all right," I insisted. "You go take care of them."

She nodded and left to do just that. Duncan stirred a bit, but I told him to rest. She'd fixed him enough so he wouldn't die, but that didn't mean he was in good shape.

Willa had gotten some bandages from Sara, who had apparently joined our effort to care for the injured, and she took over the care of Duncan, wrapping up his wounds.

When I had been yelling for Aurora, Tove left his post next to Bain to see if he could help. Once Duncan was stable, I turned my attention to Tove. He held out his hand and pulled me to my feet. I had to lean on him for support, and Loki was nearby, in case I needed more.

"You know, it's almost a shame we don't love each other," Tove said, with his arm around my shoulders. "We make an awfully good team."

"I don't know about that." I looked around the room, at all the Trylle and even the Vittra hobgoblins that had been hurt.

"Wars have casualties," Tove said, understanding what I meant. "And that's not to say I'm not sad about the lives we lost tonight, but we managed to stop a centuries-old war. Imagine how many lives that will save in the future."

I realized he was right. I mean, I had known it—that was why I'd wanted to go to war in the first place—but the devastation of it all had a way of blocking that out.

But now, standing there with Tove, I felt good. Despite the losses and the damage, we had done what we had set out to do. We'd freed ourselves, and the Vittra people, from Oren's oppressive rule. We were free.

"We did the right thing." I looked up at him, and his mossy eyes looked unusually light.

"We did." He squeezed my shoulder and kissed me gently on the temple. "I'm proud of what we accomplished."

"Me too."

"But what do you say we get out of here?" Tove asked. "Let's get our people fixed up as best we can and get them back home."

"That sounds fantastic."

"I'm going to go see if my mother needs any help." Tove let go of me and started stepping back toward his mother.

I managed to stand by myself, but Loki was only a few feet away, helping Willa set another tracker's broken leg, if I needed him.

"Hey, Tove," I said as he walked away, and he paused, turning back to me. "Just because we won't be married anymore doesn't mean we can't still be a team. I still expect you to work with me back at the palace."

"I wouldn't have it any other way." Tove grinned. "And trust me, I have *plenty* of ideas on how to run things."

I helped as much as I could with our people, but I really didn't have the strength to do much. Fortunately, Loki was working at 110 percent, and he managed to help out quite a bit. Aurora healed as much as she could, focusing on the worst cases, and the rest of the injuries were wrapped and set until we could get back to the palace and enlist more help.

As soon as we were able, we started to load up the vehicles, and began sending the caravan of Trylle back to Förening. We were careful to take those we'd lost with us, since they deserved a proper burial back home.

Even though I was hurt, I insisted on waiting to be last to leave. I wanted to make sure we saw everyone off.

I talked with Sara briefly before we departed, and she assured me that there would be no more attacks on the Trylle, not by any of the Vittra. We would convene in a few days to sign a new peace treaty, but for now, we both needed to rest up and get our communities in order.

Willa drove us home to Förening, with Duncan sitting in front beside her, sleeping soundly. Tove had decided to ride home in Bain's car, and they left right before we did. Tove had stayed until the end with us, making sure we'd gotten everyone out safely.

The sun was just beginning to rise as we made the trek back

home, and the sky above the horizon looked more pink and purple than blue.

I curled up in the back next to Loki, his arm around me, and my head resting on his shoulder. My body ached all over, but it felt good being with him. He kissed the top of my head, and I snuggled up closer to him. He'd been helping me at the palace, but we'd waited until we were alone in the car to be affectionate. Willa had raised an eyebrow at us, but she said nothing. Later on, back in Förening, I'd have a thousand questions from her. But for now, she let us have our moment together.

"I can't wait until we get home," I said.

"*Home*," Loki said and laughed a little.

"What?" I lifted my head to look up at him. "What's funny about that?"

"Nothing." He shook his head. "I just . . . I don't think I've ever really felt like I had a home before." He smiled down at me. "Not until I met you."

Loki leaned down, kissing me gently on the mouth. I'm sure he wanted to kiss me more deeply, but he was afraid of hurting me. He continued to kiss me tenderly, and I clung to him as tightly as I could as heat swirled through me.

When he stopped, he rested his forehead against mine and breathed in deeply. "I cannot wait to get home with you, Princess."

"I'm the Queen now, you know," I teased, and he laughed and kissed me again.

epilogue: four months later

The first few weeks after the battle were rough. I'd broken several ribs and dislocated my shoulder. So many of our people needed Aurora and Sara's healing powers that I refused to use any on myself. I had to heal the old-fashioned way.

Everyone was quick to point out that I healed much more quickly because of my Vittra blood, but it was still a rough couple of weeks. Some good things came out of it, though. Like Loki waiting on me hand and foot. Truth be told, he barely left my side.

As soon as I was well enough to attend, we had my mother's funeral. The entire kingdom turned out, and to my surprise, the King and Queen of the Kanin came, as well as the Queen of the Omte. They came to pay their respects but also to thank us for ending the tyranny of the Vittra.

Oren had set his sights most fervently on the Trylle, but we weren't the only ones. It wasn't until the funeral, when so many people came that the crowd overflowed into the street, that I realized what exactly we'd accomplished.

I also got to hear from other Trylle and even other tribes what my mother had done to protect them. The deals she had made, the things she gave up, and all the work she put into keeping the peace. Elora had given so much to the people, and it was deeply moving to see how much they appreciated it.

Losing Elora made me understand even more the importance of having a mother, and what had been taken from Rhys. Despite the way my "host" mother, Kim, had treated me, I knew she'd done everything out of love, love for a child she'd never even met.

Matt took Rhys to see Kim, where she's still locked up in an asylum. Matt's still resistant to the idea of repairing his relationship with her, but being willing to see her at all is a huge step.

Rhys plans to go to college near the asylum in the fall, so he can begin getting to know her. Matt says that Kim is doing a bit better, and if she continues on the road to recovery, she might be released one day.

Matt came back to Förening, though. He says his home is here, and for that I'm grateful. I know I'm an adult with my own kingdom now, but I don't think I'm ready to live that far away from my brother.

Oslinna is still rebuilding, and Matt has spent a great deal of time helping them with the process. His designs are gorgeous, and it's been really good for the Trylle people to see a mänks do something so well.

We're still working against prejudice, and I know it will be a while before they completely give in to the idea that it's okay for people to marry whoever they love, no matter if they're Trylle or not. But we're on the right road.

Before I hang up my crown as Queen, I'm certain we'll make it legal for anyone to marry whoever they love. Willa's hoping that it's sooner rather than later, of course, but she's been shopping around for a wedding dress since she was eight.

She's taken a much more active role in our society. Since I was on bed rest when we first came back, she stepped up to handle a lot of the day-to-day work with Tove. He is still one of my smartest and most trusted confidants, and he works alongside me all the time.

Shortly after the funeral, Tove and I had our marriage annulled. He insisted on it, because he said my and Loki's auras were blinding him. It turned out to be a rather complicated process, but thanks to our recent defeat of a major enemy, the Trylle people were much more willing to go along with our ideas.

Tove seems to be taking our annulment better than our marriage. Thanks to his efforts on the campaign, he managed to get Bain elected as Chancellor, which is a drastic improvement from our last Chancellor. Both Tove and Bain are working hard to improve the entire Trylle community.

Tove's met someone, although he's been very tight-lipped about who it is. Though he won't name names, I have an idea who the special someone might be. He's still afraid of how the community will react to him being gay, but I don't think it will be long before he's able to be open about it.

After we defeated the Vittra, Thomas left, joining his family in the Kanin tribe, and I don't think he'll be coming back. Finn stayed behind, taking over his father's duties as head tracker.

It's still a bit strange seeing Finn around the palace. I don't love him anymore, not like I did, although I don't think I can ever truly stop caring for him. He was my first love, and he was immensely important to me becoming the Queen I am today.

At first he was cold and distant, but the ice between us seems to be melting. We're on the path to becoming friends again, and that's something.

I've seen Finn talking with Mia, spending time with her and her small daughter. When he's around them, he seems relaxed in a way that he never was around me. Even though he did care for me, I don't think he was ever able to really relax or be himself with me. But when he's holding Hanna and laughing with Mia, I've never seen him happier.

She's giving him something that I never could, and for that I'm forever grateful. Finn deserves to be happy and to truly love someone who can love him back.

And Loki . . . well, Loki has hardly left my side since we came back, but I wouldn't let him into my bed again until he made an honest woman of me. So he did.

Two weeks ago in the garden, beneath the spring flowers, we had a small wedding, much different from my first one. This time, it was only my closest friends in attendance, including my aunt Maggie. I actually had a hand in planning it, and it was exactly as I wanted it.

But its greatest difference was that I wanted this wedding, and I married a man I desperately love.

Maggie's been staying with us for a few weeks, and it's mostly been wonderful. She still hasn't completely wrapped her mind around everything that's going on here, but she took to Rhys immediately. Thankfully, he's spent the last week keeping her entertained so Loki and I can have a little bit of time to ourselves.

Unfortunately, there's never enough time. The nights seem too short, and the sun always seems to come up too early when I'm still snuggled in bed with him. Usually he wants to sleep in as much as I do, but not today.

He opens the shades, so the morning light shines in too brightly, and I squeeze my eyes shut and bury my face in the pillow.

"Aw, Wendy." Loki kneels down on the floor next to the bed and brushes the hair back from my eyes. "You knew today was coming."

"I know, but I didn't want it to come." I open my eyes so I can look at him, smiling at me even though his eyes are pained. "I shouldn't have let you agree to this."

Loki laughs. "You don't 'let' me. I'm the King. Nobody tells me what to do."

"That's what you think," I scoff, making him laugh harder.

"But seriously, my love, are you going to get up and see me off today?" Loki asks. He takes my hand in his, kissing it. "You don't have to, of course. I can do the ceremony myself, and I know how mornings have been for you lately."

"No, if you're going to leave, I want to say good-bye." I sigh. "But you better hurry back."

"As quickly as I can." He smiles. "Nothing in the world will keep me from my Queen."

I throw off the covers and go into the closet to get dressed. We're having a ceremony to see Loki off, so I have to choose a nice gown, and I even have to wear my crown. I avoid it for the most part, since it makes me feel silly, but I have to put it on for formal occasions.

Loki is already dressed for the day. I'd felt him get up about an hour ago. I kept sleeping, though, since I've been so tired lately. I'd like to say it's because of how worn out Loki had left me after our honeymoon, and while that is definitely part of the reason, it isn't all of it.

"How are you feeling this morning?" Loki asks. He leans against the closet door, watching me as I pull on a dark emerald gown.

"Other than being sad, I'm okay." I slip the dress on, but I can't zip it up myself, so I turn my back to him. "A little help, please."

"You really ought to get a lady-in-waiting or something," Loki says as he struggles with the zipper. "These things are impossible to get on."

"That's what husbands are for," I tease.

He continues to yank at the zipper, and it finally goes up. But I know what the problem is, why my dresses are so hard to get on anymore.

From behind me, Loki reaches around, holding his hand against the snugness in my middle, and he kisses my shoulder.

"We're going to have to tell them soon," Loki says, hugging me.

"I know." I sigh. "But not until you get back, okay? I don't want to have to deal with all the talking and questions unless you're with me." I turn around so I'm facing him. "That means you'll have to hurry back soon."

"As if I need another reason to do that." He smiles and playfully tugs at my silver curl, the lock of hair that always refuses to stay in place.

Loki kisses me deeply, holding me to him, and he still makes my knees go weak. I keep expecting that feeling to fade, but every time he touches me, I feel it all the same.

We go down to the throne room for the ceremony. Sara is already waiting for us, along with Finn working as head guard and Bain working as the Chancellor. Tove is there too, mostly for moral support. Sara has been here since last night, so she can ride with Loki in a gesture of solidarity.

Loki and I sit on our thrones, waiting until everyone else arrives before beginning the ceremony. I had met with Chancellor Bain last night, and he had gone over all the right words I should say. Uniting kingdoms happens so rarely in our history, but apparently there is still a script I should follow.

Once everyone is here, Loki and Sara take their places in front of me. I stand up and do my best to recite the words that Bain taught me. I think I muddle up the middle part, but the basic idea is that we are uniting the Vittra and Trylle, pledging to work together and all that.

As part of the deal, Loki is going back to the Vittra to help them rebuild. Their society has begun to crumble since I killed the King. Sara has been doing her best to hold it together, but without intervention, it will soon fall apart.

"Since you both agree to work together in peace and respect, I say this union is complete," I say, finishing up the ceremony. "You may now . . . work together."

"Thank you." Sara gathers her skirts and curtseys to me.

"Thank you." Loki bows with a smile on his face.

"And you'll only be gone for two weeks?" I ask him.

"Two weeks is the absolute maximum, and then I'll be right back at your side," Loki assures me.

"I promise not to keep him any longer than I need him," Sara adds.

Her eyes are warm when she smiles at me. I didn't want to lend my husband out to her, but she had saved his life. And it's better if the Vittra work to become our allies instead of our enemies.

Loki kisses me, even though it isn't polite. A King and Queen are never supposed to show public affection, but Loki breaks that rule as often as he can. Although, to be honest, I don't do much to enforce it.

"Hurry back to me," I whisper.

Loki smiles. "As you wish."

As he turns to leave, I feel that familiar flutter in my stomach. Not the one out of love for Loki, but something different, something alive inside of me. I put my hand on my stomach, holding it as if to calm the baby.

The night Loki and I had spent together while I was still married to Tove had resulted in a small surprise. I'd told Loki weeks ago, and even though we were both frightened, we were both really excited. We're first-time parents, but we will also be the first royal Trylle parents. My child won't be a changeling.

I know that the idea of changelings can't go away overnight. Our society still needs a lot of restructuring before things are different and we can stop being dependent on the money the changelings bring in.

But we are working on it every day, Loki and I, and Willa, Tove, and even Finn. We are going to turn the Trylle community into something it should've been all along. A great people with a great appreciation for each other and for life.

I will make this world a better place, whether they like it or not. That's the fun of being Queen.

GLOSSARY OF TRYLLE TERMINOLOGY

aura—A field of subtle, luminous radiation surrounding a person or object. Different-colored auras denote different emotional qualities.

changeling—A child secretly exchanged for another.

Förening—The capital and largest city of Trylle society. A compound in the bluffs along the Mississippi River in Minnesota where the palace is located.

hobgoblin—An ugly, misshapen troll that stands no more than three feet tall.

host family—The family that the changeling is left with. They are chosen based on their ranking in human society, with their wealth being the primary consideration. The higher-ranked the member of Trylle society, the more powerful and affluent the host family their changeling is left with.

Kanin—One of the more powerful tribes of trolls left. They are considered quiet and peaceful. They are known for their ability to blend in, and, like chameleons, their skin can change color to help them blend into their surroundings. Like the Trylle, they still follow the practice of using changelings, but not nearly as frequently. Only one in ten of their offspring are left as changelings.

mänsklig (often shortened to *mänks*)—The literal translation for the word *mänsklig* is "human," but it has come to describe the human child that is taken when the Trylle offspring is left behind.

Markis—A title of male royalty in Trylle and Vittra society. Similar to that of a Duke, it's given to trolls with superior abilities. They have a higher ranking than the average Trylle, but are beneath the King and Queen. The hierarchy of Trylle society is as follows:

King/Queen
Prince/Princess
Markis/Marksinna
Trylle citizens
Trackers
Mänsklig
Host families
Humans (not raised in troll society)

Marksinna—A title of female royalty in Trylle and Vittra society. The female equivalent of the Markis.

Omte—Only slightly more populous than the Skojare, the Omte tribe of trolls are known to be rude and somewhat ill-tempered. They still follow the practice of using changelings but pick lower-class families than the Trylle. Unlike the other tribes, Omte tend to be less attractive in appearance.

Ondarike—The capital city of the Vittra, and site of the royal palace. It is located in northern Colorado.

persuasion—A mild form of mind control. The ability to cause another person to act a certain way based on thoughts.

precognition—Knowledge of something before its occurrence, especially by extrasensory perception.

psychokinesis—Blanket term for the production or control of motion, especially in inanimate and remote objects, purportedly by the exercise of psychic powers. This can include mind control, precognition, telekinesis, biological healing, teleportation, and transmutation.

Skojare—A more aquatic tribe of trolls that is nearly extinct. They require large amounts of fresh water to survive, and one-third of their population possess gills so they are able to breathe underwater. Once plentiful, only about five thousand Skojare are left on the entire planet.

stork—Slang term for tracker; derogatory. "*Humans tell little kids that storks bring the babies, but trackers bring the babies here.*"

tracker—A member of Trylle society who is specifically trained to track down changelings and bring them home. Trackers have no paranormal abilities, other than the affinity to tune in to one particular troll. They are able to sense danger to their charge and can determine the distance between them. The lowest form of Trylle society, other than mänsklig.

Trylle (pronounced *trill*)—Beautiful trolls with powers of psychokinesis for whom the practice of using changelings is a cornerstone of their society. Like all trolls, they are ill-tempered and cunning, and often selfish. Once plentiful, their numbers and abilities are fading, but they are still one of the largest tribes of trolls. They are considered peaceful.

Tryllic—An old language that Trylle wrote in to disguise their important documents from humans. Its symbols are different from those of the standard Greek alphabet, and are similar to Arabic or Cyrillic in appearance.

Vittra—A more violent faction of trolls whose powers lie in physical strength and longevity, although some mild psychokinesis is not unheard of. They also suffer from frequent infertility. While Vittra are generally beautiful in appearance, more than fifty percent of their offspring are born as hobgoblins. They are one of the only troll tribes to have hobgoblins in their population.

Turn the page for the new,
never-before-published bonus short story

Ever After

by Amanda Hocking

ONE

Arrivals

"But you liked it when I made it for you," Matt insisted, dumbfounded.

He stood on the other side of the kitchen island from me with a chiffon cake covered in white frosting, a solitary blue candle standing in the middle. I actually kind of hated telling him the truth, since he looked so heartbroken about it, but I wanted today to be perfect.

"Wendy was lying, honey," Willa told him. She was walking by him with a bowl full of blueberries, and she stopped to give him a quick kiss on the cheek as if to compensate for the recent disclosure.

"But . . ." Matt still couldn't seem to grasp the idea and shook his head. "Why?"

"She didn't want to hurt your feelings," Willa explained. "And now she wants everything to be just right, so the truth has to come out." She turned to face him, looking as apologetic as she could. "We all *hate* the way your birthday cake tastes."

"But you've all been eating it!" Matt went from dubious to indignant and looked between Willa and me. "I made you both cakes! I even made one for Loki, and he ate it!"

"Matt, I love you," Willa said, touching his shoulder. "And later on we can argue about the cake. But right now, we do not have time for it. People will be arriving any minute."

As if on cue, the doorbell rang in the front hall.

"I'll get it," Willa offered, grabbing a bunch of bananas to go along with the blueberries.

"I'll be right there," I told her, but I walked over to my brother first. "Sorry, Matt. I should've told you sooner, but I always appreciated all the effort you put into it. I didn't want to spoil it for you."

"It's okay." He stared down at the cake and stuck his finger in the frosting, then grudgingly licked it off. "I'm just more disappointed because I wanted to make the cake special for him."

"He doesn't need a special cake." I smiled at Matt. "He just needs to spend time with his favorite uncle."

Matt smiled then, apparently feeling better about it. I heard voices coming from the front hall, and a familiar panic took me over. I'd been frazzled all week, trying to plan a special birthday party for my son, and of course, at the last minute, everything felt like it was going wrong.

"But I have to go now," I said, already starting to walk away from Matt. "Can you grab the yogurt before you come up?"

"Sure." Matt nodded.

I grabbed the sippy cup and a bottle of grape juice from off the counter, what I'd actually come down to the kitchen for. Willa had been getting fruit to serve at the party, and we'd discovered Matt making a surprise birthday cake, so we'd had to break the news to him that no Trylle or Vittra anywhere liked his cake.

By the time I made it to the rotunda, Willa had already let Rhys and Rhiannon in. Rhys had dropped his duffel bag on the floor, but Rhiannon still had a bag slung over her shoulder.

"You guys came!" I beamed and hurried over to them. "I'm so glad you made it. Last time I talked to you, you didn't sound sure if you could make it."

Rhys grinned. "Come on, it's my nephew's birthday. Like I would miss that."

I hugged him, awkwardly because I had a bottle of juice in one hand, but he didn't care and hugged me fiercely anyway. When he let me go, I gave Rhiannon a quick hug.

"Here, let me help you with that," Rhys said, taking the bottle from me.

"I didn't realize this was so formal," Rhiannon said as she looked me over. She ran her hand through her red hair, freeing an orange maple leaf that had gotten tangled in it. "You look so beautiful."

"What?" I glanced down at myself. I was wearing a dress, but it was less formal than my normal gowns. But compared to the jeans that Rhys and Rhiannon were wearing, I probably did look dressed up. "Sorry. It's from being Queen, I guess. I've gotten used to wearing dresses, and I actually feel a bit weird when I'm not in one."

I'd been Queen for over a year and a half now, and I'd become accustomed to all the formalities that had seemed so foreign when I first came here. I was certain I had nowhere near the grace and class that Elora had, but I was getting closer to the kind of woman my mother would've been proud of.

"No, there's no need to apologize." Rhiannon waved it off. "You look lovely."

"So do you," I said, making her laugh. "But I should head up to the party. Do you guys want to get settled in first? Your old room is all ready for you."

"We should probably drop off our stuff," Rhys said and picked up his bag. "Where is the party at?"

"Your old playroom," I said as we climbed the curving staircase. "We did a little bit of redecorating, and it's worked out perfect for him."

"Well, I'm glad to see someone getting some use out of it." Rhys laughed.

"How is college going?" I looked back over my shoulder since he was following a step behind me. "Were you okay to miss a few classes to come here?"

"Yeah, college is going great." Rhys nodded. "I can't miss too many classes so I have to leave the day after tomorrow."

I frowned. "That's such a short visit. But I'm glad you could make it. I'm sure you're both busy."

"Probably not as busy as you," Rhys pointed out, and I laughed at that.

"Oh, you have no idea."

Being a new wife *and* a new mother *and* a new queen could get rather exhausting at times. I'd been running the kingdom on less than five hours of sleep a night pretty much since I was crowned. Even though we were heading into a new era of peace, there was so much uncharted territory, and that meant a lot more work on the part of the Queen.

Not that I didn't have a great support team. With Tove, Willa, Garrett, and Chancellor Bain working as my advisors, we were able to make real changes for the Trylle. I'll admit that Loki spent a great deal of time playing stay-at-home dad while I took care of business, but Willa and Matt were happy to babysit every chance they got.

I stopped at Rhys's old playroom to head into the party while Rhys and Rhiannon continued down the hall to his room to drop off their stuff. He handed me the juice back, and I thanked him.

Before I even pushed open the door, I could hear my son giggling. He had to be one of the happiest babies on the planet. He had an infectious smile and chubby cheeks. He'd gotten his father's golden eyes, and my dark unruly hair.

I went into the playroom and instantly saw what had sent him on a laughing jag this time. Using his abilities, Tove had my son floating in the air above him, wiggling him a little bit.

His arms and legs danced in the air, and he laughed so hard, his tanned skin turned red.

"Tove!" I exclaimed. I set the juice down and went over to pluck my son from the air. "What have I told you about that?"

"Sorry, Wendy," Tove said, smiling sheepishly. "He just likes it so much."

"Come on, Wendy," Loki chimed in.

He stood at the side of the room, helping Bain decorate the gift table. Bain was twisting blue and green ribbons around it, and Loki was handing him tape. A number of boxes were already on the table, covered in shiny wrapping paper. I assumed they were gifts from Bain, Tove, Willa, and Matt, since they were the only ones here so far—and of course, a few gifts from Loki and me.

"You know Tove would never let anything happen to Oliver," Loki said.

"And they entertain each other for hours," Bain added.

I looked down at the baby in my arms, and instantly Oliver started babbling. He could only say a few words, like mama and da-da, but I think his favorite word was Dodo—his attempt at pronouncing Tove. In fact, at this point, I'd say Tove was probably his favorite person, since Oliver liked nothing more than flying about the room. I could do the same thing, of course, but I always got too nervous to do it myself.

"You want to play with Uncle Tove, don't you?" I asked Oliver, and I tried to sound exasperated. But it was hard to even pretend when he looked so happy. I sighed and handed my son over to Tove. "But be careful with him, and only for a few minutes. If Maggie catches you, she'll go bananas."

Tove complied with a smile. "Understood." I swear he liked playing with Oliver just as much as Oliver liked playing with him.

Loki came over to me and slid his arm around my waist. Kissing my cheek, he told me, "Don't look so worried."

"I'm not worried," I lied and turned away from Oliver to face my husband. "I just can't believe it's already been a year. How did that happen?"

"Time flies when you're having fun." Loki grinned.

I kissed him quickly on the mouth. "I have to finish getting the party ready. Rhys and Rhiannon are already here."

I grabbed the juice from where I'd left it on the floor and went over to the food table to pour it in the punchbowl. Willa was already there, arranging the fruit she'd brought up as well as the other snacks on the table.

On Saturday, in the main ballroom, we were having a huge birthday party for Oliver. The whole kingdom was invited. Since Oliver was the first royal to not be a changeling in centuries, the Trylle had become infatuated with him.

When I first told the kingdom that I wasn't going to let him be a changeling, some were irate. Even after all this time, some still refuse to accept it. But I was adamant that we needed to do things differently, that in order to grow as a kingdom, we needed to raise our children, teach them our ways so they would be less likely to abandon us than they have been in recent years.

Eventually the Trylle conceded, I think in large part because they had come to trust me. After I defeated the Vittra King and united the two kingdoms peaceably, they'd begun to realize that I might actually be able to help them.

Of course, there had been a bit of an uproar when I announced my pregnancy in the first place, only a month after I'd married Loki, when I was already five months along. Tove's mother had initially been suspicious that the child might be his, but Tove told her in no uncertain terms that it wasn't.

For most of the Trylle, any reservations they'd had about Oliver had changed when they saw him. We had his christening ceremony when he was a few weeks old, and the kingdom turned out in droves. They all fell in love with him, the same way I had. It was hard not to.

I swear, no child in Trylle history had ever been as loved as Oliver.

While I was pleased with how the Trylle had taken to him, I wanted to have a small party with the people closest to me before his huge party on Saturday. Since I was simultaneously planning two parties, a lot of the preparation for this one had gone to Willa and Bain, who had gladly taken on the task.

After Rhys left for college last year, we'd redone the playroom for the baby. We hadn't had to change that much, but we'd filled it with all kinds of toys and touched up the cloud mural on the ceiling. Willa and Bain had decorated it this morning, draping everything with brightly colored streamers and dotting every corner with balloons.

The door to the playroom swung open, and I immediately

turned around to glare at Tove, who gently dropped Oliver to the floor. It was only Matt, carrying the yogurt I'd asked for, with Rhys and Rhiannon following behind him.

As soon as Tove set Oliver down, he squealed, then toddled over to Loki. He nearly fell in his hurry, but Loki caught him and scooped him up in his arms.

"There's my boy," Loki said and kissed him on his chubby cheeks.

Matt was asking Rhys very seriously about his studies at college, so Willa went over and took the yogurt from him. She set it down on the table behind me, then stood next to me, surveying the room.

"Well, I think the decorating is as done as it's ever going to be," Willa said.

Bain had finished with the gift table, so it appeared he felt the same. He stood next to Tove, who slid his arm around Bain's shoulders. Tove hadn't come out yet—not officially—but he wasn't exactly hiding it either. Anyone who spent any amount of time with Bain and Tove knew how much they loved each other.

"You did a great job." I smiled over at Willa. "Thank you."

"Anytime," Willa said. "When is it supposed to start anyway?"

I glanced up at the clock made of moons and stars. "Um, now, actually."

"Who's left to come?" Willa asked.

I opened my mouth to answer when Maggie burst through the playroom door with her usual zeal. Garrett came in behind her, carrying several large birthday presents.

"Where's the birthday boy?" she asked, and before Loki even had a chance to answer, she went over and stole Oliver from him. "Oh, you've gotten so big!"

"Thank you, I've been working out." Loki grinned at her, and she swatted him on the shoulder.

"I was talking about your adorable son." Maggie admired Oliver, who began babbling happily at her. "And I missed you too, Oliver."

After spending some time here at the palace, Maggie had gone back to traveling. She'd spent the last several months painting in France, which was something she'd always wanted to do but never had the chance to before. That was why she kept telling Oliver he was all sorts of things in French.

Garrett started lugging the gifts over to the table, but Bain and Tove stepped in, taking them from him. I'd asked Garrett to pick up Maggie from the airport, since the rest of us were so busy here. Also because Garrett and Maggie seemed to enjoy each other's company, and he'd been rather lonely since my mother passed away.

As soon as he'd been freed of his gifts, he went over to Rhiannon and hugged her. He'd raised her, and even though she was a mänks, she'd always felt like a daughter to him.

Willa went over to talk with her father and catch up with Rhiannon. They hadn't been close, but since Willa had started dating Matt, they had become closer. They'd never be like sisters, but they were friends.

Maggie appeared to be content speaking to my son in French the entire afternoon, but I decided to see how she was doing. She hugged me when I came over, nearly squishing Oliver between us.

"You look so beautiful!" Maggie gushed when she finally released me. "Motherhood must be sitting well with you. You're positively glowing!"

"Thank you." I gestured to her. "You look really good yourself. France suits you."

"Oh, it's marvelous," Maggie said dramatically. "You and your family really must visit sometime."

Duncan came in a few moments later, carrying the special cake I'd had made for Oliver at a bakery in Förening. It was filled with things he'd actually enjoy and lacking all sorts of processed things he'd spit up.

"Here." Matt took it from Duncan. "I'll put this over with the other food, but I'm telling you all right now that there is no way this cake is better than mine."

"I don't know," Duncan said, letting Matt take it away. "I tried a piece of cake while I was waiting for them to box this one up, and it was delicious."

Maggie asked what that was about, and Willa filled her in on the great cake controversy.

As Duncan walked around the room, he favored his left leg. He had a limp now, a reminder of the battle at the Vittra palace. He also had a few scars, but those were hidden underneath his clothes. Still, it pained me every time I saw them.

He still worked as my bodyguard and part-time nanny, but with a substantial pay increase. In fact, all the trackers working in Förening had pay raises and health care. It was part of my initiative to treat those who protected us and took care of us the way they ought to be treated.

I'd been able to make a lot of changes, but unfortunately, I wasn't able to make all the ones I'd hoped to so far. Willa's bare wedding ring finger was a sad reminder of that.

We'd managed to make some progress in making it legal for the Trylle people to love who they want to love. Tove's semi-open relationship was proof of that, as well as Willa's relationship with my brother, Matt. They were completely in the open about it now, but she'd had to give up her title as Marksinna in order for that to happen.

I was determined to make it possible for them to marry *and* have her title be reinstated. Whenever I got frustrated about things like that, Tove was quick to remind me that it had only been a year and a half. Progress takes time, and eventually, we'd get where we needed to be.

A small knock came at the playroom door, so Loki went to get it. Little Hanna stood there with her dark hair pulled up in two pigtails.

"She's going through a knocking phase," Mia explained with a demure smile.

"Oh, you better watch out," Loki said. "I hear the next phase is ding-dong-ditch."

Oliver squealed when he saw Hanna, demanding to be put down, and Maggie finally relented. Hanna ran into the room when she saw him, and they instantly started some kind of toddler banter I couldn't follow.

There weren't any other Trylle children for him to play

with, and he actually had a very limited number of playmates in general. At this point, Hanna was probably his best friend, even though she was a year and a half older than him.

"Joke all you want, but it won't be that long until Oliver's doing it too," Finn warned Loki with a grin. "And along with the knocking phase comes a talking back phase and a kicking phase."

Loki laughed. "I can hardly wait."

"Where should I put this?" Finn asked, holding out a present for Oliver.

"Here, I'll take it," Loki offered

"Thank you both for coming," I said when I went over to greet them. "I wasn't sure that you would make it."

Finn had taken the past week off to go with Mia and Hanna to visit her relatives in Oslinna. It was actually nice to see Finn taking time off to do things with his family, that he'd finally put something in front of his job. Or maybe he'd finally just found something he loved enough to put in front of duty.

"We couldn't miss the Prince's birthday." Mia rubbed her swollen belly absently. The small diamond in her wedding band caught the light when she did. "Besides, Hanna would be so disappointed if we did."

"Oh my gosh!" Rhiannon gasped. "Mia! I didn't realize you were pregnant! When are you due?"

"Three months." Mia smiled, blushing a little.

"Wow." Rhiannon shook her head, as if she couldn't believe it. "It seems like just yesterday I was at your wedding. You guys must be so excited."

Mia and Finn exchanged a look, one filled with love and joy. "We're both thrilled," she said.

Willa mentioned a baby shower, and that was it. Rhiannon stole Mia away so they could all talk excitedly about shower plans.

Loki had moved on to talk to Tove, Bain, and Duncan about a meeting we had next week with the Kanin King, and Matt and Garrett were talking to Rhys about school. That left me standing with Finn for a moment, watching Oliver and Hanna pushing around a large ball.

"Do you have a name picked out yet?" I asked Finn.

"Yeah. We're thinking Liam Thomas."

"So you know it's a boy?" I asked.

Finn nodded. "We couldn't wait to find out."

"Me neither." I smiled. "Liam's a good name. Nice and clean."

"Well, it's no Oliver Matthew Loren Staad the First," Finn teased, mocking the terrible time Loki and I had coming up with a name for our son. We'd finally settled on two middle names, because we just couldn't decide on one.

I pretended to be offended. "Hey, it's a good name."

"It is," Finn agreed, laughing a little.

"I'm really glad you guys came," I said, and looked at him more seriously. His dark eyes met mine, and I couldn't help but notice how much happier they were. Before, they'd always been so stormy, but now they seemed to sparkle.

"Me too," Finn said, smiling at me.

I turned back to watch our children playing together.

"When we first met, did you ever think things would end up this way?"

"No." Finn shook his head. "Not in a million years. But I'm really glad they did."

"Yeah, me too," I agreed.

Hanna suddenly ran over to him and grabbed Finn's hand. "Daddy, come see!"

"Duty calls," Finn said, and he smiled as Hanna pulled him away.

Finn isn't Hanna's real father, of course, but he's the only one she can really remember. When Hanna first started calling him "Daddy" all on her own, Finn actually had a long talk with Loki, asking him how he would feel knowing that if he passed on, Oliver might call his stepfather "Dad."

I wasn't there for it, but Loki'd told me about it later. He said if any man could love Oliver as much as he did and take care of him, and take care of me and love me the way he did, then that man would deserve the title. And he told Finn if that was true for him, then let Hanna call him that. So Hanna does.

Finn had married Mia a little over six months ago, and I'd honestly never seen him happier. His smile came so much easier, his laughed sounded more relaxed, and Mia seemed so much more contented. I'd gotten to know her fairly well, and she was as kind and nurturing as I'd suspected her of being when I first met her.

They complemented each other in a way that Finn and I never had, bringing out the best in each other. When I thought about it, it actually seemed silly that Finn and I had ever even tried to be together.

Hanna was busy showing Finn something, so Oliver came over, his arms outstretched. I picked him up, holding him close to me.

It was times like this when I realized what my mother had given up. If Elora really loved me—and I'm certain she did—then letting go of me must've been devastating. Even before Oliver was born, I'd felt a love for him growing inside me. By the time he was born and placed in my arms, it was almost overwhelming.

I've truly never loved anything as deeply as I love my son. And in the strangest way, I don't feel like I really came alive until I had him. It was as if an essential part of me had been sleeping, lying dormant, until he awoke it.

As much as I love all the people in my life, and even as much as I love Loki, the love a mother has for her child is completely unparalleled. Nothing in this world will ever mean as much to me as Oliver does.

I had one arm around Oliver as he sat on my hip, and I turned him around to see one of the new additions to the playroom: a large portrait of Elora, young and stunningly beautiful as she sits in the back garden wearing a blue gown, in the early stages of her pregnancy with me. It was the only picture I could find of her looking happy.

"Who's that?" I asked Oliver. I pointed at the picture, so he did the same. "Who is that in the picture?" He babbles a bit, but makes no real words. "That's Gramma Elora. And she loves you very much, even if she never got to meet you."

"Oliver!" Hanna called from behind me, and Oliver began to squirm in my arms. "Oliver!"

I kissed him once on the forehead before putting him on the ground. "Go play."

I turned around and got a good look at the room, at the people who filled my life. Maggie stood with Mia, her hand on her belly, presumably feeling for the baby. Matt, Rhys, and Rhiannon were talking.

Willa was sitting on the floor while Hanna put a pink plastic tiara in her hair, and for some reason Oliver was handing her toy blocks. Finn and Loki stood nearby laughing as Oliver started wrapping a blue streamer around Willa.

Tove had been sitting on a couch next to Bain, but he got up and went over to the kids to make the blocks fly about, and they both stared in wonderment. Duncan limped over and joined in, plucking the blocks from the air so he could juggle them.

Loki noticed me standing off to the side, and he walked over to me, still smiling, but his eyes were concerned.

"Is something the matter, My Queen?"

"No, not at all." I shook my head and smiled at him. "The opposite actually. I'm happy."

"Good." He leaned forward, kissing me tenderly on the mouth, then he took my hand and stepped backward. "Come on. Let's join the party."

TWO

Forever

Willa and Rhiannon finally sent me away. I'd been trying to help them clean up the party after the guests had gone, but they insisted I'd done enough. Loki and Oliver had already left about a half hour before I did because Oliver needed to sleep. Quite honestly, so did I, and that's probably why Willa and Rhiannon made me leave.

I walked down the long hall, pulling stray bits of confetti free from my hair and dress, remnants of the piñata. Try as he might, Oliver had been unable to break it, so Loki had stepped in to help. Unfortunately, sometimes he didn't know his own strength, and candy and confetti had exploded around the room like a small firework.

The door to the nursery was open slightly, and I could hear Loki's soft tones as he sang to our son. When he sang loud, along with the radio, Loki could be off key. But when it came to lullabies, his voice was soft and filled with love, and there was something spectacularly beautiful about it.

"Alone I walk on paths I know, looking for a friendly face," Loki sang. "I look to meet you, the one I gave my whole heart to. I want to see you once again, and dance again with you, my love."

I pushed the door to the nursery open a bit farther and peered inside, and it was just as I expected. Loki held Oliver in his arms, the baby's head resting against his chest, as Loki swayed slightly back and forth.

Loki told me his mother used to sing him that lullaby, but only when she was holding him, rocking him in her arms like they were dancing. And so he did the same with our son.

All the lights were out in Oliver's room, save for a small nightlight casting stars upon the ceiling. Loki and Oliver stood in front of the windows, the glow from the moon bathing them in blue light.

Watching Loki cradle our child like that, singing sweetly into his thick dark hair, filled me with an overwhelming love for them both.

Loki loved Oliver fiercely. Like me, he never could've dreamed of parting with him. One of the first things Loki had said after I'd told him I was pregnant was, "The baby cannot be a changeling. He's ours, and we'll raise him."

When I'd married Loki, I didn't think I could ever love him more than I did then. But watching him with our son, I'd fallen in love with Loki all over again. I'd seen more of him emerge, revealing a man who was patient and nurturing. I couldn't have asked for a better father or husband.

"Hey," Loki whispered when he noticed me sneaking into the room. "I think he's asleep."

"I would imagine." I went over and stood next to Loki. "After all that running around he did, I'm surprised he stayed up this long."

"At least he'll probably sleep through the night." Loki smiled.

"We can dream anyway," I said, and Loki laughed softly. I held out my hands to him. "Here. I'll put him to bed."

"Okay." Loki kissed Oliver's head, then handed him over to me. Once I had the baby safely in my arms, Loki gave me a quick peck on the cheek. "I'm going to go change into pajamas."

"I'll be in in a second," I told him, and he slipped away.

I held Oliver for a minute, just loving the weight of him in my arms. Mia had warned me many times to cherish these moments as they happened, because babies grow up far too fast, but I already knew it. I couldn't believe how fast the first year had gone by, that my son could now walk and even talk a little.

Carefully, I laid Oliver down in the crib. He stirred a little, stretching an arm, but he never opened his eyes.

I bent down, kissing him gently on the forehead, and whispered, "Goodnight, my little Prince."

When I went into the room I shared with my husband, he'd already changed into his pajamas, which consisted of a pair of satin pants and no shirt, and he was sitting on the edge of our bed. Many of his scars had faded thanks to his strong Vittra blood, but a few remained.

Most notable was the one on his chest, where Oren had stabbed him clean through. Sometimes, just the sight of it would bring a tear to my eye. The memory of losing him, even for a second, was still crushing.

"He went down okay?" Loki asked me. "He didn't wake back up?"

"Nope, he's totally out." I'd gone over to my jewelry stand on the side of the room and started taking off my earrings and necklace. "I think he'll sleep for a while."

My son was a darling, sweet boy, nearly perfect in every way, except for his absolute refusal to sleep a whole night through. I was lucky if he slept for four hours straight during the night. Fortunately, tonight might be one of those nights.

"He's a year old now," Loki pointed out. "He's not a baby anymore. He might surprise you."

"Maybe." I shrugged and turned back to him, thinking of what I'd said to Finn earlier that day. "Did you ever think things would turn out this way?"

"What do you mean?" Loki asked, cocking his head.

"When you met me." I walked nearer to him. When I got close enough, Loki took my hands and pulled me closer still, but I remained standing in front of him. "Did you think things would end up like this?"

"No," Loki admitted with a lopsided grin. "But I hoped."

"Even when you first met me?" I asked. "Back when you were trying to kidnap me and Kyra was beating me up?"

"Even then. Why do you think I stopped her?"

"I don't believe you." I shook my head. "How could you possibly have known that we'd end up together?"

"I didn't *know.*" He wrapped his arms around my waist, pulling me to him, and I looped my arms around his neck as I stared down at him. "But as soon as I looked into your eyes," he paused, thinking of the right words. "You'll think I'm making this up."

"Making what up?" I asked.

"What I'm about to say. It sounds silly, but it's true." He took a deep breath. "I saw my whole world in your eyes."

I smiled at him, not sure what to make of that. "What does that mean?"

"I don't know how else to explain it." He shrugged. "I looked in your eyes to knock you out, so we could safely take you back to Ondarike. But when our eyes met, I just . . . I saw *this.* Not this exactly, but I saw how much love we could share together."

"Really?" I asked.

"Well, I didn't realize then how much I could love you and Oliver," Loki corrected himself. "But from the moment I met you, even in that very first second, I was already falling in love with you."

"When did you know for sure?" I asked.

"That I loved you?" Loki asked, and I nodded. He stared upwards for a second, thinking. "When you escaped Ondarike the first time. We were standing in the hall of the dungeon, and you had stopped and were just looking at me. Then somebody called for you and you ran off, and I couldn't remember a time I'd felt so heartbroken.

"I mean, I was glad you'd escaped," Loki went on. "I knew that was the best thing for you. But I realized how terribly I was going to miss you, and we'd only spent a few moments together." He brushed back a hair from my face. "I don't think I've ever really loved anyone until I met you, Wendy."

I bent down, kissing him, and his arms tightened around me, pressing me to him with a strength I'd come to love. He pulled me down to the bed with him, then laid me down so he was on top of me.

Usually, when we had a moment alone in our chamber when we weren't both exhausted, we hurried to make love, knowing there might only be precious minutes until the baby began crying or someone interrupted us with important news about the kingdom. Duncan had walked in on us more than a few times.

This time, Loki was taking it slower. Kissing me deeply and holding me to him in a way that sent butterflies swirling in my stomach. He kissed my neck, letting his lips travel down my collarbone and making me tremble.

Then he stopped. Propping himself up on one arm, he smiled down at me and brushed the silver curl from my forehead.

"You never answered your own question," Loki pointed out. "Did you think things would turn out like this?"

"Never in my wildest dreams," I said. "I never imagined that I could ever be this happy."

"Hmm." Loki narrowed his eyes, a playful smile on his lips. "Good answer." I reached up to pull him down to me, but

Loki took my hand and pinned it back on the bed. "Not so fast. You didn't answer the other question."

"What question?"

"When did you fall in love with me?"

I opened my mouth to answer but realized what I'd been about to say wasn't quite right. The moment I knew I loved him was when we'd kissed at my coronation, but I think I'd actually fallen in love with him before that. I'd just been too afraid to admit it to myself.

"At my wedding," I said finally. "Not *our* wedding, but when I married Tove. You came and danced with me, and you made me feel . . . like I'd never felt before. I never wanted to stop dancing with you."

"Shall we dance now?" Loki offered.

"No. I think there's something else I'd rather do." I smiled and pulled him to me, kissing him deeply on the mouth.

Wake

If you enjoyed the Trylle Trilogy, you'll love *Wake,* the first book in Amanda Hocking's previously unpublished Watersong series.

Turn the page to read an extract . . .

PROLOGUE

Ours

Even over the sea, Thea could smell the blood on her. When she breathed in, it filled her with a familiar hunger that haunted her dreams. Except now it disgusted her, leaving a horrible taste in her mouth, because she knew where it came from.

"Is it done?" she asked. She stood on the rocky shore, staring over the sea, with her back to her sister.

"You know it is," Penn said. Although Penn was angry, her voice still kept its seductive edge, that alluring texture she could never completely erase. "No thanks to you."

Thea glanced back over her shoulder at Penn. Even in the dull light of the moon, Penn's black hair glistened, and her tanned skin seemed to glow. Fresh from eating, she looked even more beautiful than she had a few hours before.

A few droplets of blood splattered Thea's clothes, but Penn

had mostly been spared from it, except for her right hand. It was stained crimson up to her elbow.

Thea's stomach rolled with both hunger and disgust, and she turned away again.

"Thea." Penn sighed and walked over to her. "You know it had to be done."

Thea didn't say anything for a moment. She just listened to the way the ocean sang to her, the watersong calling for her.

"I know," Thea said finally, hoping her words didn't betray her true feelings. "But the timing is awful. We should've waited."

"I couldn't wait anymore," Penn insisted, and Thea wasn't sure if that was true or not. But Penn had made a decision, and Penn always got what she wanted.

"We don't have much time." Thea gestured to the moon, nearly full above them, then looked over at Penn.

"I know. But I already told you, I've had my eye on someone." Penn smiled widely at her, showing her razor-sharp teeth. "And it won't be long before she's ours."

ONE

Midnight Swim

The engine made a bizarre chugging sound, like a dying robot llama, followed by an innocuous *click-click*. Then silence. Gemma turned the key harder, hoping that would somehow breathe life into the old Chevy, but it wouldn't even chug anymore. The llama had died.

"You have got to be kidding me," Gemma said and cursed under her breath.

She'd worked her butt off to pay for this car. Between the long hours she spent training at the pool and keeping up on her schoolwork, she had little time for a steady job. That had left her stuck babysitting the horrible Tennenmeyer boys. They put gum in her hair and poured bleach on her favorite sweater.

But she'd toughed it out. Gemma had been determined to get a car when she turned sixteen, even if that meant dealing with the Tennenmeyers. Her older sister Harper had gotten their father's old car as a hand-me-down. Harper had offered to let Gemma drive it, but she declined.

Mainly Gemma needed her own car because neither Harper nor her father readily approved of her late-night swims at Anthemusa Bay. They didn't live far from the bay, but the distance wasn't what bothered her family. It was the late-night part—and that was the thing that Gemma craved most.

Out there, under the stars, the water seemed like it went on forever. The bay met the sea, which in turn met the sky, and it all blended together like she was floating in an eternal loop. There was something magical about the bay at night, something that her family couldn't seem to understand.

Gemma tried the key one more time, but it only elicited the same empty clicking sound from her car. Sighing, she leaned forward and stared out at the moonlit sky through the cracked windshield. It was getting late, and even if she left on foot right now, she wouldn't get back from her swim until almost midnight.

That wouldn't be a huge problem, but her curfew was eleven. Starting off the summer being grounded, on top of having a dead car, was the last thing she wanted. Her swim would have to wait for another night.

She got out of the car. When she tried to slam the door shut in frustration, it only groaned, and a chunk of rust fell off the bottom.

"This is by far the worst three hundred dollars I ever spent," Gemma muttered.

"Car trouble?" Alex asked from behind her, startling her so

much she nearly screamed. "Sorry. I didn't mean to scare you."

"No, it's okay." She waved it off and turned around to face him. "I didn't hear you come out."

Alex had lived next door to them for the past ten years, and there was nothing scary about him. As he got older, he'd tried to smooth out his unruly dark hair, but a lock near the front always stood up, a cowlick he could never tame. It made him look younger than eighteen, and when he smiled, he looked younger still.

There was something innocent about him, and that was probably why Harper had never thought of him as anything more than a friend. Even Gemma had dismissed him as un-crushworthy until recently. She'd seen the subtle changes in him, his youthfulness giving way to broad shoulders and strong arms.

It was that new thing, the new *manliness* he was beginning to grow into, that made her stomach flutter when Alex smiled at her. She still wasn't used to feeling that way around him, so she pushed it down and tried to ignore it.

"The stupid piece of junk won't run." Gemma gestured to the rusty compact and stepped over to where Alex stood on his lawn. "I've only had it for three months, and its dead already."

"I'm sorry to hear that," Alex said. "Do you need help?"

"You know something about cars?" Gemma raised an eyebrow. She had seen him spend plenty of time playing video games or with his nose stuck in a book, but she'd never once seen him under the hood of a car.

Alex smiled sheepishly and lowered his eyes. He had been blessed with tanned skin, which made it easier for him to hide his embarrassment, but Gemma knew him well enough to understand that he blushed at almost anything.

"No," he admitted with a small laugh and motioned back to the driveway where his blue Mercury Cougar sat. "But I do have a car of my own."

He pulled his keys out of his pocket and swung them around his finger. For a moment he managed to look slick before the keys flew off his hand and hit him in the chin. Gemma stifled a laugh as he scrambled to pick them up.

"You okay?"

"Uh, yeah, I'm fine." He rubbed his chin and shrugged it off. "So, do you want a ride?"

"Are you sure? It's pretty late. I don't want to bother you."

"Nah, it's no bother." He stepped back toward his car, waiting for Gemma to follow. "Where are you headed?"

"Just to the bay."

"I should've known." He grinned. "Your nightly swim?"

"It's not *nightly*," Gemma said, though he wasn't too far off base.

"Come on." Alex walked over to the Cougar and opened his door. "Hop in."

"All right, if you insist."

Gemma didn't like imposing on people, but she didn't want to pass up a chance at swimming. A car ride alone with Alex wouldn't hurt, either. Usually she only got to spend time with him when he was hanging out with her sister.

"So what is it about these swims that you find so entrancing?" Alex asked after she'd gotten in the car.

"I don't think I'd ever describe them as entrancing." She buckled up her seat belt, then leaned back. "I don't know what it is exactly. There's just . . . nothing else like it."

"What do you mean?" Alex asked. He'd started the car, but stayed parked in the driveway, watching her as she tried to explain.

"During the day there are so many people at the bay, especially during the summer, but at night . . . it's just you and the water and the stars. And it's dark, so it all feels like one thing, and you're part of it all." She furrowed her brow, but her smile was wistful. "I guess it is kind of entrancing," she admitted. She shook her head, clearing it of the thought. "I don't know. Maybe I'm just a freak who likes swimming at night."

That was when Gemma realized Alex was staring at her, and she glanced over at him. He had a strange expression on his face, almost like he was dumbfounded.

"What?" Gemma asked, beginning to feel embarrassed at the way he looked at her. She fidgeted with her hair, tucking it behind her ears, and shifted in her seat.

"Nothing. Sorry." Alex shook his head and put the car in drive. "You probably want to get out to the water."

"I'm not in a huge rush or anything," Gemma said, but that was sort of a lie. She wanted to get as much time in the water as she could before her curfew.

"Are you still training?" Alex asked. "Or did you stop for summer vacation?"

"Nope, I still train." She rolled down the car window, letting the salty air blow in. "I swim every day at the pool with the coach. He says my times are getting really good."

"At the pool you swim all day, and then you want to sneak out and swim all night?" Alex smirked. "How does that work?"

"It's different." She stuck her arm out the open window, holding it straight like the wing of a plane. "Swimming at the pool, it's all laps and time. It's work. Out in the bay, it's just floating and splashing around."

"But don't you ever get sick of being wet?" Alex asked.

"Nope." She shook her head. "That's like asking you, *Don't you ever get sick of breathing air?*"

"As a matter of fact, I do. Sometimes I think, *Wouldn't it be grand if I didn't need to breathe?*"

"Why?" Gemma laughed. "Why would that ever be grand?"

"I don't know." He looked self-conscious for a minute, his smile twisting nervously. "I guess I mostly thought it when I was in gym class and they'd make me run or something. I was always so out of breath."

Alex glanced over at her, as if checking to see if she thought he was a complete loser for that admission. But she only smiled at him in response.

"You should've spent more time swimming with me," Gemma said. "Then you wouldn't have been so out of shape."

"I know, but I'm a geek." He sighed. "At least I'm done with all that gym stuff now that I graduated."

"Soon you'll be so busy at college, you won't even remember the horrors of high school," Gemma said, her tone turning curiously despondent.

"Yeah, I guess." Alex furrowed his brow.

Gemma leaned closer to the window, hanging her arm down the side and resting her chin on her hand as she stared out at houses and trees passing by. In her and Alex's neighborhood, the houses were all cheap and run-down, but as soon as they passed Capri Lane, everything was clean and modern.

Since it was tourist season, all the buildings and trees were lit up brightly. Music from the bars and the sounds of people talking and laughing wafted in through the air.

"Are you excited to get away from all this?" Gemma asked with a wry smile and pointed to a drunken couple arguing on the boulevard.

"There is some stuff I'll be glad to get away from," he admitted, but when he looked over at her, his expression softened. "But there will definitely be some things that I'll miss."

The beach was mostly deserted, other than a few teenagers having a bonfire, and Gemma directed Alex to drive a little further. The soft sand gave way to more jagged rocks lining the shore, and the paved parking lots were replaced by a forest of bald cypress trees. He parked on a dirt road as close to the water as he could get.

This far away from the tourist attractions there were no people or trails leading to the water. When Alex cut the lights on the Cougar, they were submerged in darkness. The only light came from the moon above them, and some light pollution cast off by the town.

"Is this really where you swim?" Alex asked.

"Yeah. It's the best place to do it." She shrugged and opened the door.

"But it's all rocky." Alex got out of the car and scanned the mossy stones that covered the ground. "It seems dangerous."

"That's the point." Gemma grinned. "Nobody else would swim here."

As soon as she got out of the car, she slipped off her sundress, revealing the bathing suit she wore underneath. Her dark hair had been in a ponytail, but she pulled it down, shaking it loose. She kicked off her flip-flops and tossed them in the car, along with her dress.

Alex stood next to the car, shoving his hands deep in his pockets, and tried not to look at her. He knew she was wearing a bathing suit, one he'd seen her in a hundred times before. Gemma practically lived in swimwear. But alone with her like this, he felt acutely aware of how she looked in the bikini.

Of the two Fisher sisters, Gemma was definitely the prettier. She had a lithe swimmer's body, petite and slender, but curved in all the right places. Her skin was bronze from the sun, and her dark hair had golden highlights running through it from all the chlorine and sunlight. Her eyes were honey, not that he could really see the color in the dim light, but they sparkled when she smiled at him.

"Aren't you going swimming?" Gemma asked.

"Uh, no." He shook his head and deliberately stared off at the bay to avoid looking at her. "I'm good. I'll wait in the car until you're done."

"No, you drove me all the way down here. You can't just wait in the car. You *have* to come swimming with me."

"Nah, I think I'm okay." He scratched his arm and lowered his eyes. "You go have fun."

"Alex, come on." Gemma pretended to pout. "I bet you've never even gone for a swim in the moonlight. And you're leaving for college at the end of the summer. You have to do this at least once, or you haven't really lived."

"I don't have swim trunks," Alex said, but his resistance was already waning.

"Just wear your boxers."

He thought about protesting further, but Gemma had a point. She was always doing stuff like this, when he'd spent most of his high-school career in his bedroom.

Besides, swimming would be better than waiting. And when he thought about it, it was much less creepy *joining* her swimming than watching her from the shore.

"Fine, but I better not cut my feet on any of the rocks," Alex said as he slipped off his shoes.

"I promise to keep you safe and sound." She crossed her hand over her heart to prove it.

"I'll hold you to that."

He pulled his shirt up over his head, and it was exactly as Gemma had imagined. His gangly frame had filled out with toned muscles that she didn't completely understand, since he was a self-professed geek.

When he started to undo his pants, Gemma turned away to be polite. Even though she would see him in his boxers in a few seconds, it felt strange watching him take off his jeans. As if it were dirty.

"So how do we get down to the water?" Alex asked.

"Very carefully."

She went first, stepping delicately onto the rocks, and he knew he wouldn't stand a chance of copying her grace. She moved like a ballerina, stepping on the balls of her feet from one smooth rock to the next until she reached the water.

"There are a few sharp stones when you step in the water," Gemma warned him.

"Thanks for the heads-up," he mumbled and moved with as much caution as he could. Following her path, which she'd made look so easy, proved to be rather treacherous, and he stumbled several times.

"Don't rush it! You'll be fine if you go slow."

"I'm trying."

To his own surprise, he managed to make it to the water without slicing open his foot. When he reached the water, Gemma smiled proudly at him as she waded out deeper into the bay.

"Aren't you scared?" Alex asked.

"Of what?" She'd gone far enough into the water to lean back and swim, kicking her legs out in front of her.

"I don't know. Sea monsters or something. The water is so dark. You can't see anything." Alex was now in a little over waist-deep and, truthfully, he didn't want to go any further.

"There's no sea monsters." Gemma laughed and splashed

water at him. To encourage him to have fun, she decided to challenge him. "I'll race you to the rock over there."

"What rock?"

"That one." She pointed to a giant gray spike of rock that stuck out of the water a few yards from where they swam.

"You'll beat me to it," he said.

"I'll give you a head start," Gemma offered.

"How much?"

"Um . . . five seconds."

"Five seconds?" Alex seemed to weigh this. "I guess maybe I could—" Instead of finishing his thought, he dove into the water, swimming fast.

"I'm already giving you a head start!" Gemma called after him, laughing. "You don't need to cheat!"

Alex swam as furiously as he could, but it wasn't long before Gemma was flying past him. She was unstoppable in the water, and he'd honestly never seen anything faster than her. In the past, he'd gone with Harper to swim meets at the school, and there had rarely been one that Gemma didn't win.

"I won!" Gemma declared when she reached the rock.

"As if there was ever any doubt." Alex swam up next to her and hung onto the rock to support himself. His breath was still short, and he wiped the salty water from his eyes. "That was hardly a fair fight."

"Sorry." She smiled. Gemma wasn't anywhere near as winded as Alex was, but she leaned onto the rock next to him.

"For some reason, I don't think you really mean that," Alex said in mock offense.

His hand slipped off the rock, and when he reached out to steady himself again, he accidentally put his hand over Gemma's. His first instinct was to pull it back in some kind of hasty embarrassment, but the second before he did, he changed his mind.

Alex let his hand linger over hers, both of them cool and wet. Her smile had changed, turning into something fonder, and for a moment neither of them said anything. They hung on to the rock like that for a moment longer, the only sound the water lapping around them.

Gemma would've been content to sit with Alex like that, but light exploded in the cove behind him, distracting her. The small cove was at the mouth of the bay, just before it met the ocean, about a quarter mile from where Gemma and Alex floated.

Alex followed her gaze. A moment later, laughter sounded over the water and he pulled his hand away from hers.

A fire flared inside the cove, the light flickering across the three dancing figures that fanned it. From this far away, it was difficult to get a clear view of what they were doing, but it was obvious who they were by the way they moved. Everyone in town knew of them, even if nobody really seemed to know them personally.

"It's those girls," Alex said—softly, as if the girls would overhear him from the cove.

The three girls were dancing with elegance and grace. Even their shadows, looming on the rock walls around them, seemed sensual in their movements.

"What are they doing out here?" Alex asked.

"I don't know." She shrugged, continuing to stare at them, unabashed. "They've been coming out here more and more. They seem to like hanging out in that cove."

"Huh," Alex said. She looked back at him and saw his brow furrowed in thought.

"I don't even know what they're doing in town."

"Me neither." He looked over his shoulder to watch them again. "Somebody told me they were Canadian movie stars."

"Maybe. But they don't have accents."

"You've heard them talk?" Alex asked, sounding impressed.

"Yeah, I've seen them at Pearl's Diner across from the library. They always order milkshakes."

"Didn't there used to be four of them?"

"Yeah, I think so." Gemma squinted, trying to be sure she was counting right. "Last time I saw them out here, there were four. But now there's only three."

"I wonder where the other one went."

Gemma and Alex were too far away to understand them clearly, but they were talking and laughing, their voices floating over the bay. One of the girls began singing—her voice clear as crystal, and so sweet it almost hurt to hear. The melody pulled at Gemma's heart.

Alex's jaw dropped, and he gaped at them. He moved away from the rock, floating slowly toward them, but Gemma barely even noticed. Her focus was on the girls. Or, more accurately, on the one girl who wasn't singing.

Penn. Gemma was sure of it, just by the way Penn moved

away from the two girls. Her long black hair hung down behind her, and the wind blew it back. She walked with startling grace and purpose, her eyes straight ahead.

From this distance in the dark, Penn shouldn't have noticed her, but Gemma could feel her eyes boring straight through her, sending chills down her spine.

"Alex," Gemma said in a voice that barely sounded like her own. "I think we should go."

"What?" Alex replied dazedly, and that was when Gemma realized how far he'd swum away from her.

"Alex, come on. I think we're bothering them. We should go."

"Go?" He turned back to her, sounding confused by the idea.

"Alex!" Gemma said, nearly shouting now, but at least that seemed to get through to him. "We need to get back. It's late."

"Oh, right." He shook his head, clearing it, and then swam back toward the shore.

When Gemma was convinced he was back to normal, she followed him.

Penn, Thea, Lexi, and Arista had been in town since the weather started warming up, and people assumed they were the first tourists of the season. But nobody really knew exactly who they were or what they were doing here.

All Gemma knew was that she hated it when they came out here. It disrupted her night swims. She didn't feel comfortable being in the water, not when they were out in the cove, dancing and singing and doing whatever it was they did.